Kitchen Sink DOM

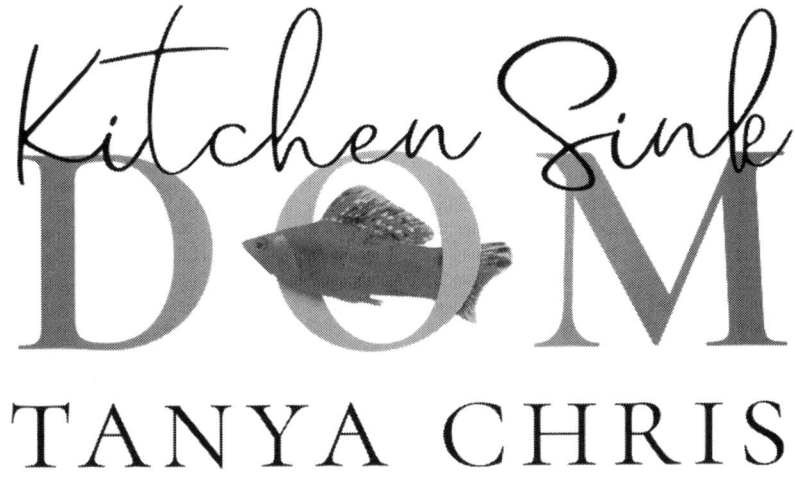

TANYA CHRIS

With sincere thanks to the members of Kate Hawthorne's Facebook group, Hawthorne's Harem, for the challenge that provided the inspiration for this book.

To see which parts of the book were proposed by the group's members, please refer to the appendix.

Table of Contents

Prologue Harrison

Harrison didn't get a lot of teenaged clients. Most teenagers couldn't afford to hire a private investigator, for one thing, and what would they even hire one for? To track down a stolen lunch? To identify the source behind an anonymous love note? But the kid sitting in one of his guest chairs was nineteen. And gay. He'd led with that piece of information, which was why Harrison had insisted on verifying his age.

"And so is my friend." Tripp raked a hand through the white-tipped bangs of his brown hair, ruffling them into a windswept look that appeared to be intentional. He had bright green eyes—lucid so far as Harrison could see, no sign of a pot haze—and a quick grin. "The one I want to talk to you about. You're gay too, right?"

"What makes you think so?"

"The sticker in your window. The rainbow one."

Harrison shrugged, essentially admitting it. He never hid his sexuality—hence the rainbow sticker—but he wasn't sure what relevance it had to Tripp's case, a case Tripp hadn't shared any details about yet except for the fact that it involved a gay friend. They were seated across from each other in Harrison's office, which was a fancy name for a storefront with a desk and a few chairs, all arranged in full view of the picture window where he'd stuck a rainbow decal. Discreetly. In the bottom corner.

He was sitting behind his desk in a giant leather office

chair, the kind boss-men had once lorded it over their peons from before they started going for more ergonomically correct nylon mesh contraptions, and Tripp sat in a smaller upholstered thing with wood arms and no wheels which, given the way he moved around, was probably just as well. He might be nearly out of his teen years, but he was a typical teenager—fidgety, scattered, and annoyingly slow to get to the point.

"Maybe we should start with my rates," Harrison suggested. Because that ought to send him scurrying away fast enough.

"I was hoping you could do it more, like, pro bono."

"You're thinking of lawyers, not private investigators. Private investigators don't work pro bono." At least this one didn't. "Does your friend need a lawyer?"

"I don't know. I don't know where he is."

"Because he's hiding from you?" If Tripp was looking for stalking assistance, he'd come to the wrong place.

"He's not *hiding* from me." Tripp blew the hair out of his eyes with an exasperated breath. "He's *missing*."

"If he's really missing, not just blowing you off, you ought to go to the police."

"I already tried the police, but I told you: Arlo's gay."

"So?"

"So they don't care."

"I doubt that's true." His opinion of the Boston Police Department's policies with respect to the LGBT community was better than that. True, he had ultimately chosen to quit rather than soldier on in the face of partners who made snide remarks right to his face and the constant fear that his fellow officers wouldn't have his back if it came to it. But the homophobia in the Boston PD was implied, not overt.

"Well, that's how it felt," Tripp said. "They wrote down what I told them, but they didn't ask me any questions, and I could tell they didn't believe me. Arlo's seventeen and he was kind of living on the street and he's gay, so they just figure he fucked off. But he didn't. He disappeared, and no

2

one's looking for him. So could you? Please? I can pay you a little."

Harrison ran a hand over his chin, brushing across his late afternoon stubble. His rates were higher than "a little," but missing person's cases weren't out of his wheelhouse. The force rarely put much effort into tracking down adults—gay or not—and seventeen was close enough to adult. Add in the fact that Arlo was homeless, and Harrison wasn't surprised the Boston PD had declined to assign a task force to his case.

It was more likely that Tripp had been ghosted than that Arlo had disappeared, but Tripp seemed genuinely concerned so Harrison texted Arlo's phone number to his contact at Verizon who pulled cell data for him when he needed it. Which wasn't legal, strictly speaking, but PIs did what they had to do, and sometimes that meant working around the edges of the law.

"Let's see what my guy comes back with. If Arlo's been using his phone, you'll know he's okay."

"If he was using his phone, he'd be using it to talk to me. You don't understand. We're close." Tripp held up two fingers and twined them around each other.

"Boyfriends?"

Tripp shook his head. "I love him, but not in a sex way. We're not compatible like that."

"Both bottoms?" Harrison asked with a grin. Not that he needed to know anything about a seventeen-year-old's preferences in bed.

"Both subs," Tripp corrected. "That's why I'm so worried about him. I think he got in with a bad Dom."

Harrison had been marginally amused by Tripp's audacity in seeking out a PI he couldn't afford to investigate a friend for blowing him off, but suddenly the situation seemed less amusing. Hearing the words Dom and sub drop so easily out of the mouth of a man who was hardly more than a boy, who had all the worldliness of a puppy, shook him. Back when he'd been seventeen, he'd had a bad

3

experience with a Dom himself. Not missing-persons bad, but bad enough that since then he'd squelched his interest in BDSM rather than risk ever feeling that way again.

"What's a kid his age messing around with that kind of shit for?"

"You think people gotta be eighteen to know they're kinky? That's not how it works."

He didn't need Tripp to lecture him on the subject because he'd lived it. But pursuing his kinky side had turned out to be a mistake, one he would rather not see anyone else make.

"Arlo's known he was submissive since he was a kid practically," Tripp said. "That's how we got to be friends, because of this online forum where people... you know."

"Which you're supposed to be eighteen to join, I'm sure." An online forum was exactly how he'd gotten himself in trouble. Anyone could check a box that said they were eighteen, and anyone could prey on the kids who did.

Tripp shrugged. "It was only online."

"Except now you think it wasn't only online, that he met someone in real life." Just like Harrison had.

"All I know is he was going to this BDSM club in the West End. It's called Hell's Bedroom, only it's basically heaven. They have everything there. All the best Doms in Boston belong to it. He texted me he was going, and then I never heard from him again."

Tripp showed him his phone. Arlo's text wasn't terribly illuminative. Lots of emojis but little in the way of facts. He was on his way to Hell's Bedroom and pretty excited about it. And then he was silent. Harrison scrolled through Tripp's return messages, which grew increasingly urgent until they ended with a final "please."

"I was on a date when he sent it," Tripp said as he took his phone back, "or I'd have called to get the deets. Like who he was going with and what they were going to do and what he was wearing and just everything. But I didn't see the text until after, and then he never answered again." Tripp looked sadly at that final message. "What if someone took him, Mr. Fisher? Or what if...?"

Tripp didn't finish his sentence, but Harrison understood. Arlo could be worse than missing. He could be dead.

His phone buzzed, indicating a return message from his source with Arlo's phone records attached. There hadn't been any activity since that last text to Tripp. No texts, no calls, no data usage. Which, considering Arlo's age, was pretty fucking drastic. Seventeen-year-olds couldn't go ten minutes without using their phone, never mind three weeks. This legitimately seemed like something to worry about.

"What about his parents?"

Arlo's line was on a family plan. There were two other cell phones on the plan that'd been recently used.

"They haven't seen him either."

"And they don't care?"

"Not much. They're drunks. They live in a semi-stoned twilight zone where nothing's very important, including Arlo. They said he'd probably turn up."

If it weren't for the phone records, Harrison would be inclined to agree. Arlo could've gotten a new number, but why would he? As disinterested as his parents might be, they were paying for his cell phone. If it'd been lost or destroyed, Arlo could've trotted down to a Verizon store and picked up a new one. The fact that he hadn't legitimized Tripp's fears.

Which brought them back to the police. If the officer assigned to the missing persons report Tripp had filed had pulled Arlo's phone records, the results should've worried them enough to take action, but that was where Tripp might be right. A gay, kinky seventeen-year-old whose own parents couldn't be bothered to look for him would be way at the bottom of the Boston PD's priority list.

"I thought maybe you could go to Hell's Bedroom," Tripp said.

5

"And ask them if they have Arlo in the dungeon?"

"There's no dungeon," Tripp answered with an eyeroll. "Not literally. But maybe you could poke around, go to the last place he was seen, infiltrate the scene of the crime. That's what PIs do, isn't it?"

Tripp obviously got his ideas about private investigators from television, where detectives snuck around in fake mustaches and took cases for the joy of it. Harrison had never worked undercover, not even while he was on the force.

"There could be a whole human trafficking ring going on there," Tripp suggested.

"I thought you said Hell's Bedroom was heaven."

"Even heaven has snakes."

That was Eden, not heaven, but Tripp was right that it only took one bad guy to make Arlo disappear, and a BDSM club had to be full of bad guys. Harrison wasn't typically in the business of rescuing maidens in distress, but Arlo was a baby gay who'd gone down a path he'd once made the mistake of going down himself and who might've paid a far worse price for it than a hit to his ego. Much as Harrison never wanted to return to that world again, he couldn't say no.

"Fine. I'll visit the club. Ask around, see what I can find out."

"Yes!" Tripp held up his hand for a high-five. Harrison looked at it until he put it back down. "Thank you," he said, only marginally subdued. "Now we just have to figure out how to get you in. It's a members-only place."

"And you're not a member?"

"I wish. I'd be there every night. But membership is wicked expensive and also, you have to be twenty-one to join."

"Then how did Arlo get in?"

"Someone must've signed him in."

Someone had signed a seventeen-year-old—who shouldn't have been at a club at all—into a BDSM bordello.

6

If Harrison were still a cop, he would raid the place. But he didn't have that kind of jurisdiction these days, and since he wasn't going to buy a "wicked expensive" membership so he could investigate a case for which he would be getting paid "a little," he would have to find another way in.

"So you're saying I need a date." He leaned back in his giant leather throne and propped his feet up on his desk.

"A playmate," Tripp corrected.

"And where would I find such a person?"

"That's what I'm always asking."

Harrison scowled at him. Nineteen wasn't much better than seventeen in his book. Tripp seemed to be doing all right emotionally, not scarred by whatever kinky sex he'd been exposed to thus far, but Harrison worried on his behalf. Young gay men had so many battles to fight as it was, so many ways in which the world tried to tell them they weren't good enough.

At least Tripp was tall-ish. At seventeen, Harrison had been coming to terms with the fact that he wasn't just gay, he was short. Insufficiently manly in so many ways. He hadn't needed some edgelord of a Dom making him feel even worse about himself.

"There's a party Saturday night," Tripp said, sobering up when he saw Harrison wasn't laughing with him. "It's at a house in Back Bay, not at the club, but there'll be members there. You can come with me, and I'll introduce you around. You can worm your way in from there, can't you?"

"I suppose." He wasn't the most personable of people, but he could probably pick up a date.

"We just have to decide if you're a Dom or sub." Tripp considered him, raking his eyes from Harrison's booted toes propped up on the dinged metal desk, over his denim-covered legs, and across the fabric of his grey t-shirt, stopping when he met Harrison's eyes which were asking him what the fuck he thought he was doing. "I'd say you're a Dom."

"And you're a sub?"

"Sub all the way." Tripp stuck out his tongue, which was pierced to match his nose and eyebrows. Harrison fiddled with the small silver ring in his right earlobe. It was the only hole he had, despite his occasional interest in getting his nipples done. So if piercings made someone a sub, he wasn't one. Except... except he'd once thought he might be.

"Don't Doms have to know how to do things? I can't just waltz into Hell's Bedroom and start swinging a whip around."

"Dude, no one's going to waltz into Hell's Bedroom and start swinging a whip around. There's so many rules. But I get your point. Beginner Dom is kind of a tough sell in terms of finding someone to play with."

"I'll bet beginner subs are a draw though. Fresh meat."

Tripp shrugged. "To some Doms maybe, but there's an art to being a sub. You'll see. If you're really going to try to play one."

He sounded doubtful. Harrison pretended not to be worried. His choice to go undercover as a sub was purely for logistical reasons, and not at all because he and the world of BDSM had some unfinished business.

Chapter 1 Harrison

For a guy who was supposedly undercover, he looked an awful lot like himself, with his nearly black hair gelled into its customary short spikes, his green eyes unfiltered by contacts, and his real nose with its pointy tip and slightly bumpy slope planted solidly in the middle of his real face. But he was dressed in clothes that felt like a costume, playing a role that made him hugely uncomfortable.

He wasn't kinky. Or, well, he was. But only in his mind, not in real life. And Tripp had him kitted up like a stereotypical submissive in tight black leather pants and a short-sleeved mesh shirt. Dark fantasies aside, he couldn't see himself this way. The shirt Tripp had picked out for him hugged his biceps the way the leather pants hugged his ass. Both were too revealing to hide a holster under, so he felt exposed not just in the sense of having a lot of flesh on display but in the sense of being unarmed.

He tugged at the leather band circling his neck as he scanned the gathering, which could be any gay house party he'd ever been to and was, in fact, the kind of gay house party he tried to avoid. A well-appointed living room, a little heavy on the ferns, a bar stocked with mid-grade alcohol, and a bunch of people, all male-presenting, drinking— though not to excess—and talking. No leashes, no beatings, no nudity beyond the ordinary, which meant there were a lot of biceps on display and more than a few sets of abs but no dicks. It was hard to believe any of the middle-class men filling this bourgeois living room were kinky beyond the obligatory leather night, never mind disturbed enough to be kidnappers. Harrison had been prepared for anything except this—to be bored.

"I hate small talk." He took a sip of his club soda, which he'd had the bartender garnish with a cherry pierced by a sword-shaped swizzle stick so it would look like something stronger, and made another sweeping appraisal of the room.

"It'll get rowdier. Give it time." Tripp had Coke in his glass, which Harrison knew because he'd stood next to him while it was being poured. As tame as this gathering might be, he didn't like that he was following a nineteen-year-old into a potentially sexual situation, even if the nineteen-year-old was taller than him and nominally his client. Very nominally. It wasn't Tripp's credit card that had paid for this ridiculous outfit.

"See anyone you know?"

"Lots of anyones." Tripp raised his glass to a guy who had to be fifty. A very good-looking fifty. "No one I recognize as a member of Hell's Bedroom yet though."

"But you think they'll be here?"

"They're not a single entity, Harry. They don't travel in a pack like the Borg."

Harry was the name Harrison used on his fake ID. It was close enough to his real name that he would respond to it, especially since his sister called him Harry all the fucking time, but right now it was just one more thing to make him cringe. This whole scene was cringe-worthy. He tugged on the band of leather around his neck again. It was tight and awful and made him feel like a dog.

"Stop fussing with that. It's obvious you've never worn a collar before."

"I don't think I'm going to be able to pull off being an experienced sub." He'd been one for twenty minutes now, and he already hated it.

"If you're going to attract a Dom, you need to appear

compliant. It'll be hard enough finding someone who wants to play with a sub who has a bunch of limits."

Harrison stopped fiddling with his collar. He was being lectured on compliance by a teenager. "Who says I have limits? I'll do what I have to do."

"Even real subs have limits, but if you're determined to sacrifice your body for the cause, I'd better steer you away from the sadists."

"Don't do me any favors." He didn't need a kid in a shredded tank top protecting him from what he would maybe enjoy? He'd enjoyed the physical aspect of what Sir Magnus—God, he really should've known better from the name alone—had done to him, which was part of why he'd felt so ashamed of himself afterward. How could he have gotten off on someone treating him that disrespectfully?

But he wasn't here to enjoy anything. This was a job, potentially a serious one. He was at this house party with a dog collar around his neck and leather bracelets on his wrists to search for a lost gay boy. Not to flirt with his interest in pain play.

"Those two," Tripp said, literally trying to talk out of the corner of his mouth. Kid had watched too many movies. "In the doorway to the kitchen."

Harrison turned slowly—maybe he'd watched too many movies himself—until he could take in the pair of men Tripp was referring to. They stood on opposite sides of the doorway, leaning against it as if they were bracing it. The one on the right would make a good brace. He was a mountain of a man with an incongruously friendly flop of brown hair and a big smile which he was aiming at the darker, smaller guy he was talking to.

"They're club members?"

"The big guy is, for sure. He and I scened together once."

Harrison felt a flash of anger that a guy that big had been messing with someone Tripp's age. Tripp might be an adult, but only barely, and he was camp enough that his

11

adulthood was hard to remember.

The guy in the doorway was closer to Harrison's own pushing-forty years and dressed casually in jeans and a simple t-shirt rather than fetish-ware. He seemed to pick up on the fact that he was being watched because he turned his eyes in their direction. Brown eyes, round and heavily lashed. They matched his smile, which only got wider when he caught Harrison looking.

Harrison held his gaze for longer than he probably should've. "The bigger one's a Dom?" he asked doubtfully. The guy seemed too friendly.

"They're both Doms. Though the bigger one..."

"The bigger one what?" Harrison managed to peel his gaze away from the man in question to look at Tripp.

"He might be a good choice for you, actually."

"You mean, like, a suspect?"

"No, I can't imagine him doing anything bad to Arlo. He's way too nice."

"Then what makes him a good choice?"

"Because he *is* nice. Nice isn't my thing." Tripp smirked knowingly, suddenly coming across as much older. "But he'd be good for you. Respectful, safe, wouldn't push your limits."

"You're saying that like it's bad. Aren't those things important? Respectful, safe, doesn't push your limits?"

"Yep," Tripp agreed without hesitation. "I'd totally trust him with you. I was kind of nervous about sending you into Hell's Bedroom as a sub, but this could work."

What the hell kind of games did this kid play that he was worried Harrison couldn't handle them? Harrison might not be as tall as Mr. Super Safe over there—or even as tall as Tripp—but he won all the fights he got invited to. There was a reason the sleeves of his mesh top were digging into his upper arms like the elastic on a too-tight pair of panties.

"Come on, I'll introduce you to him."

"Aren't the two of you exes?"

12

Tripp made an expression only a teenager faced with a clueless adult could make. "We scened once. We didn't have a relationship."

"Why not, if he's so safe and all?"

"Dude, I just told you why. Safe is important, but nice isn't my thing, and yes, there's a difference. But he's perfect for you. He's a club member, and he hasn't got anyone kneeling at his feet. We need someone who can get you into the club. That's him. Let's go."

Harrison swallowed what was left in his glass, stalling for reasons he couldn't explain. The jab about kneeling maybe. He didn't *kneel*, goddammit, but Tripp said a good Dom was hard to find, and the guy in the doorway was a Dom, good or not. So...

"I'll take it from here," he said. "Thanks for getting me in the door and pointing him out."

"Don't you think an introduction would help?"

"I don't need help picking up men."

And he didn't need the burly Dom deciding to pass him by in favor of another session with Tripp. Because Tripp probably came off as the better prospect. He was young, lanky, attractive in a messy sort of way, and he was a sub. A real one. Harrison was going to have to put on a good act to pull this off, which would include kneeling if he had to kneel.

He dropped off his empty glass at the bar and detoured to the bathroom to give himself a once-over and call his backup, a rookie cop named Cade Brixby he'd hired to stand by in case his undercover activities got him into a spot where he really needed that missing gun.

"I've got a prospect," he told Brixby as he fluffed his hair in the mirror, trying to separate the spikes into something less aggressive. Height aside, he came across as too butch, too dominant—a Dom, like Tripp had suggested. Maybe he should've gone with that instead of flirting with secret temptations.

"Description?" Brixby asked.

13

Harrison had never worked with the guy before. He came recommended, but he was young, mostly untried, and almost too good looking to take seriously. Harrison was counting on the fact that he didn't need the rookie to do anything except sit in a car playing babysitter.

"Six-two, six-three. Two hundred and twenty pounds, obvious muscle through the chest and shoulders." And ass and thighs. "Chestnut brown hair cut to ear length." *Chestnut brown?* Really? Was he a romance novelist? "Bangs covering his forehead. No visible piercings or tats."

"He sounds like a hot date."

Harrison could definitely get it up for the guy if the situation called for it, but he wasn't letting a fresh-faced uniform joke about his sexuality. "Let's remember who's working for who," he warned.

"Sorry." The teasing tone dropped from Brixby's voice. "Got a name I can run?"

"I haven't made my approach yet, but I'm heading that way now. I'll shoot you a text when I get something."

"Roger that. Be safe."

Harrison ended the call and went back to critiquing himself in the mirror. Ruffling his hair hadn't made him look any softer or put a more submissive cast in his eyes. The only part of his appearance that said submissive was that damn collar, which he desperately wanted to remove. But the collar was his entrée, his reason for approaching the hot guy with the chestnut brown hair. Tonight he was Harry, a submissive in search of a Dom. One who could get him into Hell's Bedroom, in particular. Mr. Hot and Nice was going to be that Dom.

Except that when Harrison rejoined the party, his target had disappeared from the doorway. A quick scan turned up Tripp hanging on the arm of the silver fox he'd waved to earlier. Tripp jerked his head toward the other side of the room, and there was the guy Harrison was looking for—by the bar accepting a drink from the bartender with an adorably wholesome smile. Weren't Doms meant to be

14

cold and sneery? Sir Magnus sure had been.

Nice, Tripp had said. This Dom was nice.

The Dom crossed the living room, drink in hand, and Harrison moved to intercept him. He didn't have any particular plan, but his prior experience with picking up men suggested the direct approach worked pretty well, so he didn't bother to disguise his interest, just put himself between his target and where his target was headed.

"Hey."

"Hey." The Dom gave him a quick up-down. "We haven't met before, have we? I think I'd remember you if we had."

"I don't think we've met."

"Then let's meet now." The Dom moved his drink into his left hand and stuck out his right. "I'm Cash." His hand was chilly from his drink and big, enveloping Harrison's completely but briefly.

"Harry," he said in return, remembering at the last moment to use his alias. Presumably Cash was an alias too, hopefully not one that indicated he was a pro of some sort. Harrison had dumped enough money into this job already, considering he wasn't likely to get reimbursed for any of it.

"Harry," Cash repeated. There was a bit of scruff on his cheeks and chin, so neatly uniform that Harrison was guessing he shaved with an electric razor on a low setting to give himself an intentional two-day shadow. With a lot more beard and a little more stomach, he would qualify as a bear. A teddy bear. The man was just asking to be cuddled. Harrison couldn't imagine him hurting anyone.

"Someone said you were a Dom."

"I'm more of a top than a Dom, but I might be close enough, depending on what you're looking for."

"A top, meaning you fuck people?"

"I do fuck people, if they want me to, but that's not what I meant. You're wearing a collar." Cash brushed a fingertip along the leather, reminding him of it all over again.

"Because I'm a sub," he lied.

"Are you? As in you belong to someone?"

15

"I'm in search of someone." He made hopeful eyes up at Cash, trying to convey uncomplicated interest even though his feelings were complicated. Cash had a boyish warmth to his face, despite being somewhere in his thirties, and he smiled at Harrison like Harrison was someone important to him. Harrison wished they were meeting in a gay bar and that he didn't have a missing kid on his mind.

"Ever done anything like this before, Harry?"

Harry. Ugh. He'd spent his whole life correcting anyone who tried to call him that. "I'm not super experienced, no. My friend said you'd be a good Dom to start with."

Cash's expression got even brighter. "I am. Though like I said, I'm more of a top than a Dom. A service top."

And obviously Harrison was going to have to find out what the hell that meant because Cash was looking at him like it was important. But now wasn't the time to corner Tripp for a vocabulary lesson, and Harrison didn't really care *what* Cash was, as long as Cash could get him into Hell's Bedroom.

"Okay, well, I'm a bottom. Maybe we could go somewhere?"

"Now?" Cash held up his glass, partially filled with an amber liquid Harrison could guess was Scotch based on the smell. "I don't play when I've been drinking. How about we get to know each other, see if we can negotiate something we'd both enjoy on a future date?"

"Yeah, sure." Realistically, he hadn't expected Cash to take him to the club this very minute, but it didn't hurt to try. He would have to put in some time fussing and flirting, make it seem like he was really interested in whatever Cash had to offer, which he still didn't understand. What kind of person didn't fuck because they'd had a drink? "I'm up for pretty much anything."

"Then let's grab a seat." Cash angled his head toward a sofa that'd just freed up. "Can I get you a drink?"

"I'm good." He took a seat, adjusting the collar around his neck again as the motion made it tug on his Adam's apple.

"You don't like wearing that, do you?" Cash put his drink down on a side table and reached behind Harrison's head to unsnap the leather band. "Why wear it if you're not comfortable in it?"

"I thought I had to."

"The first rule of scening with me is please don't do anything you don't want to do."

Harrison nodded like he was agreeing, but he would have to wait and see what Cash asked him to do before he could promise for real. Maybe it would be something he wanted, and maybe it wouldn't.

Chapter 2 Cash

Something about Harry was off. Cash's friend Sandi liked to joke that he was an empath, but there was nothing new-agey or mystical about the way he read people. He paid attention to them, that was all. And because he did, he could tell something about Harry was off.

It wasn't unusual for a sub to be nervous in a gathering with this many Doms, and if Harry was as new to the scene as his lack of familiarity with the lingo suggested, then he had all the more reason to be nervous. But nervous wasn't the vibe Cash was getting from him. The only word he could come up with to describe the vibe was *off.*

At any rate, Harry didn't belong in a collar. He hadn't been able to keep his fingers away from it the whole time they'd been talking. Harry had nice fingers—square with clean, blunt nails that suggested he worked a desk job—and they repeatedly swept under his collar, tugging it away from his neck, until Cash couldn't stand it anymore. He hated seeing people suffer. Removing a collar that wasn't his was pretty bad etiquette, but Harry had said he didn't belong to anyone, and he seemed thoroughly relieved to have it off.

"How'd you hear about the party?" Cash asked, fishing around the edges of whatever was going on.

"Came with a friend."

"Who's that?"

18

"Just a friend."

Cash could guess who Harry had come with because they'd been standing together when he'd noticed them across the room, but the evasion rang more alarm bells. Next to Tripp, Harry had been a vision—a hundred and fifty pounds of lean muscle packed into a pair of tight leather pants—but Cash didn't approach guys in collars. A collar meant the guy either had a master or was looking for one, and though Cash could play Dom if that was what his partner needed, he was constitutionally incapable of playing master.

But Harry had approached *him*, so here they were.

The gorgeous man sitting next to him would be a joy to play with. Cash could already imagine his light green eyes darkening to a glistening emerald, could see his dark hair matted with feverish sweat and his thin-lipped mouth hanging open as he panted out his pleasure. Harry's body wouldn't be hard to look at either. He had a lean abdomen, a nicely developed torso, and colorful tattoos running down both arms. So if he didn't want to make small talk—or not honest small talk, at least—Cash would skip straight to the point.

"What kind of a scene are you interested in?"

"You're the boss." Harry darted a quick glance up at him—anxious but also something else.

"I can't 'be the boss' without knowing what you like. Unless you want me to throw random kinks at you and see what sticks."

"You might as well," Harry said with a nerve-laced laugh. "I really don't have any idea. I told you I was new, right?"

"You're so new you don't even know what you like?" That was... intriguing. Cash's kink was driving his partner wild. Usually his partners told him what made them wild—maybe not in exact words, but he'd been around the scene long enough to understand which triggers went with which kinks—and then he executed on it. Very well, too.

19

If a guy wanted to be whipped, Cash broke out the flogger. If he wanted to be pissed on, Cash let loose. If someone wanted to be bound and gagged, Cash could turn them into a veritable pretzel. He had the skills to wield any implement, expose any vulnerability, satisfy any fetish. But as a service top, he was usually pushing buttons that had already been pretty well mapped out. What would it be like to find those buttons himself, to push them for the very first time?

Intriguing.

"I could definitely introduce you to some things." And enjoy the fuck out of it. "I'm safe, sane, consensual, and I've got a lot of experience. Your friend can vouch for me."

"My friend?"

"Tripp. That's who you came with, right? I've only scened with him once, but he's been around long enough to know how I play."

"He's nineteen," Harry said turgidly, his semi-flirtatious smile gone. "How long has he been around, exactly?"

"Whoa, there." Cash held up his hands to disavow whatever Harry was accusing him of. "The club I belong to cards people. He wouldn't have been in there unless he was of age, and as long as he's legally an adult, his exact age is none of my business. How old are *you*?"

"Do I look like a teenager?"

"I'm not the one who started with the accusations. Tripp can vouch for me. Who's vouching for you?"

Harry fiddled with the collar he held in his lap, then looked up with more conciliatory eyes. "I'll trade you IDs."

Cash chucked. Whatever. He was an open book. He took out his wallet and flashed his driver's license. The picture had only been taken a couple of years ago, but he looked like a frat boy in it. Despite his size, he gave off zero scary vibes. It was one of the reasons he had trouble attracting and keeping play partners, though not the only one.

Harry leaned forward to peer at the license, getting

20

close enough that Cash could pick up on his cologne—something rich and masculine with a heavy musk component. The scent matched his carriage. Cash took a deep inhale and tried not to hope too hard that the two of them could negotiate a scene. If he wasn't the right top for Harry, then he had no business scening with him, but man, he hoped he could be the right top.

"Cassius," Harry read out loud.

"Yeah, I know. I don't look like a Cassius, do I?"

"What would a Cassius look like? Old and Roman?" Harry wrinkled his nose.

Cash couldn't help laughing. "How about classic? Or a fighter?" He put up his dukes as if he were a pre-Mohammed Ali Cassius Clay. "I'm not either of those things, though."

"You could be classic." Harry surveyed him with obvious approval, and Cash's hopes rose dangerously high. "I figured Cash was a scene name."

"Just a manageable version of Cassius." He tilted up his ass cheek so he could wedge his wallet back in his jeans and Harry snuck a peek Cash didn't miss. "Is Harry not your real name?"

Harry grimaced. "Also a version of my real name."

"Except you don't like it, so why use it?"

"Am I making it so obvious I don't like it?"

"Yes." Perhaps that was the wrongness Cash had been picking up on. "How about I call you something else? It doesn't have to be your real name, but I'd like it to be something that doesn't make you wince. I'm not that kind of sadist. Unless you're that kind of masochist. Do you enjoy humiliation?"

Harry gave him an even more confused look than the one the term service top had brought on. This guy was really starting from zero. He had no idea what he liked and wouldn't know the words for it even if he did.

"Let's try some alternatives to Harry," Cash said. "Baby? Pet? Little one?" Each endearment made Harry scowl harder than the last. His scowl face was adorable. His lips, which were on the narrow side, pouted into plumpness, and his heavy eyebrows closed in on each other. Still, Cash would rather see him smile. "How about hot stuff? You're definitely hot stuff. No? Let's see. Puppy? Angel?"

"Harrison," he said in an exasperated rush. "You can call me Harrison. But that's my real name, so don't tell the whole world."

"All right." Cash winked at him. He didn't know what had Harrison so paranoid, but he would honor his need for secrecy. He leaned in closer and said "Harrison" right into his ear, and Harrison shivered in a way that told Cash yep, that was his name, all right, and he liked hearing it.

Cash got closer, shifting so their hips brushed together, and breathed into Harrison's ear again. Harrison might not be sure what he was looking for, but Cash was up for anything that got his partner off. He really enjoyed the way subs let themselves go so completely, and Harrison was already revealing himself to be nicely reactive. Cash trailed a finger along his inseam, starting from his knee and continuing up until Harrison swallowed and his eyes softened.

"I'd like to kiss you, Harrison."

Harrison licked his lips, then parted them in damp invitation. Cash closed the distance between them to mold their mouths together. Harrison tasted fresh and clean, no alcohol on his breath despite the drink he'd been holding earlier. His eyes fluttered shut, and his tongue came out to play. Cash cupped his jaw and felt a tremor run through it. Very nice. But he drew back to put space between them again. This was a social event, not a play party.

"So about that scene we were going to negotiate."

"You said you belong to a club?"

"I do, but I wouldn't want to bring you there, not for starters."

"Why not?" Harrison became all bristly challenge again,

his soft mood evaporating in an instant.

"The club would be a lot for a beginner to take in. I'd rather you be able to concentrate on figuring out what gets you off than worry about being watched."

"What if being watched is what gets me off?"

"Is it?"

"I... don't think so," Harrison said slowly, as if he didn't want to admit that showing off wouldn't get him off.

"That's okay. BDSM can be a hundred percent private and still be totally valid."

"But aren't there private spaces at the club? I mean, people don't fuck right out in the open, do they?"

Cash laughed. "No, definitely not. There *is* a fair amount of public nudity, or semi-nudity, at least. It's not uncommon for subs to be mostly undressed, and some of the Doms don't wear much more. But it's optional. Everything is optional."

"Now I know why Tripp said you were nice," Harrison said, making it sound like a compliment, though Cash doubted Tripp had meant it that way. He sighed. This was always the problem.

"Everything in BDSM is optional, but some people enjoy the illusion of force. Is that what you're looking for?"

"No." Harrison gave that answer decisively. "No, not at all. I think you're great. I want you to be my first."

Cash wanted that too. Very much. He couldn't resist leaning in to take another kiss, lingering over Harrison's lips longer than he'd meant to, thinking about how those lips would look parted and pleading. Together they would figure out what got Harrison's motor running, and then Cash would run it all the way up to the red line.

But not here, not yet. He drew away, determined to behave, and fished his glass off the table. He took a sip, letting the warm swirl of Scotch in his throat and chest remind him he wasn't playing tonight. "You're sure I can't get you something?"

Harrison snatched the glass out of his fingers and

brought it to his lips, seeming to breathe it in more than actually drink from it. "It tasted good on you," he said with a shrug as he returned it. "But I shouldn't." Maybe he was driving.

"I'm not far from here," Cash said to justify his own drinking.

"I know." Harrison nudged him with a grin. So Harrison had taken note of his address along with his name, had he? It made him realize Harrison hadn't actually shared his own ID in return—just looked at Cash's and changed the subject. Cash wasn't getting bad-guy vibes off him exactly, but he took in a lot of information for someone who didn't give any away.

"What do you do for a living?" Cash tried.

"I'm a tattoo artist."

"Is this your work?" He brushed Harrison's right arm, which was decorated in a tropical rainforest theme bursting with dark green vines, vibrant flowers, and an occasional animal head peeping out in a quasi-cartoonish style. The other arm was ships and skulls, as if Harrison were showcasing the fact that he had a hard side and a soft side.

"You can't tattoo your own arm," Harrison said with a frown that suggested Cash should've known better. "A friend of mine did it—another artist in the shop I work at."

"Which shop is that?"

"Oh, it's in Cambridge. Lots of foot traffic there with all the colleges. You have any tattoos?"

"Not even one. No piercings either. Pure unadorned flesh." Cash waved a hand down his body like he was showing it off, and Harrison's eyes definitely followed, lingering on his crotch where he had to admit he was rocking a chubby.

"Is that really why you don't have any tattoos? Some kind of purity thing?"

"No, that was a joke. I'm not good at picking one thing and sticking to it, I guess. Maybe you can help me figure out what I should get."

Harrison considered. "Piercings might be more your thing, since they can always come out. How about a Prince Albert?"

"Would that turn you on?"

"I've never fucked around with a guy who had a Prince Albert. Sort of a fantasy that one day I'll pull down a zipper and a dick will pop out with a big fat ring right through the head."

"Uh huh." Cash got rid of his drink before he dropped it. Turned-on Harrison was too hot. If Amazon sold Prince Alberts, there'd be one on the way right now. "And what would you do with this pierced dick?"

Harrison shrugged. "I'd have to experiment. They're pretty to look at, anyway."

"But you don't want one yourself?"

"What makes you so sure I don't have one?"

"In pants that tight? I think I'd be able to see it if you did." Cash dropped his hand on Harrison's thigh, just below the obvious line of his cock. Harrison hadn't made any move to adjust himself, so either he had a touch of masochist in him or he was too shy to shove his hand down his pants in pubic. Since Harrison didn't strike him as the shy type—coming straight up to Cash the way he had, as if a Dom were something you could fetch for yourself—it must be that he didn't mind the sensation.

"Getting pierced would probably hurt," Cash suggested, and Harrison's shudder confirmed his hypothesis. Harrison's affinity for touch extended into the realm some people would call pain. Mm. Cash loved a good masochist. They could be tortured to such exquisite heights of ecstasy. His own cock swelled harder in his jeans, and since he *wasn't* a masochist, he adjusted it. Harrison's eyes followed his hand, and the flush that'd been crawling up from the low neckline of his peekaboo shirt deepened.

"So there's really no playing here?" Harrison asked.

Cash wished he could offer a taste of something, but it wasn't advisable. "Sometimes folks get up to shenanigans in the bedrooms, but we're keeping it PG tonight. There's a cruiser down the street, staking the place out. Not that we're doing anything illegal, but you know cops. There's legal and then there's *gay* and legal."

"Shit." Harrison looked unreasonably annoyed, half rising as if he were about to leave. Cash put a hand out to stop him.

"It's fine. They're watching for something they can raid us over, but they won't find it. If you have any drugs on you, now's not the time to use them."

He was mostly joking, but Harrison's reaction had him wondering once again what Harrison had to hide. He was a contradiction, this guy. Cash was either going to enjoy figuring him out or be sorry he'd ever gotten involved.

Chapter 3 Harrison

Harrison had only taken a single step outside before he spotted the squad car. Brixby wasn't wearing his uniform, but everything from his haircut to his posture screamed cop, and there was no mistaking the black-and-white markings of the cruiser. No wonder the party guests had made him.

Harrison shook his head as he headed for the closest T station, texting Brixby as he walked with the address of a gay bar in the neighborhood. He didn't want to be seen socializing with a cop, but meeting a handsome guy for a drink fit his Harry cover just fine, and if being in a gay bar made Brixby uncomfortable, Harrison didn't really give a fuck. He was going to have to find a smarter backup—one who knew better than to bring a marked car to a stakeout.

Roger's was a welcome haven of familiarity, a dark but not wild place where two men could sit at a high-top and have a drink together without worrying about anyone giving them shit or having an orgy break out around them either. There was a television in every corner, a trio of pool tables in the back, and the patrons kept their clothes on and their hands to themselves. More or less.

Harrison went to the bar and ordered himself a beer, waving Brixby over when he saw him stride in with a swagger that telegraphed the gun belt he usually wore around his hips.

"And one for my friend," Harrison told the bartender,

smirking to himself when the bartender gave Brixby a once-over. Brixby was a hot guy, but the bartender was probably barking up the wrong tree there, not that Brixby was acting like it was a problem. His mouth was set in a slightly upturned line, as if he were willing to indulge the bartender's presumption.

"Anything else for you gentlemen?" the bartender purred as he handed over their drinks, his eyes flitting between them. Either he was angling for a tip or he was angling for a top.

The thought made Harrison remember Cash's insistence on using the word top to describe himself. Harrison considered himself versatile, but his partners usually pegged him as a top and he didn't fight that assumption very hard. Brixby came across as quintessential top too. He had a clean-cut military look with dark hair cropped short and a lot of confidence for someone who'd just royally fucked up.

Harrison tipped the bartender and brought Brixby over to a table. He took a hefty swallow of his beer, letting the stress of pretending to be someone he wasn't fall from his shoulders. Now that he'd had a taste of working undercover, he wasn't sure he liked it. And he was pretty sure he sucked at—that he'd been almost as easy to make as Brixby.

"A squad car? Really?"

"It's the only car I've got," Brixby said. "I drive it home for one of those cops-in-your-neighborhood programs."

Not surprising Brixby didn't keep a car of his own. Who in Boston did? And Harrison didn't need to add the cost of a rental to the list of expenses he would never get reimbursed for, but still.

"You couldn't have parked a few blocks over? Somewhere they wouldn't have spotted you."

"How was I going to make sure you weren't being kidnapped if I couldn't see the house?"

"No one was going to kidnap me," Harrison said with a roll of his eyes.

"Given the subject of the investigation, it's a possibility. One of those guys could've slipped you something."

"I appreciate the concern, but if my pigeon realizes I'm being followed around by a cop, it's going to blow my cover. Luckily, he took it as heavy-handed policing."

"So you made a connection?" Brixby's eyes were a startling blue, even in the low light of the bar.

"Yeah, I've got a date." He gave Brixby Cash's full name and address. "We're meeting at his apartment Saturday."

"Can't say I like the idea of you going to his place."

"Yeah, me either, but it's the price of admission. He doesn't think a club is the right starting point for a beginner, but he *is* a member. So I'll put on a dog-and-pony show for him, prove I've got what it takes for the big time, and then I'll have my in. To the club and to the...?" He groped for the word Tripp kept using.

"The scene," Brixby supplied. "But his *apartment*? You've gotta consider him a suspect."

"He offered to meet me at my place, but I don't have a cover that runs as deep as a fake address, and I'm not giving him my real address."

Brixby shook his head. "No, not a good idea. But how am I supposed to monitor the inside of a civilian's private residence? We can't even put a wire on you, not if you might be getting undressed. Are you sure about this, Fisher? If Arlo's in trouble, I want to find him as bad as you do, but not at the cost of you whoring yourself out."

"Cash is a good looking guy," Harrison said with a shrug. "Under other circumstances, I'd be happy to get naked with him."

Seriously. With Cash blowing in his ear and resting his big paw so close to Harrison's hard dick, Harrison had been struggling to remember Cash was supposed to be a job until that comment about the squad car. There was just something so intensely *interested* about him. Not interesting, although he'd been that too. But interested. Like he really saw Harrison, even through his Harry

29

disguise.

"And he's a good choice," Harrison added.

"According to who?"

"Tripp. Apparently he's a service top, not a Dom. Whatever that means."

"It means he's not actually dominant. He'll wield a whip, but only for your sake, not his own."

"And you know that because...?" Harrison eyed the blue-eyed man across from him.

"Because I'm in the scene myself."

"You could've mentioned that before."

"It's not something I'm eager to have widely known." Brixby lifted his right shoulder in a half-shrug. "Not that and not the other either."

"What other?"

"This." Brixby waved at the bar. "You're really gay, right? That's not just a cover?"

"Gay and out." And now he understood why Brixby's reaction to being ogled by a twink in a bright pink t-shirt emblazoned with the words *Roger Me* in silver glitter had been so prosaic.

"Have you got a membership to that club?" Why were they dicking around if Brixby could just flash a key tag?

"I wish. Hell's Bedroom is expensive, and you know how much a rookie cop makes. Besides, like I said, I'm not out. And I'm not ready to be out."

"I get it." He'd started his career out, and in retrospect, maybe that'd been a mistake. But no. He couldn't live like that. Better to be free of the whole thing. Still, he was glad to know his sexuality wouldn't be an issue with Brixby. He changed his mind about ditching him for a more experienced backup. He would take a rookie over a homophobe any day.

"So, which role do you play? If that's not too personal a question."

"I'm a Dom."

"And the difference between a Dom and a service top is

a Dom likes what he's doing and a service top doesn't?"

"I wouldn't say that exactly. Just that a service top is going to be more accommodating, less dictatorial. He's there to serve, despite being nominally the top."

"Sounds like a good thing to me."

Brixby laughed. "Because you're not a real submissive. A true sub wants a true Dom—someone who'll dominate them. A service top is more like a machine—like a dildo instead of a dick. A lot of subs won't play with a service top. Or they'll play with one when they need a quick fix, but it's not what they're looking for long term."

Huh. That explained Tripp's attitude. And maybe Cash's too. It'd been clear every time Cash said something about being a top that he was expecting Harrison to reject him for it, despite his gorgeous physique and the boyish smile beaming out from beneath deep brown eyes that went topaz when they tipped up to the light.

"But a service top is exactly what you need," Brixby said. "You'll be able to dictate the scene. Any decent Dom would respect your limits, but with this guy, you won't have to balance what he's looking for against what you're willing to do. Ask for whatever you'll be comfortable with."

Last time Harrison had tried BDSM, he'd been looking for pain. And he'd gotten it. There'd been a whip—a small one, not like Indian Jones—but it'd touched his body exactly the way he'd wanted it to be touched. But all the rest of it, the things that made the encounter a scene rather than just sex, had been too much. He'd come away feeling humiliated, worthless, and—worst of all—deserving of having been made to feel humiliated and worthless. Because anyone who would allow someone to say those things to him deserved to have them said.

He might enjoy it if Cash took a whip to him, but he wouldn't enjoy what came with it, and he'd learned his lesson about trusting himself to a stranger. Not to mention that he had to consider Cash a suspect. He had a hard time envisioning Cash as a predator, but the fact that he'd

31

screwed around with a nineteen-year-old Tripp meant the possibility couldn't be written off completely.

"I don't know what I'd be comfortable with," he told Brixby. "Probably none of it. But the point is to find Arlo, not for me to have a spa day. What's the least sex-like thing I could ask for?"

"Protocol, maybe? Tell him you're interested in service." Brixby punctuated the suggestion with a snort.

"What?"

"A service sub serving a service top. It's funny. The definition of pointless. But it would be safe. A little kneeling. Maybe polish his shoes or do his dishes, make him some tea. Ritual. You think you can manage that without getting so turned you end up fucking his brains out?"

Harrison laughed. "I'll try. He's hot enough, but it would be a conflict of interest."

"Dedication." Brixby winked. "It would be pure dedication." He rose, leaving behind his half-finished beer. "I'll run a background check on him before your date on Saturday."

"Thanks, but I doubt you'll find anything."

"Never know. He's watching out for cops, apparently."

"Good point." Harrison shook Brixby's hand, then sat back down to finish his beer and examine what had happened with Cash through a more personal lens.

He'd kissed Cash, given him his real first name, practically melted under the warmth of his eyes. It'd been a long time since he'd felt such an instant connection, and it seemed unfair that his job precluded him from pursuing it. Or even from being honest.

Was Cash involved in whatever had happened to Arlo? Already, Harrison was inclined to say no, but that might just be because he didn't *want* Cash to be involved.

Chapter 4 Cash

The man who rang Cash's doorbell early Saturday evening looked both more and less comfortable than the one he'd met last week. Harrison was dressed in jeans and a t-shirt, not as delectable but a whole lot more natural than he'd been at the party. He wore a pair of dark glasses, and his short hair was spiked up as if it'd been freshly styled, but his smile was queasy, suggesting there were nerves percolating under his confident exterior.

"You made it." Cash made sure his own smile was thoroughly enthusiastic. He stepped back to let Harrison follow him in.

He rented a garden apartment, down half a flight of stairs from street level, which meant his front windows were little more than letterboxes. But the back opened out to a private space that made living partly underground in a tight one-bedroom worth it.

Harrison removed his sunglasses and tucked them into the pocket of his aqua-blue tee as he inspected Cash's living space. Mr. Moo, Cash's ancient and adored cat, inspected Harrison back. He hopped down from his perch below one of the letterbox windows, the vantage point from which he watched pedestrians pass by for twenty-two out of every twenty-four hours, to stalk closer.

"Can you say hi to my friend, Mr. Moo?"

Mr. Moo tilted his head to the side as if to suggest that

greetings of that sort were beneath him. He preferred judging people to making friends with them.

"Mr. Moo?" Harrison asked.

"For his markings."

"He does sort of look like one of those cows. What are they called? Holsteins?"

"Careful. He's sensitive about his weight." Cash gave Mr. Moo a head scratch, which Mr. Moo vigorously rejected. Mr. Moo cuddled on his own terms. "I should've asked if you were okay with animals."

"Depends. What else have you got?"

"Just a hamster. Ellie. You won't see her though. She lives in the walls and only comes out at night to eat."

"You have a hamster that lives in the walls and only comes out at night to eat? I hate to break it to you, Cash, but I think what you've got is a rat."

Cash shrugged. No one ever believed him about Ellie. "She belonged to the people who lived here before me. They left a note asking me to call if I found her, but I've never been able to catch her. One day she'll trust me enough to come out."

"Mr. Moo doesn't harass her?"

"Mr. Moo's vermin-chasing days are behind him. He prefers to sit in silent condemnation now."

As if to prove it, Mr. Moo returned to his perch to resume his busy day job of watching legs go by.

"So, this is the living space, obviously." Cash waved at the room that was a combination living room and mini-dining room, overcrowded with places to sit because he liked to entertain, and decorated in a mish-mash his friend Sandi called *gay bachelor*, which meant geeky paraphernalia, lots of potted plants that he treated like friends, a smattering of sports memorabilia—mostly things that'd been given to him—and whatever jumped into his basket at Pier One while he was only supposed to be browsing.

"Colorful," Harrison commented.

"I like color."

"And art, I take it." Harrison had stopped in front of one of Cash's larger canvases, a realistic forest scene interspersed with unrealistically bright fantasy elements, almost like children's stickers had been pasted over a photo.

"That's one of mine," Cash told him.

"Yours, as in you painted it?" Harrison gave it a harder look. "It suits you. Whimsical but solid. Is that what you do for a living?"

"Sort of yes, but mostly no. I'm a graphic designer. More commercial, less whimsical." He traced a finger down the edge of the frame. "Anyway, this is the living space. I've got a nice patio, but it's probably not the best choice for a scene. It's exclusively mine, but the other tenants can see into it."

Harrison took a cursory peek through the slider that led outside.

"And then there's my bedroom, and that's about it. We can work wherever you're comfortable."

"What are we going to do?"

"How about we start by talking about it? Can I get you something to drink?"

"No, thanks. I'm good." Harrison sat on the edge of a loveseat in a way that suggested he wasn't good at all. Negotiating a scene was often an awkward, unsexy thing to do, even for people familiar with the process. For a newcomer, it could feel like peeling back your skin to put your insides on display.

Cash sat next to Harrison, crowding him a little because Harrison had responded to physical proximity at the party. "I find you very attractive."

"Thanks?"

"And I'd like to make you feel good. It doesn't have to be any more complicated than that. Give me an idea of what would make you feel good. It could be anything—kinky or not."

"Anything, huh?" For a moment, a light went on in Harrison's eyes. Cash wished he knew what Harrison was imagining that made his lips quirk upward like that, because whatever it was, that was what he wanted to do, but then Harrison swallowed and his next words didn't carry the same passion. "Maybe we could start with protocol?"

"Protocol?" That was the last thing he'd been expecting. It wasn't a bad place to start for a brand new sub, but it seemed like a strange request from the self-assured guy bristling with energy "Sure, we can do that. Let me just clarify what you're asking for. A little hands-off training?"

"You can touch me, just maybe not..."

"Take a whip to you? Fuck you?"

"Maybe not either of those things."

Pity about the fucking, but Cash would live within the boundaries he'd been set. And if kneeling made Harrison dazey-eyed, then he would enjoy seeing it.

"I'd like it if you stripped down to your underwear, if you're comfortable with that. If not, I'll work around it."

Harrison reached for the hem of his t-shirt.

"Hang on. I didn't say do it now. Just checking limits. Protocol means that once we get going, I'll be giving orders and you'll be following them, so weigh in now on what kind of orders you want me to give."

"I can't change my mind?"

"Of course you can. That's what safewords are for. But you don't want to be safe-wording out of everything I say. That's not protocol. And you don't want to be resisting me the whole way either."

Which was exactly what Harrison looked to be on the verge of doing. His hands were curled into tight fists, and a determined expression sat hard on his face. It wasn't the expression of someone happily anticipating what was about to happen. More like someone steeling himself to endure it. Either Cash was way off about what Harrison would enjoy or *Harrison* was. Logic suggested it must be Cash who was wrong, so he forged ahead.

He talked Harrison through using stoplight colors. No one ever needed to safeword out of his scenes because his only intention was to give his partner exactly the experience they wanted, but it was better to be safe than sorry. Then he went over some standard commands and responses— the whole yes-sir, no-sir, count your strokes nonsense he didn't care much about but was what Harrison had asked for.

Finally, he delved into his toy chest and found a super-soft flogger he could use to demonstrate flogging protocol without causing any actual pain. He gave it to Harrison to handle so he could get comfortable with the idea of having it applied to him, standing over him as he ran the soft brushed-leather strands through his fingers.

"Why even make a flogger that doesn't hurt?" Harrison asked when he'd satisfied himself that it wouldn't with a few test swipes across his thighs.

"It can be used for a warm-up. Or the way we're going to use it—sort of symbolically. But it *would* hurt if I kept going long enough. More like an uncomfortable warmth than a sharp sting, but the sensation would approach pain. Some people just like the way the leather feels."

Cash took the flogger back. He trailed its tails over Harrison's forearm a few times, brushing back and forth without any pressure. The hair on the back of Harrison's arm bristled, and his skin puckered tight. Harrison pulled his arm away from the flogger and gave it a brisk rub with his other hand.

"Too much?"

"No, just... weird. Makes me— I don't know."

Horny was the word that came to mind. Harrison's disinterested wariness had dropped away. His eyes followed the flogger as Cash set it down on the coffee table, watching it like he wanted it back. Cash filed the reaction the way he filed every reaction his subs had. Some went under the heading "avoid," others under the heading "repeat," and a third set landed under the heading "save to be relished in private later."

Harrison's shudder had only risen to the level of *repeat*, but Cash had a feeling he could elicit a category-three response with the right moves. Harrison was so beautifully reactive, as if his nerve endings lived very close to the surface. Cash ran a finger down the ruffled hairs on the back of his forearm and, yep, another shudder.

Now seemed like a good time to get him undressed. During a play session, Cash monitored a variety of vital signs to gauge his sub's arousal level—pupil dilation, pulse, breathing, skin tone—but cocks were the best indicator of arousal nature had ever invented, and you couldn't hide what your cock was up to once you were down to your shorts.

He set Harrison on his feet, moving the coffee table out of the way to stand him in front of the loveseat, then took a relaxed attitude against the cushions. He spread his arms wide and summoned a convincingly dominant attitude. He knew how to put on a good show, how to make a submissive tremble and twist—eager to please him and desperate to be pleased. It was all in the tone of his voice and the way he took up space—a certain careless command, the expectation of obedience.

"Strip," he ordered with a snap of his finger. "Stop," he said immediately when Harrison reached for the hem of his shirt without giving the proper response. "What do you say?"

Harrison did something with his face that looked a lot like he was trying to keep from rolling his eyes. "Yes, sir."

"All right, let's try that again. Strip."

"Yes, sir," Harrison said dutifully. Petulantly even.

Cash raised an eyebrow at him. "Try harder. We'll keep doing this until you get it right."

"Yes, sir!" That one was just plain mocking.

"Harrison?" Cash put his Dom voice away. "Do you really want to be doing this?"

38

"Yes." That hadn't been a lie. Harrison really wanted to be doing this. Odd, considering he seemed to hate it. "Sorry, sir. I'll do better."

Cash almost believed him. "All right. Last try. Strip."

"Yes, sir."

Close enough, though if Cash were a real Dom, he doubted he'd be satisfied. But he didn't stop Harrison this time when he reached for the hem of his shirt. He was too eager to get Harrison undressed—to see what was going on under his clothes. Was this turning him on? Maybe he had a disobedience fetish.

Beneath the shirt, Harrison's chest was pale white, several shades lighter than the skin on his neck. Either he didn't get outside a lot or he kept his shirt on while he was there. But his torso was worth looking at despite the lack of color—his stomach flat, his chest hair dark and neatly contained between his pecs. A trail of it led down his chest to disappear into his low-slung jeans.

"Keep going?" Harrison asked.

Cash fixed him with a look, giving him a moment to figure out where he'd gone wrong.

"Should I keep going, *sir*?" Harrison corrected.

"Let's see what you've got." He gave Harrison a doubtful look, checking for a humiliation kink. Since Harrison seemed determined to do this badly, maybe that was the point.

Harrison reached gracelessly for the button on his jeans. He flipped it open and slid down the zipper, then gave his jeans a yank. He wore boxers beneath—the old-fashioned kind, not boxer briefs—and they threatened to go with the jeans. The points of his hips flashed before he yanked the boxers back up with one hand while continuing to shove his jeans down with the other.

His pants jammed up against his shoes, which he kicked off with all the formality of having just gotten home from a long day of work. One of them skidded forward to ricochet off Cash's shin. Cash picked it up and set it to the side, favoring Harrison with a particularly disapproving look.

"Sorry." Pause. "Sir. Sorry, sir."

Cash could tell he wasn't really sorry. He stood there in black boxers decorated with red and white paisley swoops and a pair of ankle-height black socks in full defiance of any authority Cash might claim to have over him. Undressed, but not quelled. His calves were shapely, coated in the same dark hair as his forearms. His knees were a little knobby, but his thighs made up for them. Those were some kick-ass thighs. Someone wasn't neglecting leg day.

Above the kick-ass thighs, where Cash might expect a hard cock to distend the paisley boxers, there was mostly flat fabric—enough of a bulge to suggest there was something under it, but not enough to suggest that the something was interested. Which meant that as attractive as the man in front of Cash was, Cash was going to struggle to get into the scene. Because if his partner wasn't into it, then neither was he.

He ordered Harrison to his knees, then rose to circle him, doing the inspection thing that could send both exhibitionists and people with a shame kink flying. In Harrison, it produced only reluctant compliance. He assumed the positions Cash ordered him into—separating his knees or bringing them together, touching his head to the ground in subservience or bending it back to expose his throat. And oh, he didn't like that one *at all*. Posing wasn't Harrison's thing.

Obeying orders didn't seem to his thing either. The soft sack of paisley cloth between his legs remained small and loose. Harrison's eyes were little more than angry slits, and what pupil Cash could make out was as tight and flat as his abs. It was time to change activities. Cash didn't know what activity to do next, but it needed to be something that would provoke a response other than constrained fury. Because right now, Harrison was the least-interested sub in the world. And that left Cash just as disinterested.

The only time Harrison had shown a spark of true interest was when he'd been toying with the flogger, so Cash got him on his feet and brought him over to the wall, arranging him so he was leaning forward lightly in a standing push-up position. He maneuvered Harrison's body with his hands rather than his voice, trying to rub some warmth into his skin, to wake it up the way it'd been on the couch earlier, and Harrison softened a little, letting himself be positioned.

"I'm going to use this on you now." He draped the flogger's tresses over Harrison's shoulder until they tickled at his nipple. Harrison twitched, and the nipple pebbled. That was more like it. "After each stroke, do like I taught you. One sir, thank you sir."

They'd gone over it earlier, but Harrison wasn't proving to be a quick study, despite his obvious intelligence.

"Yes, sir," he said now, a light hitch in his voice as if he were finally something other than bored and restless. A guy like this, so full of energy—he needed a more active scene. Stillness got some people hot, but Cash had a feeling he would get further with Harrison using motion. He pressed a hand flat against Harrison's back to remind him to maintain position, then stepped away to give himself enough room to swing the flogger.

One very carefully applied stroke—right shoulder across to left ribcage—then a pause.

"One, sir. Thank you, sir." Rote, but right.

A second stroke, just as light, moving left to right this time, and another stilted response. Harrison's back broadened as Cash continued. He stopped hunching forward protectively, started arching into the trail of leather across his skin. His verbal responses grew less precise, slower and more mumbled, until they stopped coming altogether.

"Harrison?" Cash prompted.

An exasperated huff and then: "Fine. Sixteen."

Cash put down the flogger. For a moment, he'd thought

41

they were getting somewhere. "This isn't working for you, is it?"

"What do you mean?" Harrison spun around, breaking position without a moment's thought about why he shouldn't. He was rocking a bit of a chubby now, but he wasn't anywhere near subspace.

"What I mean is you asked me for protocol, but I don't think you really want protocol. You were enjoying the flogger a bit." He flicked it toward Harrison so the strands fanned across his stomach and cascaded over that mild bulge. "But not the scene."

Harrison chewed at his lip before muttering, "Sorry."

"No need to apologize. You like what you like, but this isn't it, so I'm not sure why you asked for it. If what you like is to be forced to do things you *don't* like, I can point you to some Doms who enjoy that kind of scene, but I'm not one of them."

"I'll make you tea," Harrison blurted out.

Tea? Cash didn't even know if he had tea. Someone had filled Harrison's mind with a certain version of BDSM that didn't mesh at all with his personality, but fine. They could try service.

"There are some grapes in the fridge. You can feed them to me if that's something you think you'd enjoy."

It *wouldn't* be something Harrison enjoyed. Cash could tell from the way he stomped off to the kitchenette. Cash took a seat in one of his furry moon chairs, and Harrison got down on his knees next to him with the colander of grapes, doing a decent job with the "kneel up" position Cash had taught him. Then he immediately ruined the effect by trying to cram a grape into Cash's mouth, as if Cash were a recalcitrant toddler. Cash jerked his head away to avoid the next incoming grape. Enough was enough.

"You're not submissive."

"Says who?"

"Fine, you're submissive. I don't get to decide that for you. But if you're submissive, then we're really incompatible because I sure as hell can't bring it out in you." He rubbed his chest, as if the ache he felt there were a physical thing, not the accustomed sensation of having his hopes dashed yet again.

He was disappointed. And worse, he'd disappointed Harrison, who might not have been excited by their scene but who looked devastated to have it end.

Harrison rocked back on his heels and splayed his knees in an ungainly posture. "Don't say that," he pleaded. "We can make this work."

Cash couldn't understand why Harrison sounded so desperate. They weren't ending a long-term relationship here. It was just a scene, and not even a good one. "I'll find you someone else to work with."

"No." Harrison grabbed his wrist like he could force him into continuing. The gesture confirmed his total lack of submission, but there was no doubting the sincerity behind it.

"I don't get it," Cash protested as he gently twisted his wrist free. "What am I missing? Help me out here."

43

Chapter 5 Harrison

Shit. He'd fucked this up. Now Cash didn't want him, and he would have to start over with trying to wrangle a way into Hell's Bedroom when Arlo might be in who knew what kind of awful situation. Harrison sure as hell hadn't been able to find him on the streets of Boston. Hell's Bedroom was his best and only clue, which meant he needed to get in there yesterday, not dick around trying to arrange another so-called playdate.

On top of being frustrated with himself for slowing down the investigation, he felt an unexpected tug of hurt from losing Cash's interest. He'd been doing his best. Kind of. Okay, not a lot. He hated all that kneeling shit. Hated it too much to fake liking it, apparently.

The only thing he'd been able to get into was the flogger. *That* he wouldn't mind more of, but he wanted to be able to sink into it, to lose himself in it—let the textured strands of black leather rain over him like a hot shower on a cool day and revel in Cash's painstaking attention until his brain went as loose as his body, not be all blah blah blah, counting strokes like a trained animal. And he especially didn't want to call anyone sir.

But he really, really needed Cash to get him into the club, and it wasn't like he could say so outright. The most he could do was be a tiny bit more honest than he had been.

"I might not be super submissive."

"Yeah, I figured that out."

"I'm a fighter, always have been. And somewhere between loner and leader. That's how I ended up in the job, I guess."

"How much fighting goes on at a tattoo studio?"

Shit. He'd forgotten about the cover story he'd fed Cash. "Somebody's got to keep the rowdy customers in line." His sister—the one who really owned a tattoo parlor—was always complaining about having to toss drunk college kids out of her store. "And there are others artists at the shop where I work. I guess you could say I'm their boss."

Cash nodded thoughtfully. "Is that why you wanted to try subbing? Some people with leadership roles enjoy the chance to let go of power."

"It was worth a try," Harrison said with a shrug, though he hadn't had any illusions about wanting to submit. When he watched videos of guys getting flogged, the visuals got him hard, but when he turned the sound on, heard all that *one, sir* shit, he got so soft he might as well be watching hetero porn.

"Well, it never hurts to try," Cash said, "but it's obviously a no." He said it definitively, as if he'd been right there in Harrison's body with him, feeling how much of a no that'd been. "I've never seen anyone less into submitting."

Harrison staggered to his feet—fuck this kneeling thing, he was too old for kneeling—and moved over to the loveseat where they'd started the evening, sagging into a comfortable sprawl. No point playing at being submissive when Cash could so easily see he wasn't. He still needed to figure out how to get into the club though.

"What about the other letters in BDSM? The ones that don't stand for dominant and submissive."

"Actually, none of them stand for dominant and submissive. BDSM stands for bondage, discipline, sadism and masochism. Sometimes you'll hear the term D/s, and in that case, the D is for domination and the s is for submission, but there are plenty of ways to play that don't require submission."

"Yeah?"

"I'd be fine with sex that didn't include any power exchange at all, as long as you were into it." Cash came over to sit on the loveseat next to him, but he left as much space between them as possible. "Next move has to be yours though. You're in your shorts, you're in my space, and I've been bossing you around in ways that did nothing for you for over an hour. It's your turn to set the rules."

So they could just fuck around? The offer would be tempting if Cash weren't a literal suspect. Besides, vanilla sex wouldn't get him into Hell's Bedroom. He needed to be kinky.

"How about bondage?" That was one of the four letters Cash had reeled off.

"Not here. Never let a stranger tie you up in their house."

Jackpot! "Not here" was the perfect answer. "Could we do it at that club you belong to? What was the name of it again?"

"Hell's Bedroom," Cash supplied. Which, of course, Harrison knew. "Sure, if you want to try. I'm not convinced bondage is going to be your thing though. Have you considered masochism?" Cash looked at him like he could see right into his soul.

"Why, um... what makes you ask that?"

"Just an idea I had." Cash floated his hand up to Harrison's chest. His fingers hovered over a nipple. "May I?"

Harrison meant to say no, but somehow he nodded instead. Firm fingers, cool and dry, closed around his nipple and pinched. Harrison's mouth gaped open from the lungful of air he sucked in as a swirl of pain rushed straight from those fingers to his groin. Cash's fingers pinched harder, and then all Harrison's air was gone.

"That's what I thought." Cash ran his fingernail over the bud he'd trapped, scoring it sharply. "You have no idea how gorgeous you are right now." Cash eyed him with avid curiosity as he toyed and teased, sparking sharp pings of arousal that ricocheted through Harrison's body like fireflies until he couldn't hold himself upright anymore. He slumped forward, not wanting Cash to stop but needing support. He even tried to say as much, to say something like "don't stop," but all that came out was a whimper.

"It's okay," Cash murmured consolingly, as he did that trick with his fingernail again. "I've got you." He tilted Harrison's body so he could latch his mouth onto his other nipple.

Ah! Teeth. Fuck. So sharp and bitey, so exquisitely good. Harrison's body vibrated as his hands groped blindly over Cash's arms. He hadn't understood it could be like this. He'd suspected, even hoped, had seen glimpses of it under Sir Magnus's whip, but he hadn't understood. Not really. Understanding was coming now. *He* was coming now.

"Cash!" he pleaded, not sure what for. "I'm going to—"

"Go ahead." Cash had to stop using his teeth so he could talk, which backed Harrison off from the edge he'd been about to tumble over. "Can you come from this? Give yourself a hand if you need more."

Harrison yanked Cash's face into his chest because what he needed more of were those teeth, the spiky points of pain that balanced the duller ache on his other side. When Cash latched on again and the pain bloomed hot and urgent, Harrison shoved a hand into his boxers and came instantly. His orgasm wracked him and wrecked him. There were tears in his eyes and come all over his hand. His left nipple tingled with each now-gentle swipe of Cash's tongue, and his right nipple was purple from the blood that'd been trapped in it by Cash's pinching fingers. It slowly expanded back to its normal shape when Cash released it. Holy hell.

"Stay there." Cash gave the restored nipple a loving kiss, then went away and came back with a damp cloth. "I could clean you up," he offered. "Or if you'd rather do it yourself..."

Harrison took the cloth and stuffed it into his boxers to swipe at the mess he'd made, keeping his gaze well away from Cash's. What had just happened, and how they were supposed to move on from it? He ought to reciprocate, right? An orgasm delivered required an orgasm be returned. On the other hand, he was working here. Not that anyone was paying him exactly.

"I can see where your mind is going," Cash said, "but don't worry about it. I liked making you come. That's kind of my kink."

"You get off on being nice?"

"Not exactly." Cash disappeared into the kitchen with the used cloth, talking over his shoulder as he went. "If my kink was being nice, I'd do volunteer work. I mean, I *do* do volunteer work, but there's nothing sexual about it. I'm a literacy volunteer down at the library. They've got a program where—"

"I feel like we're getting off track," Harrison interrupted. "You were explaining your kink, which I assume isn't literacy."

"Right." Cash came back into the room with two beers.

He held one out, and after a moment's hesitation, Harrison took it. He'd already had sex on the job. Might as well top it off by drinking on the job.

Cash clinked their bottles together and said, "Here's to orgasms," before taking a swig from his. "My kink is vicarphilia."

"Vicarphilia." Now that was something he'd never heard of. "You're into British priests?"

Cash laughed. "I'm not necessarily *anti*-British priests. Depends on the priest. But no. The vicar part comes from vicarious. Basically, I get aroused by other people's arousal. If they get off, I get off.

"That's all it takes? Someone else has an orgasm and you just... boom?"

"No, it usually requires a little physical stimulation too. I was"—Cash made a jerking motion with his hand—"while

48

you were. You were just too wrapped up in yourself to notice."

"Sorry."

"Hey, no. I was wrapped up in you too. That was amazing. You were amazing. I love sending my partner sky-high like that. It's what attracted me to the scene in the first place. I was dating someone who asked if we could kink it up a little. I didn't think it was for me until I saw how into it he got. Making people hot is my thing."

"Nice for your partner."

"Well." Cash's face fell in a way Harrison didn't understand.

That was a compliment, what he'd just said. If all Cash wanted to do was make a guy come using whatever techniques that guy liked best, he was the definition of a perfect partner in Harrison's opinion. Someone had obviously hurt him in the past, and Harrison didn't like the thought of that much.

"Anyway." Cash brightened back up. "I'm glad you enjoyed it. I'll be replaying that scene for the next few nights. And I'd love to help you figure out more about what really does it for you."

Harrison looked down at the still-sensitive points on his chest. "It would seem I'm a masochist." He'd always known it. He just wasn't comfortable with it.

"You might be," Cash said. "Or you might be a sensualist, which is someone who enjoys various sensations, not exclusively pain—anything that stimulates nerve endings and generates endorphins. You like being touched, don't you?" Cash traced a beer-cold finger down the fur of Harrison's forearm, making him shiver.

"Touch is good." Nothing had ever felt like what Cash had just done to him though. He wanted to tell Cash as much—admit how absolutely astounding that'd been and beg him to do it again—but sex wasn't what he was here for.

"It's a matter of degree," Cash said, settling back more

49

comfortably against the cushions. "More intense stimulation generates more sensation, but it doesn't all have to be pain. There are lots of ways to do sensation play. Tickling, temperature variations, pressure. I'm not convinced about bondage for you though."

"No, I want to try." Bondage was what would get him into Hell's Bedroom, so bondage it had to be, though he suspected Cash was right. Cash had a habit of being right when it came to him.

"I'll do it if you want," Cash said with an easy shrug. "I aim to please. Now, what do you need in the way of aftercare? We could call what we just did sex and have a snuggle, or we could say it was a scene, in which case you deserve some pampering."

"I should get going."

He hated how disappointed Cash looked at that answer, but snuggling was definitely going too far, and aftercare sounded like something for submissives, which they'd just established he wasn't one of. It was a relief to have the truth out there. Whatever lies he might need to tell Cash, he was grateful that calling him sir wouldn't be one of them. Because that had felt like the biggest lie of all.

"Or we could have a second round." Cash smoothed a hand over Harrison's still-bare chest, triggering another rush of sensation.

Cash was fully dressed, which Harrison decided was another thing he didn't like about this whole dominance and submission business. Why was he the only one in his undershorts? Cash had a nice body beneath those clothes, Harrison could tell, and he'd missed seeing it. The guy hadn't even gotten his fly open. Next time...

Well, next time they'd be at Hell's Bedroom where he'd have to be Harry. Let himself be pushed around, let himself be stripped, let himself be tied up.

"Hey." Cash put a hand under his chin and tilted it up to look into his eyes. "We're not going to do anything you don't want to do. Including this."

"No, this is okay. I mean, I should get going, but I don't mind you touching me." Not at all.

"Then what?"

"At the club, for the bondage... how would that go?"

"You get to have a say in that, you know. It's not just my decision. But a simple bondage scene might involve a supported standing pose. Or you could be on your knees."

"*Not* on my knees," he said before he could stop himself.

"Not on your knees then. That was traumatizing, wasn't it?"

Cash laughed like it was a joke they shared. He leaned in with an intention Harrison could see in the twinkle of his eyes and the purse of his lips. Harrison found himself drawn toward those eyes, entranced by those lips, ready for the offered kiss, but he jerked his head away before it landed.

No more kissing, no more snuggling. This was a job. His focus should be first on finding Arlo and second on not draining his own bank account to do it. Which meant getting in and out without any entanglements.

"Gotta go." He hopped to his feet and was halfway to the door before he remembered he should set a date for their trip to the club. And also that he was still in his boxers. "What's a good day for you? For the bondage thing." He fished his phone out of his discarded jeans and made a production of checking his calendar, pretending not to notice that he'd hurt Cash's feelings by ducking away from that kiss.

This is a job, he reminded himself. *An important one.*

And Cash was a good sport. Harrison had lucked out. Really. He would have to tell Tripp how right he'd been about Cash being the perfect Dom for him, because Tripp had acted like there was something wrong with Cash, and there was nothing wrong with Cash. But he wasn't a date. He was a job.

51

Chapter 6 Cash

"This is going to be fun, San."

Cash snuggled his head deeper into Sandi's welcoming lap as she scritched her sharp-tipped nails over his scalp. She'd just had them painted a luminescent pearl pink, and they felt even better than they looked. He loved having his head rubbed, and Sandi was the only one who ever did it for him now that he was too old to crawl into his mother's lap.

He sighed, happy about the scene he'd had with Harrison a few days ago and happy to be where he was now—stretched out on Sandi's plush couch.

"He's a complete neophyte. Never tried any of it. And if the way he reacted the other day is any indication, there's a lot more coming."

"Coming," Sandi repeated with a snort. They might be approaching middle age, but Sandi still had the same sense of humor she'd had when they'd met at nineteen. He could count on her for both cuddles and laughs.

It was a shame Harrison had bailed on the cuddles, but the rest of the scene had gone so well Cash refused to dwell on it. Well, not the *whole* rest of the scene, but the honest part, the part where he'd managed to unlock Harrison's chest of secrets and pull a few things out. He hoped Harrison had a huge-ass chest full of just everything and that he would let Cash keep unpacking it.

"Don't get ahead of yourself with the feelings," Sandi warned with a light rap of her knuckles on his forehead.

"Remember you told me there was something wonky about him."

He had. After the party, when his head had been full of Harrison but also full of questions, he'd swung by her place to spill it all out to her, and she'd listened like she always did, with humor and hugs. Cash's kink meant he tended to be the caretaking partner in his sexual relationships, so Sandi was a crucial part of his self-care—the person he turned to when he needed to be selfish.

"I knew there was something off about him," he agreed now, "but that's all been figured out. His name is Harrison, not Harry, and he might be a masochist, but he's definitely not a sub."

"Why though?"

"He doesn't need a reason to be who he is."

"I mean why lie about it? Why say your name is Harry if it's Harrison? Why go through the whole rigamarole of dressing up in a collar if you can't stand the thought of getting on your knees?"

"Stop being rational. I'm trying to have happy thoughts here. Maybe this time..."

He wanted more than a play partner, more than a hot scene here and there. Sexually, his love life was great. Being part of the kink community meant he had innumerable opportunities to witness people in the throes of desperate arousal. He didn't even have to take part in the scenes to enjoy them, although it was better when he did—more personal. There was always a demo going on, something to watch, someone who wanted to be watched. He could feed off their arousal while they fed off his. Sexually, his life was a smorgasbord.

But he'd been eating buffet food for a lot of years now, and the appeal of quick-and-easy had worn off. He wanted someone he could take home and enjoy at leisure. Someone who was his—both in and out of the bedroom. Not someone he only got to borrow for the night because he knew how to tie a knot or work a sounding rod.

"Honey." Sandi's hand stroked down the side of his cheek.

"I'm getting ahead of myself again, aren't I?"

"I don't know what's wrong with these people. You give them everything."

What was wrong was that he wasn't a Dom. He only *acted* like a Dom. His lovers started out happy enough, appreciating his skills and the way he used them, but eventually they started complaining that something was missing. Something big enough that they moved on.

"I get it," he told Sandi, because he couldn't begrudge anyone for trying to find what they wanted, whether it be true love, a soulmate, or just the perfect kink matchup. "If your kink is submitting to someone else's will, then that person has to actually *have* a will." And he didn't.

He could put guys on their knees all day, and if kneeling made them breathless and red-faced, made their eyelids sag and their pupils blow, then he would never get tired of doing it. But if his partner didn't want to kneel, then fuck if he was going to make them. Kneel, stand. He didn't care.

And that right there was the problem. He couldn't pretend that being called sir did something special to his cock—or to his ego. He couldn't chortle with glee at the prospect of punishing a submissive's slip or take pride in having a perfectly behaved slave crawling at his heel. No offense to people who enjoyed that sort of thing, of course. He was down with whatever. But it was his very willingness to be down with whatever that disqualified him in most submissives' eyes.

"But Harrison's not like that," he reminded Sandi. "He doesn't want to be dominated, only topped, which I can do. This might work."

"I hope so." She bent down to drop a kiss on his forehead, and her ample breasts swung forward to tap him on the cheek before she straightened back up. "You deserve love, honey. It's not your fault men are trash."

"If men are trash, why do we both date them?"

"Lord help me if I know. It's the best argument for sexual orientation being born into us I've ever heard. I'd be a happy lesbian, let me tell you. I'd wear yoga pants and watch the Hallmark Channel and never worry about another thing."

"Do lesbians watch the Hallmark Channel? Isn't that aimed at straight women?"

"Women are women. We like love."

"Well, so do I." He knew he shouldn't get his hopes up about Harrison, but goddamn. Everything about the man was delectable, from the buzzing energy of his personality to the intensity of that orgasm he'd had. Those pebbled nipples eager for his nails and teeth, the hard length hidden behind his sedate boxers, the sexy tangle of tattoos running down his arms. Harrison was perfect, and Cash was already lost.

It was a shame people couldn't pick who they were attracted to. Men weren't really trash, of course. That was a joke and probably a bad one. Truth was, he'd never minded being gay—what with the whole being attracted to men thing—but it was too bad he couldn't be attracted to his best friend, with her soft curves and flowing red hair, instead of to a restless, buff stranger with challenging green eyes.

Cash had bonded with Sandi in Freshman Composition when a TA with a stick up his ass had insisted on using everyone's full and legal name. Cassius and Cassandra—both of them cursed by fanciful parents to carry around names bigger than their personalities. They'd sworn to alibi each other if the TA ever turned up missing and had been partners in thought-crime ever since.

Even at nineteen, Sandi had been maternal. She hadn't blinked at the big reveal of his sexuality, and when he started exploring the wide world of kink, she didn't blink at that either. They'd been out of college by then, Cash in his first serious relationship getting his eyes opened in a big way.

He'd been instantly hooked. Well, not instantly. When John had draped himself over his knee, he'd been uncertain at first, had felt foolish bringing his hand down on his boyfriend's shapely unmarked ass, had felt cruel when John thrashed and squeaked and acted as if he wanted him to stop. He *had* stopped—because he wasn't cruel, couldn't be. But once all the frenzied motion died down, he noticed what he'd been too freaked out to notice before—the hard dig of John's erection into his thigh and the fact that John's thrashing had been an attempt to rub off on him.

And that'd changed everything. He'd reapplied himself to John's ass with a vigor that made him wince in retrospect. They hadn't discussed limits, safewords, anything. He'd been a complete neophyte, and John's experience had been limited to a few light spankings, but Cash had educated himself fast after that, had learned everything John needed him to know, only to lose him to a "real" Dom after they found the scene and John discovered himself.

Well, Cash had discovered himself too. He didn't need power exchange to enjoy sex, but when he was able to send someone past aroused right into the stratosphere? Nothing beat that. Nothing.

"Hey." Sandi gave his forehead an experimental tap. "Don't fall asleep on me. You promised me dinner." Sandi's maternal nature didn't extend to cooking. That was his job.

"I wasn't sleeping. Day dreaming, maybe."

"I'm glad you've got someone to sigh over, honey. I hope he turns out to be worth it. But you hear that growling?"

With his head in her lap, he could hardly miss it. He got to his feet as commanded. "Give me half an hour." He dropped a kiss on top of her head, then trotted down the stairs to his apartment. He loved everything about his place, but especially the garden and the fact that Sandi was right above him.

"Hey, Moo Moo." His cat was waiting for him at the door when he opened it. "You're hungry too, aren't you? Come on, we'll do you first."

Mr. Moo followed him with something that looked like obedience but was really command. It was dinner time, and he would be fed. Even with his cat, Cash played service top. His ownership of the black-and-white junior king-of-the-jungle was in name only. Mr. Moo knew who owned who.

"I'm working on it," he complained when Mr. Moo tried to trip him as he moved from refrigerator to counter. "You'd think you didn't have a bowl full of food already." But not wet food. Not the good stuff. Cash tapped a tablespoon of wet food into Mr. Moo's dish and stood back, spoon in hand while the cat devoured it.

"If you didn't butt your head in there so fast, I could dish up the whole thing at once."

As usual, Mr. Moo ignored his entirely valid point, thoroughly wolfing down the first spoonful before turning his head up to insist that his second serving be delivered.

"All right, that's all you're getting." Cash tapped out another spoonful and put the rest of the can back in the refrigerator. He diced up a hunk of cheese and placed it on the plate in the corner for Ellie, then washed his hands and set to prepping dinner, a whistle on his lips and his mind on what he was going to do to Harrison next Saturday.

He still had his doubts about bondage. There was so much energy in the guy that Cash couldn't imagine him being still like that. And while some people appreciated enforced stillness, he couldn't see Harrison enjoying enforced anything. But there was no doubt Harrison was excited for their scene. He'd pushed hard to schedule it ASAP, frowning when Cash wasn't able to work it into his schedule for a whole week.

Maybe Harrison was just eager to see him again. Cash smiled at the thought, but his mind immediately corrected his optimistic assessment. Harrison had been angling to get into Hell's Bedroom from the very beginning, and the more cynical part of Cash—the part he tried to keep tamed because life wasn't fun when you looked at everything from the worst possible perspective—said Harrison was only using him as an entrée, that as soon as Harrison made contact with other people in the scene he would jump ship to someone who suited him better. The way John had.

Cash shook the thought off. It would be good to get down to the club again regardless. He paid dues every month—a not insignificant part of his discretionary income—and he hadn't been getting his money's worth lately. Since the previous owners had sold out to a corporate conglomerate a year ago, the vibe had changed. There were fewer people he recognized, less a sense of community and more a sterile cookie-cutter feel. Not for the first time, he considered canceling his membership. Maybe there was a better way to meet the man of his dreams.

"All done?" he asked Mr. Moo when the cat stalked off without so much as a thank you. Ingrate. He picked up the saucer from which Mr. Moo ate his daily ration of wet food and dumped it into the sink along with the bowl he'd used to mix up his gourmet hamburger blend, though the word hamburger was an insult to his patented patties made from ground sirloin and savory spices and grilled to a dripping-red perfection.

His phone buzzed while he was firing up the grill, and he fished it out to see Harrison had texted.

"Can I ask you something?"

Resisting the urge to make a smart reply—because he could sense Harrison's hesitancy in the formal text—he texted back "always." His phone rang almost instantly.

"It's about the dress code," Harrison said without preamble.

"There isn't a dress code."

"I'm not a sub, but I'm *playing* the sub, right? So does that mean, um…? You're going to tie me up, right? So…?"

"Just say what you want to say."

"Do I have to get naked?"

"No. Is that definite enough for you? You can strip down to your shorts, like you did the other day, or you can stay all the way dressed. The rope doesn't care what you're wearing, and I can work around whatever you have on."

"But people will be expecting—"

"Fuck people."

"I don't want to stand out."

"Really?"

The guy had a wild splash of tattoos down both arms and an attitude that said *mess with me and I'll fuck you up.* But when Harrison didn't answer, Cash softened.

"Generally speaking, male subs are shirtless and barefoot. There's no rule, but if you want to blend in, that would do it. You don't need a collar because no one owns you, and you can leave your pants on or take them off. You'll see plenty of both."

"Thanks. I just wasn't sure what to expect."

"There's a wide range of experiences, and they're all valid. You'll likely see some pretty far-out costumes. Full nudity, pony tails attached to butt plugs, hoods and gags and leashes, leather and vinyl and sequins and sparkles." Last week, Cash had played voyeur for a sub with fake fur wrist cuffs and an exhibition kink. "But you'll also see guys who look just like you in jeans and crew cuts. And you'll be with me. Which means it doesn't matter what anyone else thinks. If you please me, that's all you've gotta do. And Harrison? You please me, okay? However you are, I like it."

A soft wash of breath came over the line. "Sorry. Mini panic attack."

"It's all right. I'm happy to answer any questions you have. And remember, I'm going to be right there with you."

"Yeah. It'll be fine. I'm looking forward to it." Harrison rang off with no more leave-taking than there'd been greeting, leaving Cash staring at his phone in bemusement. Harrison was the worst sub ever. Which meant maybe Cash could keep him.

Chapter 7 Harrison

"Out of the chair," Taylor ordered. "I'm trying to clean that."

Harrison picked his ass up out of his sister's tattoo chair. "There's nowhere else to sit."

"Because it's my place of business, not your living room." She shooed him farther away from the chair, then attacked it with a spray bottle of disinfectant.

He hitched a hip against the counter where her instruments were arrayed and crossed his arms over his chest, cataloguing her brisk movements. He was there to absorb tattoo parlor atmosphere, the better to fool Cash and anyone else he might need to feed his faked-up backstory to. Other than occasionally allowing Taylor to give him free ink, he didn't spend much time in her shop. The two of them had a relationship that worked better when it was infrequently exercised.

"Why are you hanging around here anyway?" she asked as she swiped at the disinfectant she'd just sprayed. "You got another project in mind?"

"Not at the moment." He didn't get tattoos for the sake of getting them—maybe because he had such free and easy access to them. He needed to be inspired, and nothing was inspiring him right now. Cash, on the other hand, was a blank slate apparently.

"Why then?" Taylor elbowed him out of the way as she worked around to the other side of the chair. Her work space was tiny, no bigger than it needed to be, everything at hand. It wasn't set up for visitors.

"Maybe I need moral support."

"And you're going to get that by annoying me? Why are you here, Harry?"

"Harrison," he corrected automatically. "You know I hate that."

"You call me Tay all the time."

"Because it's an abbreviated version of your name. Like if you called me Har."

"Hair is *this*." She gestured at the coiled mass of black piled high on her head. Taylor went for a goth vampire look complete with deep cleavage, burgundy bee-stung lips, and an extensive network of black tats. She really rocked it. "Harry is my little brother."

Little brother. She was only eleven months older than he was—Harrison being an oops-breast-feeding-isn't-birth-control-baby—but she'd worked every day of that age difference for every day of their lives. As a child, he'd eagerly anticipated the moment he would finally outgrow her, except that moment had never arrived. She was the same two inches taller than him she'd always been, making her tall for a woman at five-nine and him on the short side for a man at five-seven. It was only two inches, but it was never going away. No wonder he wasn't keen on submitting. People had been expecting him to do it his whole life.

"If you're done avoiding the question, you could answer it. What's going on? You need money?"

"Jesus, Taylor. I don't need money." Handling Arlo's case for free wasn't helping financially, but he wasn't as bad off as all that. "I'm just here to observe. I'm working undercover as a tattoo artist for a job I'm doing, and I'm trying to soak in enough atmosphere to fake it, if you must know."

"You're not giving anyone tattoos, are you?"

"No, I'm not giving anyone tattoos. It's a missing persons case. The tattoo thing is just my backstory. You have to have a backstory."

Taylor huffed out an unimpressed breath then made a barking noise that was a tic, not a commentary on his job. Felix, the African parrot who inhabited a perch over the reception counter, let loose with a string of expletives, cycling through the word fuck in all seven of the languages he could say it in.

Taylor's verbal tic was just a noise, not an obscenity. Despite the way the media portrayed Tourette's Syndrome most verbal tics *weren't* obscenities, but Felix's litany definitely was. She'd trained him to go off whenever she ticced so her noise would get lost in the resulting cacophony. It was easier on her to have people laughing at Felix's vocabulary than explain her condition to one customer after another.

When Felix stopped squawking, they both went on as though nothing had happened. Taylor's tics were old news.

"Is working undercover safe?" she asked with a frown.

"It's safe enough." He didn't know what kind of cesspit he was heading into, but he was old enough and street-wise enough to look after himself now. Besides, Arlo had cuddly curls and eyes so big he came across as an anime version of himself. If that was what you were looking for in a vic, Harrison was the last person you'd choose.

"Doesn't *sound* safe. Missing people, undercover."

"I'll have backup."

But Brixby wouldn't be in a position to help much. While Harrison had been in Cash's apartment, Brixby had been stationed at a café down the street pretending to enjoy a coffee drink while he waited for Harrison to emerge. If Harrison hadn't ever emerged, Brixby would've known who to blame for his disappearance, but it wasn't like he could've prevented Harrison from being raped or tortured, if that was what Cash had wanted to do.

The setup worried Brixby, which was why the two of them had an appointment with one of his department's techs the next morning, but it didn't worry Harrison.

Technically, he couldn't eliminate Cash as a suspect in Arlo's disappearance, but personally he'd already decided Cash had nothing to do with it.

"Fine," Taylor said with a huff. "Don't listen to me. As always." God, she worked that older sister routine so hard, as if she had some huge fount of elderly wisdom. "But if you're in my space to learn about tattoo parlors, then let's see you do something." She handed him the spray bottle and stripped off her black latex gloves.

"I can learn by watching."

"I don't think you can. Go on. Learn." She waved him toward the machinery she'd been wiping down, and he reluctantly took over with her watching him like a hawk to make sure he did it exactly to her specifications.

Taylor took her license seriously. She'd developed a new tic in her right shoulder just as she'd finished her apprentice hours and had painstakingly started over, teaching herself to work the tattoo machine with her left hand. He was proud of her for being a badass bitch, but sometimes he wished she could've been a little sister who needed him instead.

THE NEXT MORNING, HE MET BRIXBY on the sidewalk in front of the West End station. Brixby had his full uniform on, including mirrored sunglasses, and looked every inch the asshole cop, but he pulled off the glasses when Harrison came sauntering up and gave him a smile that overrode his height and breadth. Harrison had spent ten years on the force, but he'd never filled out his uniform this well. He was wiry rather than broad and too short to be physically intimidating, which was why he tried to make up for it with attitude. If there was one thing he'd learned growing up with Taylor, it was how to hold his own.

He shook Brixby's hand, then followed him into the cool interior. The precinct house was new, freshly built on the foundation of an old one where Harrison had once served himself. The new building was much more inhabitable—bright, airy, open, perfectly temperature-controlled, and clean—but it lacked the brick-and-ivy charm of the old one.

"Gina will figure something out for us," Brixby said as he rapped on a door before opening it to reveal an office that looked like a leftover from the old building. Bits of tech—jumbled and disassembled—were arrayed across a metal rack; paper folders were piled high enough to be a fire hazard on the two guest chairs; the desk was covered with the remains of several days' worth of lunches; and a coat rack held enough scarves and sweaters to outfit the entire precinct. The chair behind the desk was empty, aside from a pile of tiny screws, but a white woman stood next to it, removing more screws from a contraption Harrison couldn't name and adding them to the pile. Those screws were goners. He could see it already.

The woman didn't look up, but she did gesture them in with a flick of her hand. Her grey hair was pulled back in a severe ponytail, and a lollipop stick protruded from the corner of her mouth.

"Gina Harlow," Brixby said. "She's our tech guru. Gina, this is Harrison Fisher, a PI who's assisting us on one of our missing persons cases."

That was a good way to put it. Arlo's disappearance was as much Boston PD's problem as Harrison's. He stretched out a hand, which Gina acknowledged with a quick upward flick of her eyes.

"One sec," she said around the lollipop. "I've almost got this open."

"It's not a bomb, is it?" Brixby joked. At least, Harrison hoped he was joking.

"Probably not. Never know though, do you? There." She must have found the magic screw because the whole thing popped open to reveal a tangle of wires. She poked through them with the blade of her screwdriver, then gave the contraption a disappointed scowl. "Not a bomb. Oh well."

She swept the screws into a coffee mug and sat down. "Sit, sit. Just move whatever."

Harrison evaluated the mess on the chair closest to him and decided to stand. He didn't want to be responsible for disrupting what was obviously an elaborate filing system.

"Anyone want a lollipop? I've got a million of them. Ex-smoker, you know." She offered a wide bowl filled with Blow Pops, which they both declined. "What can I do for you?" she asked as she frowned into the bottom of her coffee cup like she expected it to contain coffee instead of screws.

"Fisher's gonna be working undercover inside a building I can't gain entry to. I need a way to track him. If he leaves the building, I want to know he left and be able to follow him."

"There are apps for that," Gina said with a dismissive wave.

"He's not going to have his phone on him." Brixby had already warned Harrison about that—that phones were generally prohibited inside a BDSM club. "No weapon either. He might not even have clothes." Brixby gave him a smirk, which he didn't bother to react to.

"We'll get you some booty shorts," Brixby had said when Harrison had asked him about the dress code. "A good compromise between subby and discreet."

Nothing about the Lycra booty shorts they'd picked out felt discreet to Harrison. He would be less provocative in his own underwear, which, by the way, wasn't going to fit under those shorts.

Gina didn't even raise an eyebrow at the fact that he might be naked, simply tapped her chin with a short-nailed finger. Her unpainted lips pursed above it. "Can he wear jewelry?"

"He could wear a collar," Brixby suggested.

"I don't want a collar." He fucking hated collars. "Jewelry works. What've you got?"

"Let's see. Something with GPS. Hmm." She rummaged through a trunk shaped like a pirate chest, except that what came out of it wasn't treasure but random gadgets. "Pretty sure I've got something in here. Aha!" She lifted a broach shaped like a sunflower. It was bright, yellow, and huge.

"That's, um, fancy," Harrison said. "Maybe something more masculine?"

With a mutter about outdated gender roles, Gina turned back to her magic box and resumed digging, but everything that came out was either techno-futuristic, like a Star Trek transponder, or oddly dated, like the sunflower broach.

"How about this?" Brixby reached under the neck of his uniform shirt and tugged out a chain, at the end of which a bronze medallion hung. "It's a Saint Michael's medal," he told Harrison, holding it out where he could see it. "Patron saint of emergency responders."

"It's got GPS?" Gina leaned forward to peer at it.

"No, of course not. But can't you move the GPS from that sunflower thing onto this?"

She took the medallion from him and brought it over to a bright halogen lamp in the corner. "Would make it heavier, but I could attach it to the back."

"I think I can manage it being heavier," Harrison said, relieved he wasn't going to have to pin a sunflower broach to his booty shorts. "You don't mind?" he asked Brixby. "It looks personal."

"My mom gave it to me when I joined the force, but it's there to provide protection, so let it provide protection."

"It's supposed to be protecting you, though."

"I'd rather protect you, Fisher. Let me do this."

Harrison didn't need to be protected, and he was tired of people trying to tell him what to do. Between Taylor and Brixby, he was surrounded by fucking Doms and he wasn't even at a BDSM club yet. Meanwhile, Gina was over in the corner with what looked like a soldering iron.

"She's going to ruin it," he warned Brixby.

"It'll be fine," Gina said with a dismissive shake of her head. A stream of dark smoke twirled up to the ceiling.

"Don't you love the smell of smoke?"

Um, no. Wood smoke, maybe, but not whatever toxic waste she had going on.

"I romance it sometimes," she said. "Like, wouldn't it be nice to have a cigarette?"

She turned off the soldering iron and held the pendant up by its chain. The medallion twisted freely, not looking much different from when Brixby had handed it over. Harrison reached for it, but Gina batted his hand away.

"It has to cool. I'll give it to you in a to-go container."

She shuffled through the food remains on her desk and came up with an aluminum tray holding the remnants of what might be enchiladas and a napkin that was only half soiled. She used the napkin to swipe at the food remains then dropped the pendant into the tray. "Bring it back when you're done with it, and I'll pop that disc off. It'll be good as new." She handed Harrison the aluminum tray like she expected him to hand her twelve-fifty back.

"That's a strange woman," he said when he and Brixby and their to-go container were out in the hallway.

"Yeah, but she knows her stuff. Look." Brixby held out his cell phone where the pendant registered as a dot on his tracking app. "Go somewhere, and I'll practice following you."

The metal had already cooled to a temperature that wasn't unpleasant, so Harrison fastened the chain around his neck. Gina's work was remarkably tidy considering the circumstances under which it'd been done, the chip adding a barely discernible thickness to the back of the medallion. He felt very James Bond wandering the crowded North End streets, mingling with tourists who were following Paul Revere's historic ride as Brixby followed him.

Finally he took a seat on a bench and texted Brixby to go away, wishing the medallion had an off button. Not that he had plans to rob a bank between now and tomorrow night, but he didn't need to be monitored, just like he didn't need to be protected.

Chapter 8 Cash

Harrison was dressed like, um, wow. He'd been hot in the leather pants he'd worn to the party, but those shorts were something else. Cash had meant it when he'd said Harrison could dress however, but Harrison was more concerned about fitting in than seemed in character for him.

Well, anyone might be nervous in a new situation. Cash made a point of telling Harrison how good he looked as Harrison stuffed his street clothes into the locker he'd been assigned along with his shoes and his phone, leaving just those shorts and a burnished bronze medallion.

"I like the medallion. Suits you better than the collar did."

"It's okay to keep it on, right?" Harrison fingered it nervously.

"I already told you—everything's all right. You don't like being controlled, so I'm not going to try to control you."

Harrison's shoulders dropped, the edgy tension he'd been brimming with dropping with them. "Thanks. I can't tell you how much this means to me."

It was one of those moments when he sounded a hundred percent sincere, reminding Cash that he didn't always.

"I'm going to enjoy it," Cash assured him. "Assuming you do. Come on, let me give you a quick tour, and then we'll figure out where to set up. Are you thinking more public or more private?" He led the way through the door onto the main floor of the club as Harrison pondered the question with his typical reticence.

"Public, I guess."

"There are a lot of stations in here." He pointed out various benches and pillories and connection points in the ceiling and floor as they roamed around the Center Ring of Hell, which was what they called the open space in the middle of the club.

"It's, um, different than I expected." Harrison's gaze darted around like he was trying to see everything at once.

Cash remembered how he'd felt the first time he'd come to a place like this—excited, but overwhelmed. There was a study hum of activity, punctuated by the harsh crack of a whip and the sharp screams of the whip's target coming from the St. Andrew's cross in the middle of the ring. Cash recognized the guy with the whip—a sadistic fuck named Sebastian, much sought after by the club's pain sluts. Cash could swing a whip as well as Sebastian, but he didn't get chased the same way.

Harrison was already feeling Sebastian's lure, apparently. He drifted forward, parting the circle of spectators to get a front row view. Cash wedged his way in behind him.

"We could do that," he offered.

"*That?*"

He couldn't tell if Harrison was horrified or intrigued. Not disgusted, at any rate. He hooked his chin over Harrison's shoulder to sight down his flat abdomen to the bulge his dick made in those skin-tight shorts. More intrigued than horrified, he decided. He put his hand on Harrison's stomach, and when Harrison didn't flinch away from it, he spread his fingers, claiming as much skin as he could touch.

"You might want to work up to a bullwhip, but yes. Something like that."

The whip cracked, the guy on the cross shrieked, and

Harrison's abdomen rippled as if he'd been struck himself.

"Maybe." Harrison swallowed like he had a mouthful of something he'd been chewing on. Cash brushed a kiss across his cheek. His skin was hot and a little damp. "I mean, I don't know. You were going to tie me up."

"We don't have to do that. We could just watch, even. You're enjoying this." He smoothed his hand a little lower, fingertips brushing under Harrison's waistband.

"No. I said I would." Harrison turned around, bringing their chests together. The warm bulge of his cock brushed against the top of Cash's thigh, but his expression had changed from excited to resigned. "Let's do it."

"Get it over with, you mean?" Because that was how it sounded. "Fine. Let's do it."

He found an overhead clip-in point on the edge of the outer ring, on the south side near the demo spaces which weren't in use at the moment. The location would minimize traffic, but not eliminate it entirely. He lowered the suspension point down to where Harrison could easily grab it, not wanting to challenge him with a physically stressful stance for his first experience, and positioned him under it while he unpacked his bag.

"It's green."

It took Cash a moment to realize Harrison was referring to the rope he'd brought, not giving a stoplight color. "Is that a problem?"

"No, just... I figured it'd be black. Or white."

"The green matches your eyes."

Harrison rolled the eyes in question. "Such a romantic."

"You have beautiful eyes." He went over and chucked Harrison under the chin, earning him another eyeroll. "Grab that handle up there. I'm going to wrap your chest up to your arms and then onto that point. The rope will help keep you upright, but you won't actually be suspended. Feet on the ground at all times."

"But I won't be able to let go?"

"Not once I've got you strung up. Are you okay with

that?"

Harrison nodded, but the bulge between his legs was nowhere near as prominent as when they'd been watching Sebastian flay the man on the cross. Once again, Cash didn't understand why they were doing what they were doing if it wasn't what Harrison really wanted. If Cash were a real Dom, he would insist on taking Harrison in a different direction, but as a service top, and one with a kink for pleasing his partner, he didn't have any experience dealing with a sub who was being coy about his tastes. So bondage it would be.

He started with Harrison's torso, wrapping him snugly, but not tightly enough to restrict his breathing. Ideally the lattice work would feel like a hug—comforting rather than punishing. It certainly looked pretty. He appreciated the beauty of Shibari and the meditative process of laying each strand so it was flush and tidy, plus the wrapping process allowed for plenty of skin to skin contact as he tweaked each placement.

Harrison's breathing was shallow, nervous, his skin a little pale, but he arched into the places Cash touched him. He was supposed to be standing still, not trying to guide Cash's hands with his body, but Cash didn't rebuke him, just held him, supported him, layered the rope with murmurs of praise. The lattice he was building crawled higher up Harrison's chest, then over his arms, straightening and supporting him, making him into a decorative offering that was nearly complete.

They weren't doing anything daring or interesting, weren't making any noise that extended beyond the tight circle of their focus on each other, and so they hadn't drawn any attention. The buzz of the club faded into the background as Harrison started to slip under, not into anything deep like subspace, but beneath the surface of his mind. His eyes flickered shut as he stopped trying to follow Cash's every move, and his weight came more fully onto the ropework.

"There you go," Cash murmured, keeping his voice soft and low. "How's this feel?" He trailed his hand from Harrison's wrists all the way down his arms and sides to where the rope ended at his waist, just above those flirtatious shorts.

"Tickly," Harrison muttered—almost a complaint except his voice was equally soft and low.

"Do you like it?" Now that his work was done, he stepped back to survey it. Harrison was a thing of beauty—decorated in delicate green crisscrosses from the waist up. His eyes opened, searching for him, and Cash had been right about the green bringing out their color. "Harrison?"

"Harry."

Right, right. That was Harrison's scene name. It was hard to call him something that made him bristle, but Cash had to respect his desire for anonymity.

"Sorry. Harry." Sure enough, that provoked a scowl. "I asked if you like how it feels." He'd already learned that Harrison ate up touch, and bondage was, in a way, an absence of touch, a sealing off, a separation. That was why he hadn't expected Harrison to enjoy being tied up, but maybe he processed the tickle as touch.

"Are we done?" Harrison asked, rather than answer the question.

"I'm done trying you up, yes."

"What happens now?" The languor was disappearing from his voice fast.

"Typically we enjoy it for a space of time."

"How long?" Harrison's eyes flickered away from him to something behind him. Cash turned to look over his shoulder and saw his friend Francesca there with her sub, Ilona, obediently kneeling at her feet. He turned back to Harrison. This wasn't the time to be social, and Francesca wouldn't expect him to be.

"I can take you down right now if you want."

"No, it's fine."

Fine. Not exciting or arousing or calming or safe. Just

fine.

"I'm going to start unwrapping you."

"I said it was fine," Harrison gritted out, his eyes still focused over Cash's shoulder. There were more people back there now.

"No one's going to touch you," Cash assured him. "They're admiring my work because you're gorgeous in it, but I can ask them to leave."

"Whatever."

"*Not* whatever. This is about you." When he touched Harrison's side, Harrison flinched from it. "Harry?" Oh, fuck that. "Harrison," he said, low and urgent.

"I'm fine," Harrison insisted, looking less fine every moment. He tugged on his wrists, but there wasn't any slack to play with, then twisted away, rotating so he faced the back of the room, away from where the spectators were gathered. Cash waved an annoyed hand at the crowd, and Francesca picked up his cue and started prodding everyone to move on.

"They're leaving, all right? It's just you and me now."

"It's not," Harrison growled. He tried to look over his shoulder and lost his footing so the rope took his full weight for a moment. The ropework held, and was dispersed enough that it shouldn't have hurt, but Harrison flipped into something like panic, flailing around as Cash tried to help him regain his feet.

"I need you to stay still for me a moment."

This wasn't even a little bit about power exchange anymore. This was just needing to get Harrison out of bondage. Cash reached for the last tuck of rope and started to unwind it, but Harrison was breathing way too hard. Cash could feel the quiver running through his every muscle. Fuck, he had to get him out of there. He pulled the blunt-tipped scissors from his back pocket and got to work on the wraps that kept Harrison attached to the clip-in point overhead, slicing through multiple strands with quick snips.

"You can let go now," he said with a firm arm around Harrison's waist in case the sudden lack of structure knocked him off his feet again. "Lower your arms and I'll get all that off you."

A few more snips had Harrison's arms completely free, then Cash started demolishing the decorative work around his torso.

"It's fine," Harrison said, embarrassed now.

"You keep saying that, but I don't think it is."

There. The last wraps dropped in pieces to their feet. The ground around them was littered with random lengths of emerald green rope, like a leafy bower had been deforested by an unskilled arborist wielding a chainsaw. Harrison stood in the middle of the pile of fallen greenery, shell-shocked and shaking. Cash guided him over to a bench along the wall without bothering to deal with the mess. One of the club's cleaning staff would take care of it. He needed to take care of Harrison.

But Harrison wouldn't let him.

"Don't," he said, shrugging him off when he tried to cuddle.

"How about some water then?" He looked over at where he'd left his bag, near the green mess. He didn't want to leave Harrison alone to fetch it.

"I'm not thirsty." Harrison rubbed his temple. "Fuck."

"What happened there?"

"Nothing. I said I was fine. You should've left me. We should've done whatever comes next."

"Nothing had to come next."

"Those people... they were expecting something. Who were they?"

"My friend Francesca was there—the little Korean lady who looks like she could kill you with her eyes alone. And she had her sub Ilona with her. Ilona was the one kneeling. I guess that's obvious." He was babbling, but he wasn't sure what to say. He'd never had anyone safeword on him before. Not that Harrison had used a safeword—not a verbal one—

but Cash had cut him down with scissors, so it counted. "Some other people came later, but I was paying attention to you, not them. Was it being watched that bothered you?"

Harrison shook his head, but it felt like another lie. "Maybe I am thirsty."

"Okay, great. I mean, I've got water. Can you sit here for a minute while I get it? It's over there."

"I'm not a child."

Right. Not a child. Not a sub either. Cash didn't have a formula for this. He might not be the world's most dominant top, but he gave good aftercare—lots of snuggles and praise. And even the least submissive bottom enjoyed being fussed over after a scene. Except this one.

"Here you go." He fished a bottle out of the bag he'd retrieved and handed it to Harrison without opening it for him or trying to hold it for him, even though he could see Harrison's hand shake as he raised the bottle to his mouth. "I've got some food too. I don't really know what you like—"

"You brought a picnic?"

"A picnic?"

"Why do you have food?"

"Oh! Because after a scene, sometimes a sub—or bottom, whatever terminology you prefer—will experience a drop in blood sugar. Because of the intensity. That seemed like it got pretty intense for you." He rooted around in his bag and came out with a container of grapes, remembering almost fondly how Harrison had tried to choke him with a grape last week. Instead of returning the favor, he held out the Pyrex dish and let Harrison help himself.

"I just didn't know what they were expecting," Harrison said after he'd munched on a few of the grapes. He wasn't shaking anymore, but he sat several feet away from Cash on the bench, far enough away that they could be straight co-workers. "I want people to, you know, think I belong here."

"Fuck gatekeepers though. No one gets to say who belongs in the kink community. You don't have to like being tied up in public to bottom." Or be dominant to top. "You belong here. And Francesca will like you because I like you. She stopped to appreciate my ropework, that's all. And once one person stops, other people stop. You wanted to do the club thing," Cash reminded him.

"I do," Harrison said very insistently. "Thank you for bringing me. I'm sorry I fucked this up so bad, that I keep fucking it up so bad." He dropped his head into his hands and added—more to himself than to Cash—"Fuck, I'm fucking this up so bad."

"No, hey." Cash took the bottle because Harrison was about to pour its contents onto the floor and slid along the bench until their hips touched. "You haven't fucked anything up." He draped his arm around Harrison's back and rubbed lightly between his shoulder blades. Harrison leaned into him a bit. "I had a feeling bondage wasn't for you. Or exhibitionism. I don't know why you keep picking things you're going to hate." He laughed as if he were joking, but it was really, really true.

Harrison turned to him with serious eyes. "I won't anymore."

"Does that mean you're going to give me another chance?"

"Arc you really willing to give *me* another chance?"

"Of course. You're too cute to kick out of bed for eating crackers. Or for hating bondage either." He hip-checked Harrison and offered the dish of grapes again. "Have some more of this."

Harrison wasn't shaking anymore, so that was good, but he still looked sheepish as he plucked out a few more grapes.

"I'm pretty sure I could do a scene that would totally rock your world if you'd let me call the shots. Not in an ordering-you-around sort of way," he clarified when Harrison opened his mouth to object. "I get that you don't want that. I just mean let me use my expertise to make some choices for you. You can always call red if you're not feeling it."

"Here?"

Cash didn't know why Harrison was so insistent on being at the club, but if that was what Harrison wanted, he would find a way to make it work.

Chapter 9 Harrison

He'd flubbed being a sub. Again. But Cash still hadn't given up on him. Cash's nice-guy kink ran deep, apparently. Harrison worried it made him a target. Someone might use him, lie to him, take advantage of him. Exactly the way *he* was doing.

Working undercover was for the birds. When he'd been on the force, he'd looked forward to someday getting an undercover assignment, but it turned out he hated it. The lying part anyway. Because it also turned out that he liked Cash—maybe a lot—and that he was interested in what Cash had just offered him—more than a lot—but he couldn't go down that road. He needed to focus on why he was at Hell's Bedroom, which was to search for clues to Arlo's disappearance, not get his rocks off.

He might not enjoy being undercover, but he knew how to run an investigation. His first order of business should've been to scope the place out, but he hadn't gotten more than a vague sense of it earlier, too overwhelmed by the prospect of what was about to happen and too drawn to that whipping scene.

First, there'd been a locker area, where he'd stripped off most of his clothes and parted with his phone. The locker area had been shielded from the reception desk by a partition that kept it semi-private, but it was co-ed. Once they passed into what Cash called the playroom, Harrison understood why Hell's Bedroom didn't bother to separate the changing area by gender. Because on this side of the security door, there was such a mish-mash of genders and levels of disrobement (or hyper-robement, in the case of a person encased head-to-toe in latex) that there wasn't any point in pretending modesty on the other side of it.

He'd barely begun to take in the extensive collection of Things To See when his attention became fixated on a man whose back was covered in a dark tattoo. He was dressed in black leather pants and wielded a whip long enough to do serious damage. Someone was fastened to an X in front of him, and his whip had whistled and cracked, striking the man who grunted, screamed, and occasionally sighed. Harrison had been magnetically drawn in that direction, desire warring with concern.

Other than his own brief experience with Sir Magnus, he'd never seen a whipping outside of videos, where the act always seemed schlocky and rehearsed, with so much ritualized submission it turned his stomach, distracting him from... this. This raw action playing out in front of him. If the man on the cross was counting strokes, Harrison couldn't hear them. He couldn't hear anything over the crack of leather against flesh and the thud of his own heart.

If he'd been more honest with Cash, they could have done something like that instead of what they had done. Which had been all right at first. When it'd felt like just the two of them and Cash had been touching him, brushing him all over with the rope like he was painting him with it. But then Cash had stepped away, and he'd become conscious of the spectators. The rope had stopped feeling like it was adorning him and had started to feel it was constricting him, binding him with an insistence he had to break free from. Only to find out he couldn't.

"I'm sorry about your rope." Over where he'd been tied up, someone in white coveralls was sweeping strands of green confetti into a pile. The whole place was so tidy, so bright. He'd expected something far more dungeon-like but it seemed almost like a supermarket. A supermarket of kink.

"Don't worry about the rope," Cash said. "I've been carrying these scissors around for years and never got a chance to use them. It was kind of exciting. Like hai-yah!" Cash whipped the scissors out of his pocket and brandished them. Harrison couldn't help laughing at the geeky display. "Anyway, that's why we carry scissors. Sometimes people in bondage freak out. You're not breaking new ground there."

"But everyone saw it." He was supposed to be making contacts, particularly with the sort of Doms who might kidnap a young sub. Like that hotshot with the whip. But his attempt to blend into the scene had failed miserably.

"They've seen it before and they'll see it again. Hi." Cash glanced up to greet the man who'd appeared in front of them—a white guy with a mustache, dressed in black jeans and a black tee featuring the Hell's Bedroom logo over the pocket.

"Everything okay here?" the man asked.

"He's asking you," Cash said with a nudge. "I'm just going to step over there for a second. I won't be far."

"Why?" Harrison complained, but Cash had already left—not out of sight but out of hearing, leaving Harrison to face the stranger in black alone.

"Everything okay?" the man repeated.

"Yeah, sure. Why wouldn't it be?"

The man gestured to the shreds of rope being dumped out of a dustpan into a trash container. "We like to check in when a scene ends badly, make sure everything's been handled well."

"Cash handled it just fine. The rope freaked me out, that's all. He didn't do anything wrong."

"Good to hear. Remember, you can file a report at any time." The man walked away, hands clasped behind his back, to observe a scene where a woman was making a man dressed in a puppy suit fetch a stick.

"Who was that?" Harrison asked when Cash rejoined

him on the bench. "A security guard?"

Now that he was looking, he saw several similarly dressed people at different spots around the floor. If the bright cleanliness of the place had been a surprise, finding out the club was patrolled was even more of one. He'd really been imagining a den of iniquity where young men could be spirited off in a dusky cloud of smoke by Doms who didn't give a fuck about their feelings. Instead a uniformed security guard had checked to make sure the world's nicest man hadn't hurt him. He needed to completely recalibrate.

"A dungeon monitor, if you want to use scene terminology," Cash said, "They're here to make sure no one's being forced to do anything they don't want to do. They've never had to check in with one of my subs before. Oh, sorry," he corrected when Harrison scowled reflexively. "Bottom, I should say. Or do you not like that word either?"

"I don't care. Whatever." He should adopt the term sub while he was at the club. That was his cover, after all. "I just feel bad I got you in trouble."

"I'm not in trouble. Unless you said bad things about me while I couldn't hear you. "

"What would happen if I did?"

"Did you?"

"No, of course not. Just curious." If Arlo had been feeling threatened in some way, might he have gone to Security?

"Depends how bad it was, I guess, but eventually they'd revoke my membership. Not for needing to cut someone out of bondage, but if I wasn't honoring safewords. That sort of thing."

"You think they keep records?"

"I wouldn't know. Like I said, I've never been reported before. Are you worried?"

Harrison shook his head. He was making Cash suspicious by harping on the subject, so he changed it by asking for a more thorough tour of the facility. Maybe there were darker corners he hadn't seen yet, spots where an

81

abduction could reasonably happen.

"Yeah, sure," Cash said. "Let's watch a few scenes. Unless you don't have any voyeur in you."

"More voyeur than exhibitionist," he admitted ruefully. Even walking around in these shorts made him uncomfortable. He knew the shorts framed his lower body really well and that there was nothing about his upper body to be faulted, but his interest in having lustful eyes on him was reserved for people he found attractive in return. It didn't extend to the world at large.

Cash kept in contact with him as they walked, steering him with touches, checking in physically as well as verbally, even though Harrison didn't need to be coddled. He'd had a moment of claustrophobia, not a major meltdown, but when he made that point to Cash, Cash only said. "I like touching you, and you like to be touched. But I'll stop if you want." Which made him realize he didn't want Cash to stop.

The offer Cash had made—to show him what he would really like—repeated itself in his mind as they watched a scene with two men, one over the other's lap with his pants down and his ass hanging out. The Dom was whaling on his sub's bare ass to the accompaniment of a bunch of admonishments, which Harrison tried to tune out. The men were playing out a daddy/boy thing, and Harrison only wanted the smack—the rising red and the breathless moans that leaked out between the words.

"That guy likes getting spanked, huh?"

"Mm. A lot. His name's Emmett. He's fun." Cash was behind him with his arms wrapped around Harrison's bare waist. His lips brushed over the top of his ear, and Harrison shuddered from the press of moist heat as Cash's erection ground lightly between his ass cheeks.

"You'd want to do that to me?"

"Would it get you hot if I did?"

"It might." He was hot now, his cock making a noticeable line in the tight confines of his shorts.

"What do you like best about it?" Cash's hand dipped

below his waist, gliding over the front of his shorts, unerringly finding the line of his cock. Harrison wondered whether he minded being fondled in public and decided he didn't.

"I like the crack. It sounds like it hurts."

"I'll bet it does. You can see how red his ass has gotten. They've been going for a while, I think."

It would add up, wouldn't it? The burn would get worse, the way it had when Cash had been tweaking his nipples, twisting them and tormenting them. Harrison wriggled back against Cash, and Cash brought a hand up to toy with his nipple as if reading his mind.

"Tell me more," Cash whispered into his ear. When he licked over his earlobe, Harrison nearly melted. His cock throbbed like liquid pleasure, his nipples rose to urgent peaks, and that tongue sent shivers of fire through him.

"More about what?" he mumbled, unable to follow the conversation anymore.

"About what's getting you so hot right now."

"You." He had his eyes closed. Only the soundtrack of slaps penetrated from the scene in front of him. Maybe he wasn't either an exhibitionist or a voyeur. Maybe he just wanted Cash to touch him.

"Ah, I'm interrupting?"

"A little," Cash responded to the woman who'd just spoken. His lower hand moved off Harrison's cock, and the upper one splayed across his chest in a gesture that was comforting rather than arousing. "But I did want to introduce the two of you."

And Harrison wanted to be introduced. That was what he was here for. He hauled himself upright, taking his weight off Cash to face the woman, who turned out to be the one who'd been watching them earlier.

"Harry, this is Mistress Francesca."

"Ma'am," he acknowledged, trying to adhere to protocol. Francesca was dressed in a red leather catsuit. Her dark hair flowed from a high ponytail, and her lips were painted a matching crimson red. She wore heels high enough to break an ankle but still only reached his chin.

A woman knelt by her side, dressed mostly in her own white skin with a few touches of pink lace that had been arranged more for effect than coverage. Harrison glanced down at her, not sure if he was supposed to acknowledge her or not. She wasn't acknowledging him. Francesca probably expected him to be down there on the ground with her.

"Nice to meet you, Harry. That's my girl, Ilona, but she's not allowed to talk right now, so you'll have to forgive her manners." Francesca had Ilona on a leash, the end of which was wrapped securely several times around one palm. She used her other hand to tilt Ilona's head up, though Ilona's eyes remained fixed downward. "A pretty thing, isn't she?"

"Very," Harrison agreed politely, though he didn't particularly think so.

Francesca was prettier in his opinion—a bold and lively portrait of womanhood. Ilona was so expressionless she seemed almost robotic. Or catatonic. Even if women were Harrison's thing, she wasn't. She was definitely of age, but was she truly willing? Was she even capable of being willing? He'd been thinking of Arlo's disappearance as an abduction, a struggle, but it could've been more subtle. A seduction or a drugging. Given the open atmosphere and heavy security, it seemed unlikely Arlo had been kidnapped right off the Hell's Bedroom floor, but he could've met someone here and willingly followed them elsewhere.

"Shall we grab a drink?" Francesca asked. "Unless you were going to scene more."

"No, I was just showing Harry around. I think he's had enough scening for tonight."

"He didn't enjoy the ropes?" Francesca addressed the question to Cash, as if Harrison weren't there to answer for himself, as she led them around the edge of the circle in the direction of a neon sign that read BAR with hipster succinctness.

84

"It was the crowds." Cash glanced over at him, seeking confirmation. He shrugged. If Francesca wanted to leave him out of the conversation, let her do it. He could probably learn more by listening than by talking.

"My apologies for being part of the problem then. I'd only intended to admire your handiwork, not to intrude." She stopped in front of a conversational grouping of couches and took a genteel seat on the edge of one of them, her posture as upright as if she were in a straight-backed chair.

Cash plonked down onto another couch with a lot less grace. Ilona parked herself at Francesca's feet, a position from which she'd yet to waver. She sat on her heels, her back straight but her head down in a pose Harrison thought he remembered from his training the other day. He got down on his knees next to Cash and tried to mirror it.

Cash rifled a hand into his hair, tugging until he turned up to him. "Really?"

"I'm fine here, sir."

Cash frowned at him, but Harrison resolutely turned his head forward, dropping it slightly to mimic what Ilona was doing. The motion made Cash's fingers tug, and though Harrison wasn't a fan of being on the ground, Cash's fingers sifting through his hair—pulling lightly, then more sharply, then lightly again—almost made up for it.

"Where did you find him?" Francesca asked.

"At that house party. Jealous?"

She laughed, a tinkly sound that was exactly what Harrison would've expected from her. "I don't think we'd suit, but I hope he suits you."

"I think he might."

Harrison couldn't help glancing up at that. Cash sounded so hopeful, and here Harrison was treating him absolutely shamefully.

"Oh, hell," Francesca said, calling Harrison's attention to her again. Her gaze was focused somewhere to his right, and when he followed it, he saw the Dom who'd been using

85

the long whip earlier. "Maybe if we pretend we don't see him, he'll pretend he doesn't see us."

"Behave," Cash chastised. "Can't we all get along?"

"We can all get along with *you*, but that's not saying much. Doms are territorial by nature, darling. We must stake out our space."

"This is neutral space. A bar, in fact. And if no one is going to wait on us, I'll— Oh, here we go."

A waiter dressed in a thong and a pair of heels showed up at the same time as the Dom with the whip. He wore it around his neck now, with the butt tucked into his back pocket and the length of it draping over his chest like a thick, black snake. Harrison had a hard time looking away from it as the waiter took their orders. Francesca ordered for Ilona, but Cash looked at him pointedly until he asked for a seltzer.

"I think your sub likes me," the new Dom said. He hadn't sat down, choosing to loom over them instead. He stroked the whip like it wasn't just any old snake, but his particular pet snake.

"He likes your whip," Cash corrected. "Harry, that's Master Sebastian."

"So nice to meet you, Harry." Sebastian unwrapped the whip from around his neck and draped it around Harrison's so that it puddled in his lap. "I'd be happy to acquaint you with it very thoroughly."

Harrison couldn't help running a finger down the supple leather, wondering what it would feel like touching his body in a much more aggressive way.

"Back off," Francesca warned Sebastian. "Harry is here with Cash."

"From what I saw, Cash wasn't doing it for him."

"You should keep your eyes on your own scene."

"I was concerned for Harry," Sebastian said with a shrug. "Am I wrong to want to teach all the pretty subs how good submission to a real Dom can be?"

"And you wonder why we don't get along," Francesca

86

said to Cash with a huff. "You shouldn't let him push you around."

"He's not touching me," Cash said drily, sounding like the only adult out of the three of them. Was this their idea of dominance? Petty bickering over someone—*him*—who could make his own choices, thank you very much?

He lifted the whip off his shoulders and handed it back to Sebastian with a dismissive, "No, thanks."

Chapter 10 Cash

When Harrison returned Sebastian's whip to him, Cash couldn't help feeling relieved. He knew Harrison coveted the whip—maybe even more than he realized—but Cash could wield a whip himself.

Francesca snorted, amused by Harrison's gesture, and the waiter showed up with their drinks just then, easing a situation that could've turned tense. Sebastian was a long-term acquaintance—not exactly a friend—and he was known for being a gold-plated ass who fucked with people on purpose. Cash wished he could say that knowing Sebastian's game meant he was immune to it, but it wouldn't be true. Sebastian was a gold-plated, *talented* ass. He knew exactly where to hit.

Francesca held Ilona's glass up to her mouth, watering her in tiny sips before even touching her own drink, but Harrison took his seltzer directly from the waiter and held onto it himself. Which was a relief. Cash could do the pet routine for a sub who wanted it, but it would be yet another thing Harrison wouldn't enjoy even if he asked for it. Like the way he was down there on his knees right now.

"Where did *your* sub go off to?" Francesca asked Sebastian. "If you had satisfied him as thoroughly as you're always bragging you do, you wouldn't be over here trying to poach Cash's."

"I satisfied him so thoroughly I made him comatose. He napped on me for a while, then I bundled him into a cab to finish sleeping at home."

"I didn't recognize him," Cash observed. So many new faces lately, a lot of churn, especially amongst the subs. As if no one could settle.

"He's newish," Sebastian said. "Not anyone I'm attached to, but maybe it'll get there. He takes a whip well, at any rate. You're sure?" he taunted Harrison, extending the whip in his direction. "If this is what you want, you can get it better from me."

"Stop."

Cash raised his eyebrows at Harrison's no-nonsense response. Harrison was such a contradiction—kneeling without being prompted one minute, picking fights with Doms the next.

"Stop *what*?" Sebastian prompted. He was angling for the word sir, trying to remind Harrison of his place, but that wasn't how Harrison took it.

"Stop acting like Cash can't give me what I need."

"You know he's not a Dom, right?"

"Who says I want a Dom?" Harrison put his glass down on the table in front of him—a little too vehemently—then got to his knees with a wince. "Ouch. You know what? Kneeling sucks." He slumped onto the couch next to Cash, which was where Cash had wanted him in the first place. Made him easier to touch.

"Look at that," Sebastian said. "A single session with Cash, and the humble sub walks a proud man once more."

"I didn't say I was a sub. And you can stop talking about me like I'm not here. All of you."

"Are you a switch?" Francesca asked. She hadn't ignored Harrison to be rude. She'd been following protocol, which said you didn't directly address another Dom's sub— one of those territorial things that had her and Sebastian at each other's throats. Sebastian knew the rules, which meant he knew exactly which ones to break to piss people off.

"What's a switch?" Harrison asked.

"That means sometimes you top and sometimes you bottom," Cash explained.

"Versatile?"

Cash laughed, while Francesca looked merely confused. "Not exactly. Remember, topping in BDSM means running the scene—inflicting the pain, giving the orders. Not necessarily fucking."

Harrison bunched his eyebrows together. "Then I don't think so. Why aren't you a switch though?"

"Cash should be a sub," Sebastian said with a dismissive wave. "Service top. What even is that?"

Harrison tensed, looking for all the world like he was about to go after him.

"It's weirdly easier serving from the top," Cash said, patting Harrison back down onto the cushions. He handed over the Scotch he'd ordered for himself. Something more mellowing than seltzer seemed to be in order. "But I've tried subbing, and it was all right. I'm definitely not a masochist, though. I can't see the appeal."

"I suppose Sebastian thinks he could get you to see it," Francesca said.

"I wouldn't care whether it appealed to him or not," Sebastian said. "I'm all about the fuckery. Giving someone exactly what they think they want bores me. Where's the challenge in it?"

"Thank God we're not all you." Francesca stifled a yawn, then rose to her feet. "We have to be toddling along. You may say goodbye, pet."

"Goodbye, Master Sebastian," Ilona said obediently. Then, "Bye, Cash."

"And Harry," Francesca prompted.

"Bye, Harry."

"Bye, Ilona. It was nice to meet you."

A firm tug on the leash had Ilona scurrying to keep up with her mistress as Francesca strode away, perfectly steady on those spiked heels. Sebastian took the couch she'd vacated. He propped his feet up on the low coffee table and leaned back with his drink in hand.

"What do you do, Harry?"

"I run a tattoo parlor."

"Explains the ink, then. Nice work. I've been thinking of getting more myself." He rotated to show off his back, as if Harrison could've missed it earlier. Sebastian had a mandala, all black with very sharply delineated lines, and Harrison made a noise like he appreciated the work.

"Cash doesn't have any tattoos," Sebastian said as he turned to face them again. "But maybe you've already discovered that for yourself."

"He mentioned it," Harrison said, not giving Sebastian the answer he was fishing for, which was whether or not the two of them were sex partners as well as play partners. That scene where Cash had tortured Harrison into a nipple-gasm meant they were at least nominally sex partners, but the only action Cash had gotten tonight was a little over-the-clothes groping.

He'd been aroused watching the spanking scene with Harrison, who was so clearly enjoying it, but those sexy feelings had evaporated. Now he was back to worrying both about being inadequate and about what the hell was going on with Harrison—whether he was confused or outright lying. He wished Sebastian would leave them alone so he could get some of it figured out.

"What do you do?" Harrison asked Sebastian in return. "Aside from whip people and fuck with them?" His question sounded a bit like flirting, and Sebastian's wink said he'd taken it that way.

"My day job allows for a bit of fuckery too. I'm a prosecutor for the State of Massachusetts. I enjoy punishing bad guys as well as subs."

Harrison's interest in Sebastian disappeared in a flash. He turned very pointedly to Cash and said, "You were giving me a tour."

Cash took a swallow from the glass Harrison had returned to him and rose. Had Harrison gotten in trouble with the law at some point? Tattoo parlors were sometimes fronts for less-than-legal activities, and Harrison had reacted strongly to finding out there was a cop in the vicinity at the party, but he hardly seemed the type. More cop than robber, with that upright posture and those challenging eyes.

Whatever the reason for it, Cash didn't mind getting away from Sebastian. BDSM wasn't supposed to be a competitive sport, but too many of Cash's partners—potential and otherwise—had made it clear they preferred the gold-plated ass to him. Sebastian was commanding and evil and impossible to please and oh so scary. Cash got it, already.

Harrison had wandered away without even saying goodbye, so Cash gave Sebastian a quick shrug and joined him. They walked the floor side by side, stopping to watch whatever caught Harrison's attention, which Cash catalogued. Pain play was a yes. Tickling a possibility. The Wartenberg wheel a happy medium. And, oh, electrostim. Cash would have to dig out his equipment when he got home.

"I have one of those." He nodded at the TENS unit a Domme had hooked up to a guy's balls. Her sub jiggled nicely in his bindings, too turned on to do more than moan at her.

"What's it feel like?"

"Depends how high I crank it up. It can feel like a tingle, like a million fingers running sweetly over your skin, or it can feel like getting electrocuted—a real zap. Most people find the sensation pleasant at lower settings, and some find it pleasant at higher ones. Want to try?"

"Yeah. I mean, maybe," Harrison corrected, for some reason reining in his original, and believably honest, response. "Would we do it here?"

"We wouldn't have to. I've got everything we need at my place."

"I'd rather do it here."

Cash sighed because honestly, what was Harrison's fascination with the club? "Harrison—" he started, but his attempt to initiate the conversation they really needed to have about whether Harrison wanted him or Hell's Bedroom was interrupted by a stern voice coming from directly behind them.

"Lap that up, faggot."

Harrison swiveled fast enough to give himself whiplash. Cash turned too, though he already had an idea what he would find. These public exhibitions were borderline non-consensual. Not because the guy dressed in women's lingerie on all fours next to a puddle hadn't consented—he probably had—but because *Cash* hadn't consented.

"Get your worthless face down on the fucking floor and drink it like the piss-licking pansy you are." The guy's Domme put a pointed heel on the back of his skull and pressed resolutely downward until his forehead touched the floor.

"Don't." Cash stopped Harrison from moving toward them. "It's just a scene. It's their thing."

"She has no right to use those words."

"I know. I get it. But it's not about us, not really."

The man in lingerie—Cash vaguely recalled his name was something innocuous like Bill—stuck his tongue out and took a tentative lap at the puddle on the floor, which would only be colored water since club rules prohibited bodily fluids in the public areas.

"Faster. Drink it up, you little bitch."

"And now she's insulting women."

"It's a scene," Cash repeated, taking a firmer hold of Harrison's arm because he seemed ready to go over there and interrupt it. "But we don't have to watch it. Come on."

Most of the time, he liked watching other people's scenes. It was half the reason he came to the club—to play voyeur, to soak in the excitement and feed it back. But no matter how much he knew the guy on the floor had been really, really into that, he couldn't get into it himself. The words hit way too close to home.

"So we can strike humiliation off your list," he said when he'd gotten Harrison far enough away that they couldn't hear the Domme's voice anymore.

"Yeah, strike that all the way off. If I put on women's clothes, it'll be because I look good in them."

"*That* I could get into. You in some lingerie?" Cash slid a hand across the booty shorts that were nearly as revealing as lingerie would be. "What are you wearing under here? I can't feel anything."

"Because there's nothing to feel."

"Ooh. See, that's hot—you getting all sexy for me. Come home with me. Let me peel these off you." It had been a less-than-perfect date up to that point with every step forward matched by an equal step back, but he was still disappointed when Harrison shook his head.

"Early day tomorrow."

"At a tattoo parlor?"

"Gotta get things set up. There's a lot to sterilize and, um, other stuff. Open the cash register."

"Sure." Cash knew a brush-off when he heard one. Well, nothing interested him less than an uninterested partner, so no meant no. "Let's get you home then."

He headed for the doors that led out of the main area, letting his longer strides make Harrison scramble to keep up with him. Out in the locker area, Cash retrieved his cell phone while Harrison donned his street clothes.

"Can we come back another time?" Harrison asked when he'd reassembled himself into the tough guy who'd shown up, his sexy shorts disappearing beneath an ordinary pair of Levi's.

"Why? You didn't like scening here. I'm not even sure you like *me*."

"I do. Like you. Not always the rest of it, but I'm still figuring things out." Harrison peered up through his eyelashes, briefly flirtatious.

"So what have you figured out?"

Harrison let out a frustrated breath. "I know I'm sending mixed messages. The truth is I was hoping to run into someone—a friend I haven't seen in a while. I'm worried about him." Harrison pulled up a picture on his phone and handed it over. "His name's Arlo. Ever seen him?"

"You've got young friends."

Harrison had been with Tripp at the party, and here he was flashing a photo of a teenaged blond-haired, blue-eyed cherub.

"Maybe friend isn't the right word. He used to hang around the tattoo parlor all the time."

"Looks too young to get tattoos."

"The point is, have you seen him?"

"Looks too young to be *here* too." Cash handed Harrison his phone back with a shake of his head. "Maybe I'm just getting old. I've seen a few kids who seem too young to be here lately, but they're pretty strict about who they let in."

"What if he had a fake ID?"

"Possible, I guess, if he was here as someone's guest. They card guests, but they don't run background checks on them. Anyway, I haven't seen your friend. If I had, I'd probably have reported him. How old is he?"

"Seventeen," Harrison said, like his mind was elsewhere.

"Shit, I *am* getting old then. That kid doesn't look older than fifteen."

"Who would you have reported him to?"

"One of those security guards you talked to earlier. They handle any kind of infraction. But I didn't see him, so I didn't report him."

"Right," Harrison said, still lost in thought somewhere. "But somebody else might've."

"So your reason for being here was to look for that kid? You're not interested in me or in any of this?"

"What?" That startled Harrison out of his contemplation. "No, I am. I'm just saying that if we're going to do another scene, could we please do it here? That way maybe I'll run into Arlo." Harrison turned his full attention on him, favoring him with those sparkling green eyes and a lustful smile. "I really do like you."

It was one of those moments when Harrison seemed sincere, so when he leaned in, Cash came forward, drawn toward that smiling mouth. But before he could get there, Harrison stepped back, leaving Cash once again a little short of where he wanted to be.

Chapter 11 Harrison

Harrison buttoned his suit jacket before following Brixby through the heavy bronze door that led into Hell's Bedroom. His wardrobe as a private investigator wasn't usually this formal, but he was trying to distance himself as far as possible from Harry-the-sub who'd been in the playroom last night. With his hair spiked up, a pair of generously heeled dress shoes, and the posture of a man who meant business, he came across as closer to five-nine than five-seven. And he had a uniformed police officer at his side. Hopefully no one would recognize the sub in booty shorts behind the tailored clothes.

"We'd like to speak to your head of Security," he told the woman at the reception counter, flashing his PI license at her quickly enough that it would come across as a badge. It was a move he'd mastered years ago, and having a cop with him added to his credibility.

"I have two police officers here who would like to speak to Mr. Knight," the receptionist told someone on the phone, apparently having fallen for it. A few minutes later, a man dressed in the black jeans and t-shirt of a Hell's Bedroom security guard arrived in the reception area.

"If you'd come with me," he said. All very calm, very professional, as if they had nothing to hide.

The guard ushered them through a door to the side of the leather-covered, chrome-studded double doors that led to the playroom. Behind the more prosaic blond wood lay an office suite so innocuously generic you could imagine Hell's Bedroom was an accounting firm. Industrial blue-swirled carpet, cream-colored walls, and blue-tinged LED fixtures. Harrison had been in a hundred buildings exactly like this.

Dozens of cubicles lined the corridor, separated by fuzzy. blue-speckled fabric, each one housing someone staring listlessly at a computer screen. Harrison was surprised by how many office workers it took to run a BDSM club. Once again, his preconceptions were being challenged. If he'd realized what kind of an establishment Hell's Bedroom was, he would've started by talking to Security instead of dressing up in silly shorts and allowing himself to be tied up. Though it would've been a shame not to have met Cash.

At the end of the corridor, their escort tapped on the door of a walled office and opened it in response to a vocal acknowledgement. Inside, a bald-headed Black man of imposing bulk sat behind a wood laminate desk. Everything about him screamed ex-cop.

"Horace Knight," he said as he rose to offer a hand. "Head of Security for Hell's Bedroom. What can I do for you, gentlemen?" He gestured at his guest chairs, and all three of them took a seat.

"I'm looking for someone," Harrison told him. "An underage kid I have reason to believe visited your club." He pulled a printed photo of Arlo from his breast pocket and handed it over. "If a patron reported him, that report would make its way to you, right?"

"Sure would." Knight studied the photo carefully, then turned to the computer on the credenza behind him. "You got a name?"

"Real name is Arlo Gandry, but he'd have used a fake ID, I assume."

Knight grunted agreement as he typed something into the computer that made a photo pop up. The guy on screen was more disheveled than the one in the photo—his curls matted with sweat and his eyes red like he'd been crying—but the facial structure matched. High cheekbones, bow lips. An innocent angel.

"That's your man, right?"

"Looks like."

Knight swung back around and flipped through a rolodex. He pulled a driver's license from it and skated it across the desk to them. The name on the ID read Townes Gandry, and the man in the photo was at least ten years older than the guy Harrison was looking for, but they resembled each other superficially.

"A relative, maybe," Knight said. "The ID's real, but it's not Arlo's. I gave the clerk who checked him in hell for it, but our employees are human. Mistakes get made."

Harrison fingered the ID, agreeing with Knight's assessment. Valid ID, wrong person. "How did he come to your attention if he made it through check-in?"

"Someone on the floor questioned his age, and one of my guys brought him in to see me. I logged the incident, confiscated his ID, and had him removed from the premises. I can print out a copy of the incident report if you'd like."

"You're very organized," Brixby observed.

"The corporation that owns the place had some security software installed. It's good stuff." A few clicks, the low whir of a laser printer, and Knight was handing over a printed copy of what had been on his screen. In the upper, right-hand corner was a black-and-white copy of the photo—Arlo's mug shut. Under the heading Vouching Member was the name Bob Jones.

"What can you tell us about Bob Jones?"

"Been a member ten years and no complaints before this one. Said he didn't know how old the kid was. They always say that."

"You get this a lot?"

"Depends on how you define a lot. One a month maybe? Most of them get caught at the door."

"You got records for all those incidents?"

"Only the ones who make it inside."

"Feel like sharing?"

"What do I get in return? You don't have a warrant or you'd have flashed it by now. I'm being cooperative out of the goodness of my heart." Knight's grin suggested he had more of a sense of humor than he'd demonstrated thus far. The guy was by the book, and Harrison was pretty sure it was the right book.

"All right, I'll level with you. I'm working a missing persons case with a possible kidnapping slant."

"This kid?" Knight tapped the printout with Arlo's picture on it. "We don't have him, if that's what you're thinking. Could he have met someone here?" Knight shrugged. "Maybe. But he didn't disappear from here. I had him put out on the sidewalk myself."

"Who runs this place?"

"A shadowy figure using the club to populate his harem." Knight laughed. "Nah. Kidding. Place is owned by DDD, Inc. They got their headquarters out in San Francisco, own a bunch of clubs across the country. We have a local manager here, name of Luke Olsen. Quiet guy, dots all his i's."

"It's always the quiet ones," Brixby said.

"You can talk to him. Least, I can't stop you from doing it. Personally, I'd be talking to Bob Jones."

"We will." Harrison didn't need Knight telling him how to do his job, ex-cop or not. "But right now we're talking to you. This Olsen, is he a kinky dude?"

"Lord, you wouldn't think so. Could be wrong, but I think he's your typical corporate suit. Hired for his anal-retentive accounting practices, not his way with a whip."

"How about you?" Brixby asked. "You in the scene?"

"Now you're getting personal," Knight admonished with a stern wag of his finger. "But no. From what I've heard, this place used to be all-in-the-family before it got bought out, but DDD's policy is to run it like a business. My guys

100

are on the floor to do a job, not get their jollies. We watch, we don't play."

"So you came in with the change in ownership?"

"Me, Olsen, the whole staff changed. And I'm telling you, DDD runs a tight ship. Every infraction gets logged and handled according to the rule book." Knight pulled a binder labeled Code of Operations from his drawer and dropped it on his desk with a hefty thud. "If someone's prowling the floor looking for victims, they're not doing it with our cooperation, and they're damn subtle about it."

Harrison exchanged a look with Brixby. Hell's Bedroom was starting to feel like a dead end. Arlo was a seventeen-year-old homeless kid. There were a lot of places he could've disappeared to, and even his own parents didn't seem to care which one it might be. When Harrison had dropped by to interview them, he'd found them as Tripp had predicted—half drunk and completely uninterested in Arlo's whereabouts.

"You said if I gave you something, you'd share more of those reports with us," he reminded Knight, not prepared to walk out without *something*.

"I can do that. Let's see. In the year I've been working here, we've had four people with fake IDs make it past the front desk." The printer whirred again, and Knight handed over a stack of papers, then rifled through his rolodex and pulled out ID cards to match. "I'm going to want a receipt for those IDs if you're taking them."

"We're taking them." Harrison had Brixby write out receipts while he flipped through the reports. Four incidents over a year seemed pretty reasonable, but if something systemic was going on at the club, it would hardly be logged in their security system.

"Tidy operation," Harrison observed when he and Brixby had been shown back out onto the street.

"Too tidy. Kink for profit. Can't say I like it. So what's next, boss?"

Harrison looked down at the raft of papers in his hand.

101

Their visit hadn't been encouraging as far as implicating Hell's Bedroom in Arlo's disappearance, but it'd been fruitful in terms of giving them leads to pursue. "I'll talk to this Jones guy, the one who signed Arlo in. You see if you can find anything on these other kids. Maybe we can turn up a link between them."

He caught a ride from Brixby back to his office where he ate the soggy peanut butter and jelly sandwich he'd left in his mini-fridge yesterday while he used his no-name desktop to pull up the white pages service he subscribed to. He was scanning through a stunningly long list of Bob or Robert Joneses who lived in the greater Boston area when his phone pinged with a text from Cash, confirming their date for tomorrow.

That would be good news except his interest in getting inside Hell's Bedroom wasn't all that strong anymore. He'd gotten what he'd gone there to get—the name of the guy who'd signed in Arlo. He no longer needed to have a cattle prod attached to his balls or whatever it was he'd agreed to. He winced a little at how eager he'd been to let Cash do something so clearly outlandish.

Cash said it didn't have to hurt, that it could be enjoyable even. Like a massage. But a massage wasn't what Harrison was after. He wanted something like what Cash had done to his nipples that day, how intense it'd been when he came. He'd tried to do it to himself since then— twist a nipple with one hand while stroking himself off with the other—but it hadn't been the same. Self-preservation kicked in, told him to stop. Cash might not be a sadist, but he was capable of being ruthless in a way Harrison couldn't be to himself.

He looked at his phone, at that message, at the hopeful cheer somehow evident in the digitized words, and didn't know what to do. If he'd never started down the road of lying to Cash, he would be eager to pursue this—both the relationship and the kink, at least the way Cash practiced it, which was a hundred and eighty degrees from the way

Sir Magnus had treated him.

But what kind of relationship could he and Cash build on a foundation of lies? Until he found Arlo and closed the case, he couldn't come clean about what he'd been up to because at any moment something might lead him back to Hell's Bedroom.

Which meant he would be foolish to throw away Cash as a contact. He might need him again later. Prudence suggested he continue to string him along. Yeah, prudence.

"Let's just do it at your place," he texted back. "I'll be more comfortable."

Cash sent an immediate agreement, so there. It was more of a date than a job. But it was also an effective compromise.

Chapter 12 Cash

Cash was still grinning at his phone when Mr. Jackman arrived. Harrison asking to move their date from the club to his apartment felt like such a positive sign, like the barricades Harrison kept putting up were crumbling and Cash would finally be allowed to really please him.

He pocketed his phone and turned his smile up to Mr. Jackman who was making his slow way into a wooden chair in the library carrel next to him. Cash could only watch. Mr. Jackman would smack his hand if he tried to help. The white-haired Black man might be over eighty, but he wasn't ready to make any concessions to his age yet. He'd signed up for the literacy program after retiring at eighty-one, and the two of them had been working together for about a year and a half now.

"I want to learn how to use this," Mr. Jackman had said at their first session as he placed a late-model smartphone on the table. "See this here? That's my grandson. I can read his name, all right. It says Bill Jackman." He pointed to the text next to a picture of a man in his mid-thirties that actually read William Jackman. "He posted that picture of his daughter, my great-granddaughter Keisha. I want to know what it says about her. She's at a swim meet. I can see that. But what's it say?"

Cash had helped him decipher the words about Keisha's lap times and type a slow but proud comment in response. Their partnership had started from there.

"Always promised myself I'd learn to read someday," Mr. Jackman had said when Cash asked him why now, why at eighty-one, why after he'd already retired. "Dropped out of school at sixteen, but I was only faking before then, you understand. Too busy surviving to ever pay much attention in class, didn't see how it was relevant. Napped more than anything, result of working third shift. But I got time now, all the time in the world. So you teach me."

Today, like always, they started with Mr. Jackman's Facebook feed. The secret to teaching adults how to read was using material they actually wanted to read, and Mr. Jackman was all about family with six children, fifteen grandchildren, and a growing handful of great-grandchildren. By now, he didn't need much help making his way through his family's posts, but he enjoyed the chance to show off his progeny, and there was always a new word or two to sound out.

The hour passed enjoyably, as it always did with this particular client. Mr. Jackman was steady and determined in his learning, the discipline that'd taken him from high school dropout to head of a family full of college graduates obvious in everything he did. And Cash himself was in such a good mood it couldn't be hidden.

"How are you smiling at this?" Mr. Jackman asked, pausing in his struggle to read aloud from an article one of his sons had linked to. The article detailed the latest murder of a Black man by a trigger-happy cop and definitely didn't warrant a smile.

"Sorry, I wasn't smiling at that. It's awful."

"It's awful, all right. Sometimes I think I was better off when I couldn't read. They don't say about this stuff on the TV."

"Both true facts," Cash agreed. "I have to limit my consumption too." If he read every infuriating article on the internet, he would never leave his house, both for lack of time and because the world would be too depressing a place to venture out into. "How about we find a more cheerful

105

subject?"

Mr. Jackman thumbed his phone off. "How about you tell me what's got you smiling like that today? Don't think I can't guess. I've been a young man. I can see you got your mind on a lady."

"I'm not so young." He'd never discussed his sexuality with Mr. Jackman. It wasn't something he made a habit of hiding, but there wasn't any reason for it to come up either, and Mr. Jackman was from a generation that wasn't typically open to the idea. Cash didn't want to hinder their efforts by triggering any prejudice he might have.

"You're young from where I'm standing," Mr. Jackman said, "but not so young you shouldn't get on with it. I was twenty-three when I married my Margaret, God rest her soul, and I still wish I'd done it five years earlier." He touched the watch he wore on his right wrist. Cash had noticed he had a habit of doing that when he talked about his late wife.

Mr. Jackman caught him looking and nodded. "It was a gift from her. Twenty-fifth anniversary. That's gold, you know. Eighteen karat."

"It's beautiful." Elegant but weighty. It suited him.

"Bought it out of her housekeeping money she'd been squirrelling away that whole twenty-five years. Not to save up for a watch, no. Her momma told her when we got married that she oughta have a flee fund."

"A flee fund?"

"In case she needed to run from me. Case I hit her or some such. A woman oughta always have a way out, her momma told her. When Margaret gave me this, she said she didn't figure she needed a flee fund no more, not after twenty-five years of seeing how I never raised a hand to her."

"That's, um, I don't know what to say about that."

"Neither did I. That's a kicker, ain't it? That a woman would need such a thing. So I took and got the watch appraised and worked overtime until I made back the cost

106

of it, and I gave it to her. Told her God willing you ain't never going to need it, but if you do, you better have it. She took that money to the grave with her," Mr. Jackman said with a chuckle. "No idea where she stashed it. Figure one of these days I'll turn over a mattress and there it'll be—the flee fund she thank the Lord never had any cause to use." He laughed again, slapping his thigh with his hand so uproariously Cash couldn't help joining in, even though it was a macabre subject.

"All right," he said when they'd settled down in response to a glare from a nearby patron. "Let's get back to the reading."

"Nah, son. I've had enough for the day. That's a good story to end on—better 'n any of them on the internet. You go get ready for your date. And make sure she's a good one. My grandkids say happy wife, happy life, but they got the wrong end of it. Get yourself a good wife and make her happy 'cause she deserves it. Then both of you be plenty happy."

"Good advice, Mr. Jackman. Thanks." He refrained from helping as Mr. Jackman wobbled to his feet and headed for the exit with a slow but steady stride.

Cash went straight for his phone to make sure Harrison hadn't changed his mind, but the last message from him was still the one suggesting they meet at his apartment instead of the club. Their date wasn't until tomorrow, though, so despite Mr. Jackman's exhortations, Cash couldn't do anything to get ready right now except go through his toy chest like a kid on Christmas.

So many toys, so many ways to use them. But they'd only talked about e-stim, that was all. Of course, e-stim did go very well with sounding. So well, in fact, it could hardly be considered e-stim *without* a sound. No harm in getting everything cleaned and prepped. Just in case.

God, it was going to be a long night.

"HOW DOES IT FEEL?"

"Tingly." Harrison squirmed on the chair Cash had him strapped to. His arms were bound behind his back, loosely enough that he could stand up and slip them right over the top if he wanted. The purpose was to keep him from instinctively interfering with what Cash was going to do to him, not to really restrain him.

"Tingly in a good way or tingly in a bad way?"

"Tingly like there's fingers running up and down my dick."

"Wait until we add the sound."

"We're adding sound? I don't even know what that means."

"Let's see how this goes first."

So far, it was going well. Harrison was gorgeous naked, a sight Cash hadn't had the opportunity to appreciate before. His chest hair got heavier as it went lower, becoming a forest of short, black tangles as it reached his groin where it'd been trimmed back to display his cock and balls to their best advantage.

His cock had been at attention even before Cash got all the pads in place and turned on the device. They hadn't bothered with any D/s preliminaries. No ceremonial kneeling or honorifics. Just Harrison stripping down, asking questions about the device and how it worked while he undressed, and Cash practically salivating as Harrison's gorgeous body was revealed to him piece by piece.

Harrison's cock was still at attention, but now there were two adhesive pads wrapped around his shaft—one just below the head and another at the base. Wires connected the pads to the box in Cash's hand.

"You're sure this is safe, right?"

"A hundred percent," Cash answered as he cranked the intensity higher. "Even if I went to max, it would only hurt, not damage. These devices are made to be used on people."

"Not on people's dicks though." Harrison jerked as a stronger pulse hit him. "Oh. I like that."

"Medically, they're meant to manage pain, but I would guess that at least as many units are sold to horny men as people looking for pain relief. It's safe, I promise. Relax and enjoy." He turned the dial that made the pulses last longer, and Harrison moaned when the next one hit. "Still pleasure, or are we up to pain yet?"

"Pleasure," Harrison moaned. "Fuck, it's like getting a handjob from the inside. I should buy one of these."

"That's what I'm saying. People do. I'm going to turn this up a smidge higher." The intensity should be edging into pain now, but Harrison's sharp inhale as the next pulse hit and his long exhale when it passed, said otherwise. "I bet I could make you come just like this."

"Do it," Harrison ordered. He was so *not* a sub.

"Not just yet." Cash sat down on the coffee table in front of Harrison and used his feet to nudge Harrison's legs wider so Harrison's balls dropped into the valley between his thighs, ripe and available. "This is a dual channel device."

"What does that mean?" Harrison's eyes went glassy as a shudder wracked his body. Cash dialed up the pulse length just a bit, drawing it out until Harrison gasped, then turned both dials back to where they'd started. He wanted to talk to Harrison about some options, and he couldn't do that if Harrison wasn't fully coherent.

"It means I have a second set of electrodes. They would work better if your balls were completely shaven, but..."

"My balls?" Harrison asked with a greedy lick of his lips. "What would that feel like?"

"Want to find out?"

"Okay, yeah. Yeah, let's do it."

Cash snickered. This was beautiful—Harrison sweaty and so, so eager. His dick stood at a forty-five degree angle, and there was already pre-come dripping from it, a steady strand stretching toward the floor. Watching a man's dick drool was about the sexiest thing Cash could imagine. Some guys naturally produced more pre-come than others, and though it wasn't anyone's fault if their body didn't make gallons of the stuff, he liked what he liked. And he liked this.

He leaned down and touched his tongue to the bottom of the strand, following it all the way back up to its source. His tongue tingled when it made contact with the head of Harrison's cock, as if Harrison's cock were vibrating for him. It would be so easy to suck him down, to get them both off. But he wanted more.

"I can attach both of the other pads to your balls," he said. "Or if you're feeling adventurous..."

"Oh, God. What now?"

Cash held up the sounding attachment, a metallic rod about six millimeters in diameter. "Ever tried sounding?"

"You know I haven't tried a goddamned thing." Harrison kicked at Cash's feet. "Where have you been all my life?"

Waiting for you, he wanted to answer, but that was way too corny. If waving an electrically charged, vibrating metal rod he intended to insert into Harrison's piss hole wasn't enough to scare Harrison off, a statement like that probably would.

"This is kind of advanced, but if you're liking the e-stim, I think you're going to like this too. We can always stop if you don't."

"Quit explaining and get to it."

Cash couldn't help grinning. He'd stuck sounding rods into other guys' dicks before—and they'd all been willing—but none of them had ordered him to do it. He started by applying the adhesive contacts to Harrison's balls, one to each. Then he turned the intensity back up on both channels and let Harrison twist that for a while, watched his mouth gape open, listened to the beautiful sounds coming from it. Cash's own dick was hard and aching, insistent about being touched, but he knew what it wanted better than it did. It wanted this—the glory of a desperate man begging for more.

"I'm going to insert the rod first," he said, leaving the intensity where it was but slowing the rate. "Then I'll switch one of the electrodes over to it, if you're still feeling game."

The sounding attachment for his e-stim device wasn't long. It would only intrude a few inches into Harrison's urethra, so despite teasing Harrison about this being adventurous, it really wasn't. The sound was slim too. Not slim enough to risk tearing Harrison's urethra, but not so thick as to be intimidating. Some of the sounds in his kit would have Harrison opening his eyes a lot wider than they were now.

Harrison's eyes were a little wide though. "So that goes in me, huh?"

"Like butter. Watch." He'd already gotten the metal rod slicked up with antiseptic lube, so he added a drop to the top of Harrison's cock, then touched the tip of the rod to it, opening the entrance and pushing lube down into it. "Feel all right?"

"Tickly."

"Yeah, it's weird at first, but you don't have to be a masochist to enjoy this, just like with the TENS. It's more sensation than pain. Here we go." He let gravity do the work, lightly guiding the sound as it sank. When it was fully buried, he pulled it back out and repeated the motion a few times, giving Harrison time to process what he was feeling.

"That's so weird."

"Good weird though, right?"

"Dirty weird. No one's supposed to be touching me there. Mm." That last noise was caused by Cash dialing up the intensity on the e-stim. Harrison's entire groin was alive and crackling now, inside and out.

"Ready for this?" He disconnected the electrode from the head of Harrison's cock and held it up for him to see.

Harrison nodded with a brightness in his eyes that was either determination or anticipation as Cash connected the electrode to the end of the sound. Harrison reacted immediately. The crackle of electrical current made him jerk, and he thrust his hips up as if he could chase it—could find it and meet it. But it was inside him. Pulses raced through him, wracking him from the inside out.

"Did I mention it vibrates?" If Cash wasn't so turned on he was about to swallow his tongue, he would've laughed at Harrison's reaction.

"Oh, shit" followed by "oh, fuck" followed by "oh, God."

Yeah, Harrison was loving it, loving it as much as Cash had hoped he would. Cash's heart and cock both swelled. He'd found the perfect mechanism to bring Harrison to a spectacular orgasm. Harrison was never going to forget this, not if Cash could help it. He played the TENS like an instrument, changing up the frequency and duration and intensity as Harrison's ass churned on the wood chair fast enough to start a fire.

"Jesus, Cash. What happens if I come with that in. Oh fuck, I'm going to. I'm going to come right now."

The answer to Harrison's question was "nothing dramatic." His ejaculation would either seep out around the probe or force the probe out. But Cash wasn't ready to let him come yet. He cranked the intensity higher so the sensation would edge closer to pain, and Harrison let out a short shriek in response. His arms jerked forward, reaching for the device, but the cuffs around his wrists kept him from it. He relaxed with a moan when the pulse stopped, then jerked upright again when the next one hit.

"Thought you weren't a sadist," he gritted out.

"Am I hurting you or driving you wild?"

"Both. Let me come, Cash. Ah!" That pulse seemed to run all the way through him. "It's good that way too," he panted. "It's good when it hurts, but I don't know if I can come like this."

"Let's try this then." He wanted to drag it out longer, but he couldn't deny himself the spectacle of watching Harrison come any longer. He turned the dial up on the pulse length, maxing it out so the next burst hit and held.

Harrison jerked with it, and then there it was: the first jet of come squirting out from around the rod.

Harrison screamed like someone executing a particularly challenging karate move as the sounding rod squirted out. It clanked to the floor where Cash would deal with it later. He didn't want to miss a single moment of this orgasm that had Harrison twitching in ecstasy over and over until he slumped back in his seat with a long sigh of surrender.

"Enough," he said when the next jolt hit.

"Shh, let the aftershocks work." Cash had already turned the intensity down. Way down. Now he set the frequency on high and the length on low and let the gentle, eager fingers of the TENS unit massage the last drips of come out of Harrison's cock until he was practically weeping, then Cash got down on his knees between Harrison legs to free his wrists and remove the electrodes.

He stayed between Harrison's knees to nuzzle into his groin where the warm, fresh scent of come lurked, sweet and yeasty. He licked the drips running down Harrison's shaft as he stroked himself off, not even bothering to push his shorts down, just squeezing to the memory of Harrison's orgasm. He didn't need to linger over his own orgasm because Harrison's had been his too. He just had to dismiss the buzz of need so he could revel in the soft glow of satisfaction. A few short seconds later, he was wiping his hand on the leg of his shorts.

"That's really all you want, isn't it? Just to get me off."

"Not *just* to get you off. To make you crazy, *then* get you off. To make you high, then get you off. But yeah, I'd get you off all day, any day, however you'd let me."

"Well, come on, get up. You're all shaky and messy down there." Harrison helped him to his feet, as if Cash were the one who'd been electrocuted, and settled him on the couch, then put his boxers back on—which was fair since Cash was fully dressed himself—and plopped down next to him.

113

"Phew. That just about did me in."

"Good." That was all Cash could manage. He toppled Harrison over so the two of them sprawled lengthwise across the sofa with Harrison's slighter body resting on top of his. He should get up, get Harrison something to drink, try to talk him into staying for dinner so he could meet Sandi. But first, a nap. Just a short one.

"You know a Dom named Bob Jones?"

"Huh?" Cash opened his eyes, realizing Harrison's body wasn't as limp on top of his as his was under Harrison's.

"From the club. Bob Jones?"

"No idea. Bob is too common a first name." And he didn't usually know last names. "But it's not ringing a bell. Why?"

Harrison wriggled his shoulders in a sort of shrug. "Heard there was a Dom at Hell's Bedroom by that name, that's all. Thought you might know him."

"Oh."

So that was where they were at. Cash had thought that'd been a really excellent scene. He'd thought Harrison had been as into it as he'd been. But they couldn't even have ten minutes of post-scene snuggle before Harrison started searching for a Dom who would suit him better.

"Hey." Harrison propped himself up on an elbow that dug into Cash's chest. "What's wrong?"

"Nothing. I just don't know him. Sorry."

"Did I say something to upset you?"

"Not at all." It wasn't anything unexpected, wasn't anything new.

"Cash." Harrison leaned down to examine him closer. Or maybe....

Oh. Harrison wanted to kiss him. Cash tilted his chin up to accept Harrison's mouth, but at the last moment, Harrison pulled away.

"I should go."

"You're leaving?" Obviously he was, since he was on his feet. "I was thinking of grilling something on the patio. My

114

friend Sandi would love to meet you."

"Another time, maybe." Harrison was putting his clothes on. All of them. One piece at a time, shutting himself back up when for a while there he'd been so open.

No matter how good that scene had been, there was something wrong between them. In all the time they'd spent together, Harrison had barely touched him back. To some extent, it was the nature of their roles, and when Cash was in the throes of a sexual encounter, he was too focused to keep score, but this wasn't the relationship he wanted outside of a scene.

He wanted a man who would kiss him. Not to mention one who preferred him to any other Dom in the world. And it seemed Harrison wasn't going to be that man.

Chapter 13 Harrison

Harrison jogged up the stairs leading out from Cash's apartment onto the street, fleeing from cuddling and dinner and meeting each other's friends, from mind-blowing orgasms and wild experimentation and kisses. From Cash.

The only part of that encounter that had been remotely work related was when he'd tried to fish for a clue to Bob Jones's identity. And that hadn't paid off. The more practical way to figure out which of the hundred Bob Joneses in Boston was his pigeon was to see if Knight could point him in the right direction. It was well past normal business hours, but BDSM clubs were all about second shift, and Knight answered when Harrison rang his office phone.

"As I'm sure you can imagine," Knight said after Harrison explained the reason for his call, "we owe our members a certain confidentiality."

"Look, you already told me who signed Arlo in. Suppose his name had been Archibald Longbottom the Third. I could've pulled up his address in a heartbeat. So what's the difference? Save me a few dozen unnecessary visits where I explain to every Bob Jones in Boston what Hell's Bedroom is and why I'm bothering them about it."

Knight sighed. "And you never tell anyone where you got the information from, right?"

"Just between us."

There was another sigh followed by the sound of keys clacking, and then Knight's voice, which was deep enough to be called subterranean, recited an address. Harrison typed it into the notepad app on his phone.

"Got it. Thanks."

"Try to leave Hell's Bedroom out of it from now on, huh?"

"Trying," Harrison agreed. He texted the address to Brixby, who was working swing shift, and asked him to run a trace. Then he hopped a cab over to the precinct house to meet him. Arlo had been missing six weeks now. His case deserved some urgency.

"Forty-five and Caucasian," Brixby said about Bob Jones when Harrison met him on the steps of the building. "Five-ten, according to his driver's license.

"Meaning he's five-eight."

"Lives out in Brookline," Brixby said without laughing at Harrison's joke. Brixby was tall enough that he'd probably never worried about his height. "Want to take a ride?"

"Yeah, let's go say hi to Mr. Jones."

Having a cruiser was pretty handy. For the most part, Harrison managed without a car, only renting one when it was absolutely necessary and he had a client who would cover the expense, but if you didn't have to pay for parking, he could see the appeal of being able to hop in and go wherever you wanted. Until they hit the first of what would likely be hundreds of stop lights.

"Learn anything new from Minton?" Brixby asked.

"Minton? Oh, Cash."

"Yeah, Cash. Part suspect, part Dom. Part love interest?"

"I already ruled him out as a suspect."

"Sure, boss. Not a suspect. Let's call him a witness. How'd your interrogation session go this evening?"

"I didn't tell you I was spending time with Cash." He'd agreed to wear the medallion until the investigation was

117

over since Brixby had sacrificed a family heirloom to keep him safe, but he hadn't agreed to have his every move watched.

"Don't you think you should've?"

"I didn't ask you to monitor me when you're not working for me either."

"I set up the app to alert me when your signal wanders into certain sections of town. I was about to charge over there to rescue you."

"Which I definitely didn't ask you to do. The light's green, by the way." If they hadn't been in a cruiser, the guy behind them would've been honking already.

Brixby eased his foot off the brake. "Not kidding, Fisher. How am I supposed to tell the difference between dating and kidnapping? Seeing you now, I can guess which it was. You look like you've been taken apart and put back together wrong."

Harrison ran a hand over his hair. Was it sticking up on one side or something?

"Tell me you didn't get laid."

"None of your business."

"Then tell me it was good."

"What did I just say?"

"Come on, I'm working a BDSM case and not getting any myself. Let me live vicariously." Brixby's attention was fixed straight out the window, but he had a big goofy grin plastered across his face.

On the force, Harrison's sexuality had been a topic best avoided. Having a partner tease him about it was new. And having a partner who was an expert in this odd way of life he might have rejected too hastily after a single bad experience at seventeen was a benefit he probably shouldn't pass up.

"He electrocuted me."

"With a violet wand?" Brixby didn't seem surprised by the concept of sexual electrocution.

"That's not what he called it. It was sort of—"

He used his hands and words to describe the layout of the box and the nature of the pads that'd been attached to him until Brixby said, "Oh, a TENS unit. Much nicer than a violet wand. Unless you like that sort of thing, which maybe you would. Never say never."

So then he had to have Brixby explain what a violet wand was. It was a wand that was violet, so good job on the naming. Much better than TENS, which probably stood for something but he couldn't be bothered to Google what. But as far as violet wands went, their reasonableness ended with their name.

"Like a taser," he said when Brixby had finished explaining. "It's basically an old fashioned taser."

"Sexier, but not dissimilar. Like I said, never say never."

Harrison thought violet wands might be a never, but two weeks ago he'd been dead set against all of this.

"There was also..." He couldn't figure out how to finish that sentence without using words too intimate for a police cruiser. "A thing."

"A thing?"

"In my, um..." He looked down at his crotch.

"*In* your... or *on* your..."

"In."

"Oh, a sound. Sure. How'd you like that?" Again, Brixby's casual response reassured Harrison that none of what he and Cash had done was too far out there.

"Cash said it was just a short one," he answered, rather than explain how he'd liked it, which was really a lot. How many new spots on his body could Cash find to touch if Harrison let him?

"Yeah, sounds can get long. Thick too. Sounding can be a real fetish or just, you know, a way to get off. I guess that's true for anything." Brixby laughed, still acting like this was all super normal. Driving in a squad car talking about sliding metal rods into your dick. Totally normal. Harrison had fallen down a rabbit hole, and a metal rod had been shoved in after him.

119

"How about you let me know when you're planning to spend time with Cash and when you expect to be done? Then I won't worry."

"I don't know why I'd see him again anyway. We've found the guy Arlo was last seen with."

"Never say never," Brixby repeated with a grin as he pulled up in front of a modest one-story house, set back a ways from the street.

Harrison examined the cottage, which was clad in light blue siding that could use a power wash. The yard had been landscaped in the past, but the landscaping hadn't been maintained. The rose bushes flanking the house were fading in the July heat and while the smell of fresh-mown grass drifted through the air, it wasn't coming from this place.

"I just hope Arlo's somewhere we can get him back from," Harrison said. "Not six feet deep in this guy's backyard."

"Are we knocking?"

"We just pulled up in a Boston PD cruiser. If he's in there, he knows we're here. Let's start by knocking." He got out on his side and Brixby got out on the other, donning his hat and hitching his gun belt up to be maximum cop, which made Harrison realize he was dressed in the shorts and t-shirt he'd worn for his date with Cash. He was glad he'd brought Brixby along to give him a more official air.

The door opened fast enough to confirm that Bob Jones had indeed seen them pull up. He was white, only barely middle-aged but already balding, and definitely not five-ten—five-nine, if Harrison was feeling generous—slim with a gut, the kind of guy who didn't carry weight anywhere except his stomach.

"Mind if we come inside?" Harrison executed his patented license-flashing move. Jones debated the question for a moment before backing into his house, inviting them in with a gesture. The front door opened into a small vestibule that led to the living space, where a large television blared a typically grim news report.

Jones went over and clicked it off. "What's this about?"

"Arlo Gandry."

"Arlo Gandry," Jones repeated. He settled onto one of a matching pair of delicate chairs upholstered in light blue satin that put Harrison in mind of a Victorian drawing room. Harrison let Brixby take the other one and seated himself on a different blue thing that was reminiscent of a fainting couch, choosing to perch on the edge rather than recline.

"I never knew his last name," Jones said, "but I know who you mean."

"When was the last time you saw him?"

"I couldn't give you a date."

"Could you give us an event? Maybe something happened the last time you saw him that sticks out in your mind."

Jones set his lips in a firm line. "Why exactly are you here again?"

"Because no one's heard from Arlo since he was with you."

"He wasn't *with* me. He was just *there*. Obviously you know where. But not with me."

"You signed him in."

"Only because someone had to. He asked me if I would, and I did. I should've known better." Jones crossed his arms over his chest, managing to look put out by a teenager's inconvenient disappearance. "I never saw him after we got into the playroom. He had his pursuits, and I had mine."

"You weren't his Dom?"

"Do I *look* like a Dom?"

"No," Brixby answered immediately, as if Jones had the word sub tattooed on his forehead. "And neither was Arlo, so why sign him in?"

"I remember how it was before I became a member. The club makes it hard on subs, you know." Jones pursed his lips into an expression that had Harrison understanding

121

why Brixby was so sure he wasn't a Dom. "They're prejudiced against us. Doms only need one member recommendation to join. Subs need three. It took me a full year of playing nice for whatever Dom was willing to sign me in before I earned the right to show up on my own schedule and pick my own partner. Arlo wanted in, so I signed him in. I might be sexually submissive, but fuck the power structure."

"Did you know he was underage?" Harrison asked.

"Not until Security hauled me in to talk to them. I didn't card the guy."

"You didn't think it was advisable to know who you were fucking around with?"

"I *told* you. I wasn't fucking around with him. Our parts don't match up that way. *He* gets it." Jones nodded at Brixby, who shrugged as if to agree.

"So you knew him well enough to know which way his parts went."

"I met him at a play party and gave him some tips—who's got a hot hand, horror stories about who to avoid, that kind of stuff. Arlo wanted to go deep. Twenty-four seven deep, which is too rich for my blood. I have a life." Jones waved at his ice-blue living room with its dozens of twinkling thingamajigs and oceans of brocade upholstery. "I have no desire to live under someone's heel."

Harrison made a mental note to ask Brixby about some of the terms Jones had just used. "Where'd you take him after he got thrown out?"

"I didn't. I was mid-scene when he got pinched, and Security knew better than to interrupt us. By the time I was done, he was already gone. I never saw him again."

"No one has seen him again."

"I'm sorry to hear that. He seemed like a good kid. Person," Jones corrected quickly. "I didn't know he was a kid. Anyway, I hope he's okay, and my bad signing him in, but I have no idea where he is now. Security put him out. Whatever happened to him after that, it didn't happen at

Hell's Bedroom."

Harrison had already semi-reached that conclusion after talking to Knight. Now, after talking to Jones, he wondered if it was possible that Arlo's interest in BDSM was a red herring, one he'd overreacted to because of his own personal issues. Maybe he should be working Arlo's disappearance like a regular missing persons case, which, given that Arlo was nearly eighteen and nobody was paying Harrison to do this, meant not working it at all. Brixby had managed to get Arlo's official missing persons case reassigned to him, but his sergeant wouldn't like him putting a lot of hours into it, and Harrison couldn't keep paying him out of his own pocket.

He left Jones with Brixby's contact information and got back into the squad car dispiritedly, wishing a gay teenager's life was worth as much in media points as an eight-year-old girl's. There would be no Amber alerts for Arlo.

"What did Jones mean by twenty-four seven," he asked when Brixby had started the car and turned the squawk box back on.

"Lifestyle BDSM, sort of consensual slavery. What you and Cash have been doing is scening. In twenty-four seven, the scene never ends."

"Why would Arlo want that?"

"He was young. He might've changed his mind once he got a taste of it. As a concept, it's romantic. In actual practice, it's a lot of damned work."

"All that bowing and scraping," Harrison muttered, unable to imagine the hell of living that life.

"I meant for the Dom," Brixby said with a laugh. "Lifestyle BDSM is like owning a very needy dog. But sure, for the sub too, depending on how demanding the Dom is. Most of us aren't ogres, you know. More like caretakers."

"Like Cash."

"Sure, same principle."

"Then why does Cash get so much shit?"

"Not sure I can explain it, but I understand why he's not for everyone. If you were interested in having someone dominate you, you'd understand too. As it is, the most you want is someone to hurt you a little." Brixby smirked. These conversations always seemed to transition from Arlo's disappearance to Harrison's sex life really fast.

"Cash makes me feel things. I never said anything about pain." The e-stim hadn't hurt. Much. And the other day with his nipples, that'd been... good. Painfully good. Goodly painful. "I don't understand why people want to be abused, how they can get off on it."

"Careful with the judgement. You want what you want. Let other people want what they want."

Fine, he wouldn't judge. He still didn't get it though. He tapped his knee with restless fingers as they made their slow way back downtown.

"What's next?" Brixby asked a few stoplights later.

Harrison debated calling the whole investigation off, but he couldn't quite bring himself to do it. Whether Hell's Bedroom was involved or not, Arlo was still missing. "You find any of those other kids from the incident reports Knight gave us?"

"Two of them. One sixteen, one seventeen, both trying to get an early start on their kink careers like Arlo, except that they're alive and well and right where they're supposed to be. I gave them a lecture about waiting until they're eighteen to explore and didn't rat them out to their parents. You think I should've?"

Harrison shook his head. Parents could be shitty. Shittier even than random Doms. "What about the other one?"

"Fake ID, not very well done. One of our data techs matched the photo to a mug shot from Rhode Island of a woman named Jessica Chambers. Who's nineteen, as it turns out. I don't know why she was using a fake ID, but maybe because she's got a passel of outstanding warrants in Rhode Island. Sounds like a drug problem, based on the types of things she's been hauled in for. Prostitution, et cetera."

Harrison nodded. He was familiar with the trajectory drug addicts tended to take, especially young ones without an adequate support system. It started with petty thievery and almost always ended with them selling themselves. A nineteen-year-old runaway with a drug problem using a fake ID at a BDSM club sounded like bad news.

"Did you look for her?"

"Not as hard as I'd like. Technically, I'm on patrol, right?" Brixby ginned conspiratorially. "I haven't made detective yet. But the time I've had to put in on it hasn't turned her up. What do you say we drop in on Nicholas Popinjay? That's the guy who signed her into the club. It's not outside my job duties to have a little chat with the man."

Popinjay. Harrison snickered to himself. A lot easier to find than Bob Jones. Almost as good as Archibald Longbottom. He pulled up the address of the only Nicholas Popinjay in the Greater Boston Area, punched it into Brixby's GPS, then sat back for the ride to Beacon Hill where Popinjay lived in a Victorian brick rowhouse on a picturesque cobblestone street no bigger than an alleyway. Harrison was glad they didn't have to find a legal place to park. For all its quaint appeal, Beacon Hill must be hell in the winter.

The door to Popinjay's townhouse was opened by a white woman Harrison assumed was his wife. In the hopes of having something to hold over Popinjay's head in exchange for his cooperation, Harrison kept the reason for their presence vague. Popinjay, when he came to the door, reacted like a man who'd half expected a visit from the police, flushing a deep red that could be either anger or guilt.

Despite it being nearly nine o'clock, he still wore a suit. His tie was undone, but it hung around his neck, and his feet were shoeless but clad in black socks. The narrow set of his eyes had Harrison regretting his own informal state of dress. This was the kind of asshole who only respected people he saw as social equals. Harrison pulled himself up taller and gave back a glare that dared Popinjay to fuck with him.

"Something happened at work today," Popinjay told his wife. "Nothing to be concerned about. They're here to take my statement. I'll bring them up to my office so we don't bother you with it."

"Should I make coffee?" she called after them as Popinjay practically towed them through the lower floor, up the stairs, and into a room overlooking the street.

"Not necessary," he yelled back before shutting the door firmly behind them. The room he'd brought them to featured a large dark-wood desk, which he took a seat behind. The only other place to sit was on a low black leather couch, so Harrison and Brixby sat next to each other on it like they were about to get busy in the back seat of a Caddy.

"Was it necessary to come to my home?" Popinjay asked them.

"If you were expecting us, you could've come down to the precinct and saved us a trip," Brixby answered.

"I wasn't expecting you. I have no idea why you're here."

That seemed unlikely, given how quickly and decisively he'd reacted to their presence, so Harrison only raised an eyebrow.

"I can guess," Popinjay admitted. "It's something about the club, something about what I've done at the club. It's all consensual. Security is very strict. If someone changed their mind, that's on them. They consented at the time, and that's all I'm going to say without a lawyer present."

Well. Someone had a guilty conscience about something. Harrison just wasn't sure the something in question had anything to do with his case. "We're here about Jessica Chambers."

"Who?"

"The young woman with the fake ID you brought to

Hell's Bedroom."

"Oh. Her." Popinjay waved a hand as if he could make her vanish. *Had* he made her vanish? "Look, I had no idea she was underage. In fact, for all I know, she wasn't. Security said her ID was fake, but that doesn't prove she was underage. There are a hundred reasons to be carrying a fake ID."

He was right about her not being underage, but he was so defensive about it, Harrison doubted he believed his own story. "Want to name a few of them for me?"

"The kind of life she led? I'm not surprised she'd want to keep her real name to herself, and I didn't ask for it either. But underage?" Popinjay shrugged. "You wouldn't think so. I mean, you've seen her, right?" He held his hands out in front of his chest, cupping them to suggest large breasts. "Natural, too."

"So you've touched her breasts? Or just looked at them?"

"Ha!" Popinjay wagged his finger in their direction. "I see what you're trying to get me to admit, but I met her at a strip club and I saw 'em there. So if you want to talk to someone about her being underage and flashing her tits, talk to them."

"Which strip club was that?" Brixby pulled out his notebook.

"Titaranasaurus off Tremont. You ask them. She worked there. As far as I'm concerned, she was plenty of age."

"All right," Harrison said with a shrug. "Let's say she was of age. How'd you end up bringing her to Hell's Bedroom?"

"She was interested. And she had a good attitude."

"Meaning she let you do whatever you wanted to her?" Brixby asked with a hard edge to his voice.

"I'm the Dom, aren't I? That's how it works. But don't worry, she was a kinky motherfucker. Wanted it more than I did. Wanted to live with me, if you can believe." Popinjay snorted. "As if I'd bring that kind of trash home."

Harrison clenched his fists. The sneer in Popinjay's voice was so exactly like what he remembered from Sir Magnus. And like that woman at Hell's Bedroom too, the one who'd been forcing a man to drink piss while she used words she had no right to use. Disdain like that was too psychologically damaging to be sexual, and no one could convince him otherwise. He'd enjoyed himself with Cash earlier, but he was beginning to see why Cash didn't call himself a Dom. Doms were people who thought you owed them your self-respect.

Brixby had tensed as though he were equally pissed, but for all Harrison knew, he spoke to his subs the same way. "When was the last time you saw her?" he asked.

"That night. After Security booted us, I left her on the street outside the club, and I haven't looked her up since. I'm not going to blow my membership at Hell's Bedroom over a hooker."

"Was she a hooker?"

Popinjay wagged his finger again. "Just an expression. You've got nothing on me. I had no reason to believe she was underage, and I never gave her a dime. Not outside of tips. Everything I did was perfectly legal."

Legal, maybe, but shitty all the same. Still, for all Popinjay's shittiness, Harrison wasn't seeing a tie-in to Arlo.

"Know anything about this kid?" He handed over his phone with the photo of Arlo loaded.

"That's a guy." Popinjay handed it back. "Got a mouth like a chick, but he ain't one."

"No one said he was."

"So why would I know anything about him? I don't swing that way. No offense to whoever, but I'm not at Hell's Bedroom to scope out the male subs."

"If you don't know him, how do you know he's a sub?"

"Come on. Mouth like that? Fucking police. Always trying to trick you into saying something to implicate yourself. I don't even have to talk to you." Popinjay stood up like he was done talking to them, and after a moment, Harrison stood up too. Popinjay was an ass, but as far as Arlo went, he was probably a dead end.

Back out on the street, they talked about where to go next.

"Jessica and Arlo may have made it out of the club, but they don't seem to have made it far," Harrison observed. "Last anyone saw either of them, they were on the curb outside. I hate to say it"—because he'd just promised Knight he would try to keep his investigation out of Hell's Bedroom—"but the club is still the best lead we've got.

"You think someone followed them out of there?"

"Feels like it. Wait for a vulnerable kid to get pinched by Security, pick them up from the sidewalk after they've been turfed."

"So we've got a predator stalking Hell's Bedroom."

Harrison nodded. "Maybe we do."

The place had seemed friendly, communal, almost wholesome with Cash at his side, but Popinjay was a good reminder that not all Doms were Cash.

Chapter 14 Cash

"Should I tell Harrison to go fuck himself?" Cash dropped his phone on the counter and grabbed the salt and pepper shakers to season the salmon steaks he was prepping for the grill. "I asked you a question," he said pointedly, but Mr. Moo still didn't answer. Maybe because his attention was on the salmon, but maybe because the answer was obvious.

Cash should tell Harrison to go fuck himself. Since barreling out of here after their e-stim session, Harrison had been completely incommunicado until a minute ago when he'd sent a text asking for a playdate at the club.

"He only wants me for my membership," Cash said to Mr. Moo. And Ellie, if she was listening. He never knew whether she was behind the wall or not. "I should've realized it from the beginning." All that business about experimentation had been so much bullshit. Cash was just a means to Harrison's end, whatever *that* was. It wasn't him, as usual.

"And you know I can't give you salmon," he added. "Because it's full of bones that might choke you. But I can give you this nice can of salmon-flavored whatever-this-is."

"I'd rather have the good stuff."

For a moment, Cash thought Mr. Moo had answered him in a voice pitched as high as his demanding meows. But it was Sandi, of course, come down from her apartment with a pitcher of margaritas.

"You're getting the good stuff," he told her as he served Mr. Moo from a can that at least *said* salmon. "Take that out to the patio. I'll be right there." He switched the music over to the outdoor speakers, then carried the plate of salmon to the grill.

"What was that about Harrison wanting you for your membership?" Sandi asked as she filled a glass and handed it over.

"You heard that, huh? I thought it was just me and the Moo."

"Well, if you want a *person's* opinion..."

"He texted today, asking if we could go to the club. I haven't heard from him in three days, not since he ran out of here like his ass was on fire and the sidewalk was a swimming pool, but he wants back in the club, all right. What do I tell him?"

"Tell him no," she said, as if it were that simple. "I know you saw something in him, but you have to admit warning bells have been ringing this whole time."

Loud and clear. Any honest reaction he managed to squeeze out of Harrison was inevitably followed by a dishonest one, and this request to go back to the club was the final straw. Cash needed to respect himself more than this. If what Harrison wanted was a club membership—or a more classic Dom—then he could find someone else to play with.

"You're disappointed," Sandi observed.

"Goes without saying, doesn't it?"

"You had a good scene the other day." She knew because she'd heard it. Or so she'd teased him when she'd come down afterward and found him half bemused and half ecstatic, still reeling both from how good it'd been and from Harrison's abrupt departure. "You're lucky it's only me living above you. Someone else might've called the cops."

That was what Cash aspired to—sex so good his neighbors called the cops. And he'd had it. For half an hour.

"Offer him a compromise," Sandi suggested. "Say no to

131

the club, but yes to him. Maybe he doesn't understand the message he's sending when he asks to go there. There could be any number of reasons for it besides you being a sucky Dom. And that's *you* saying you're a sucky Dom, not me. I know what kind of shit you fill your head with."

Cash used the excuse of needing to flip the salmon steaks to avoid making eye contact. Sucky Dom was exactly where his head had gone. But there was that kid Harrison had asked about. Arlo. Could that be it? Or was he giving Harrison too much benefit of the doubt because of how badly he wanted the guy he caught glimpses of in between evasions?

"Ask for what you need, Cash. It's allowed to be about you sometimes."

All right, fine. He went inside and found his phone and used it to send Harrison a text saying exactly what Sandi had suggested: no to the club, yes to seeing him. When he hadn't gotten an answer several minutes later, he left his phone on the counter and returned to his station at the grill. The lack of response must've shown on his face because Sandi didn't say anything, just topped off his glass.

"How's work?" she asked to change the subject.

"No more interesting than ever."

"Oh, don't sulk. Do you know what you need? A better playlist. This 80s stuff you listen to warps your brain. Honestly, Cash, you were barely alive in the 80s."

"It's upbeat."

"Upbeat and fake. Everyone's having fun, but they're all lying. I'm going to play you some good soul-crushing music, the kind where you can wallow in your misery and know you're not alone. Eventually you'll get sick of the dank, shake it off, and start over fresh. Where's your phone?"

"In the kitchen. I hate emo," he called after her. He could shake off his funk without wallowing in it. Maybe he would go down to the club alone. That would be a good fuck-you to Harrison. *See? All this could've been yours if you'd played nice with me.*

"Maybe it's not as bad as you think." Sandi held his phone out to him as she came back through the slider. "One missed call from a Harry Harrison Sub."

"I don't know his last name," Cash muttered to explain Harrison's contact record. "I'll call him back later."

"I don't get to listen?"

"You wish." He pocketed the phone before she could make good on her threat to change the music. He liked this song—a classic Boy George.

Where had all the genderbending gone in mainstream media? The 80s had been a brief queer heyday before toxic masculinity and misogyny had taken over again. Sometimes he wondered if his style of topping would've been more acceptable then. Maybe Doms hadn't always had to be so hard and insistent. Maybe there'd been a time when subs had liked having a soft boi beat them.

HARRISON HADN'T LEFT A VOICEMAIL. There was only the missed call record to show he'd called at all, no text or other message indicating he was agreeing to Cash's stipulation. Cash could probably leave it there. He'd said what he'd said, and the next move was Harrison's. But he didn't leave it there.

After Sandi toddled off, back through the slider and up to her own apartment, taking her empty pitcher with her, Cash found himself brooding over his phone, looking at Harrison's name on the screen as if he could read something into it. The twilight around him was brightened only by the light streaming through his neighbors' windows, and he knew when Sandi made it home because her living room light popped on, casting another rectangle of pale yellow over his garden.

A breeze teased at the wisteria decorating his gazebo, then whispered through the rose bushes and clumps of day lilies. It was a night for sharing, with the moon rising overhead and the warm weight of tequila in his chest, quiet now that he'd shut off his tunes in consideration of the hour. He had a hamster and a cat and a best friend, but thinking about what he didn't have led to him calling Harrison despite his determination not to.

Sure enough, he'd barely made it through pleasantries before Harrison started pushing the idea of their next date being at Hell's Bedroom.

"Why are you so fixated on going to the club?"

"Why are you so determined to keep me out of it?"

"Because you didn't enjoy playing in public."

"We could get a private room."

"I have a private room here."

"You said it was dangerous to let strangers tie you up."

"Why would I tie you up? You don't like being tied up. And am I still a stranger? I thought— Fuck, never mind what I thought. If you don't trust me, you don't trust me."

"I do. Shit. Cash." There was silence on the line while Cash waited for Harrison to say something that made sense. "You said it would be good for me to get to know people in the community."

"I did?"

"I think that was you," Harrison mumbled. "Anyway, it would be, wouldn't it? I'm a social kind of guy. I want to make kinky friends."

Cash reminded himself that he didn't know Harrison well enough to be sure that was a lie. Maybe Harrison was a social butterfly in non-sexual, non-kinky situations. But when Cash had invited him to stick around for dinner with Sandi, he'd practically run. And he'd been ready to either fight Sebastian or fuck him but he hadn't seemed too keen on talking to him. Francesca either.

"We could alternate," Harrison wheedled. "One time my way, one time your way. That's fair, isn't it? If we go to the club, I'll let you do whatever. You can pick how we play. Whatever you like."

And Harrison still wasn't getting it, wasn't getting that

134

Cash needed *him* to like it.

"Ever try Daddy kink?" he asked, intentionally picking something he knew Harrison would hate.

"Daddy like, um, calling you Daddy?"

"Yeah, like you crawl around with your thumb in your mouth and call me Daddy. And I call you baby. Or boy. Maybe change your didey for you. How does that sound?" He waited, hoping Harrison would admit it sounded awful.

"Sure," Harrison said after a moment, his voice sticky with how much he meant no. "We could try that."

"Or maybe humiliation kink. Took me a while to get good at that one, but trust me, I can do it."

"I don't even understand how that works."

"I just tell you what I think of you, Harry. What awful, awful things I think about a disgusting little worm named Harry while you beg me to stop even as your dick gets harder and harder because the most shameful, disgusting thing about you is that being humiliated turns you on, doesn't it?"

"Um..."

"Doesn't it, Harry?"

"Sure. Yeah. I'm turned on."

Liar. Harrison wanted to pretend, did he? Fine. Cash would call his bluff.

"I'll meet you there Saturday. Wear those booty shorts again. I want to be able to check out my boy's ass."

"Cash?"

"This is what you want, right? What you're asking me for?"

There were men out there who wanted to be talked to the way he'd just talked to Harrison, and Cash hadn't been lying when he'd said he'd taught himself how to do it, but Harrison didn't like it, and Cash couldn't keep it up any longer. Tequila swam in his head and churned in his stomach, feeling like the worst idea ever except for this idea of meeting Harrison at the club so he could humiliate him or dress him in nappies. So he could punish him. For refusing to tell the fucking truth.

"I have to go." He hung up without any further warning and made a dash for the bushes in case the contents of his stomach came up. He stood there—heaving, waiting—but the nausea receded without producing any results, and the ding of an incoming message called him back to the present dilemma.

"At 8?" Harrison had texted.

Whatever it was Harrison wanted, he wanted it badly enough to subject himself to a whole lot of what he didn't want. Cash agreed to the time, then powered his phone all the way off. He would meet Harrison at the club Saturday, then resign his membership. It would put an end to this argument. And probably to their relationship.

CASH LOWERED THE BLINDS in the private room he'd booked. Whatever was about to happen, they didn't need any witnesses to it. Harrison was dressed identically to the last time they'd been at the club—shiny black short-shorts with nothing beneath them and a medallion swinging against the coating of fur on his chest—but he regarded Cash with a distant suspicion that was new. Cash had betrayed his trust with that little scene on the phone. A non-consensual, viciously unkind scene he was angry at himself for letting Harrison goad him into.

"Let's not do this," he said, weary of the battle.

He'd been half-drunk that night. Sober, he couldn't summon the desire to punish. He should've followed his instincts and not returned Harrison's call. He definitely shouldn't have agreed to meet him.

"You wanted to get into the club, you're in the club. Just... go. Do whatever. Find whoever. I'm going to stay here."

He lowered himself into one of the wooden chairs set along the wall. It would make a good spanking chair, his mind uselessly told him. Harrison lurked by the door, his back against the wall and his head tilted, as if Cash were the one being confusing.

"I thought you were going to do things to me."

"Like what? Order you to crawl across the floor and suck my dick?"

"I guess. Is that what you want?"

"No, Harrison. That's not what I want. None of this is what I want, and I have no idea what you want."

Harrison looked the other way, as if what he wanted was in the far corner of the room. "You haven't even tried me."

"Get on your knees then."

Harrison did it. He got on his knees.

"Crawl over here."

He did that too.

"Take my dick out and suck it."

There was a physical stutter, as if Harrison might not do it, but then he reached for him, his fingers going for the button on his jeans, then the zipper, drawing it down slowly, reluctance evident in every movement, as if touching Cash's dick was the worst punishment he could be inflicted with. Worse than kneeling, worse than crawling.

He separated the folds of denim and burrowed beneath the waistband of Cash's briefs to pull out his dick. A limp, wholly uninterested dick Harrison regarded like he'd never seen a dick before.

"Go on," Cash ordered. "I told you to suck it." He steeled himself for the psychic pain of being swallowed by an unwilling mouth, but Harrison apparently couldn't make himself go that far.

"You don't really seem into it," he said instead.

"Does it matter?"

"Why are you telling me to do this if it's not what you want?"

"Why are you making me tell you to do this if it's not what *you* want? Why are we doing this, Harrison?" He

137

pushed Harrison away and zipped himself up with rushed movements. His dick had never been so soft. His heart had never been so hard. "I don't know what you want here, but it's sure as hell not me."

Chapter 15 Harrison

Harrison fumbled for the medallion hanging around his neck. He wasn't a religious man, either by upbringing or by nature, but he needed a touchstone, something to guide him as to how to proceed. He'd made a royal mess of this, failing at every turn to convince Cash he belonged at Hell's Bedroom, succeeding only in hurting Cash's feelings.

The other day on the phone, when he couldn't see the expression on Cash's face, he'd believed the cruel words and the horrible tone behind them, had believed Cash could want that, could want to hurt him. Calling him Harry when Cash knew how he felt about being called Harry. Diapers, Daddy. If anyone was going to be the Daddy in Harrison's bed, it was him. No one got to play at being bigger than him.

But now that Cash was in front of him, he could see the truth in Cash's limp dick, in the hard-and-hurt set of his eyes, in the light tremor of his half-clenched fists. Cash was hating this as much as he was. They'd pushed each other to it. Or no. This was all his fault. His lies, his inconsistencies. He'd forced a kind man to be cruel, had turned Cash into exactly the kind of Dom he'd spent his whole life avoiding.

"I'm sorry."

Cash stood up, his penis already tucked away again. "Not your fault I can't get it up."

"I think it is."

"Yeah, maybe it is." Cash turned for the door as if he might disappear through it.

"Can we talk?" Harrison asked, stopping him before he could get away.

"Are you going to tell me some kind of truth if we do?"

"If you're still willing to listen. Can we go to your place?"

"Seriously?" Cash's face was so hopeful it broke Harrison's heart.

God, he didn't deserve for Cash to give him a second chance. Third chance. Whatever number they were up to. He didn't deserve for there to be a possibility of something real here, but he was going to fight for it, whether he deserved it or not. For Cash's sake. Because *Cash* deserved it.

He went over to Cash and took both his hands. "I'm sorry," he said again. He had to go up on his toes to do it, but he pressed his mouth against Cash's, a brief promise of a kiss that had Cash breaking into a bright smile.

"You'll tell me the truth from now on?"

"Promise. Take me home, and I'll tell you everything."

"SO BRIXBY'S UNIT RAIDED TITARANASAURUS. They found an underage girl and a couple of undocumented immigrants, but they didn't find Jessica Chambers. No one's seen her since the night she got thrown out of Hell's Bedroom, just like no one's seen Arlo. He's male, she's female. He's gay, she's straight. Hell's Bedroom is the only common denominator we've got. And that," he said in conclusion of what had been a half hour summary of the case to date, "is why I wanted to go to the club tonight. I don't know what I'm looking for, but I was hoping to find something."

So where did that leave them? Harrison wanted a chance to explore a real relationship with Cash, who looked stormy—not mollified by the truth. More like pissed about it. Which he had every right to be. Harrison had perpetrated an ongoing and egregious deception. They'd had *sex*, for God's sake.

"Are you mad?" he asked, though he could already tell the answer was yes.

When they'd arrived at Cash's apartment, Cash had steered him over to a canvas side chair instead of the comfy loveseat. Cash was on the loveseat all by himself today, his arms crossed over his chest and a fierce expression on his face.

"You are. You're mad about me lying to you. Of course you are."

"Dude, that's your job. I get it." Cash unwound his arms and used one hand to rake through the floppy mess of his hair. "I'm mad someone might be using my club to kidnap people, not because you're trying to stop it. And I'm mad at myself for not realizing there was a problem. Things have been different since the change in ownership. I've known it. I just haven't been able to put my finger on it."

"Different how?"

"More strangers, more extreme exhibitionism. There was a woman down there a couple of months ago—a sub I'd never seen before—being chased. She was literally screaming for help."

"And you didn't help?" He would've expected better from Cash.

"I reported it. Security called them on the carpet for non-consensually involving other people in their scene, but everything was fine, supposedly. Just some rape play that got out of hand."

"Do you remember the date?"

"God, no. May-ish? That range."

Harrison made a note of it. He would ask Knight to look up the incident report, see if they could find the woman in question. "What else have you noticed? Since the management change, you said."

"The place just has a different vibe. Lots of security, lots of rules, more of a sterilized feel."

"Isn't that a good thing? Sounds safer, if anything."

"Hell's Bedroom used to be a community. We policed each other, I guess you'd say. New Doms got mentored. Subs were brought in under someone's protection. So yeah, there are more rules and stricter enforcement of the rules now, but it feels less safe, less like everyone has each other's back. That incident I mentioned? In the past, I'd have checked on the woman myself. I've been around long enough to know the difference between a person screaming 'help me' for the fun of it and someone who really needs help."

"What did your gut tell you?"

"That she needed help. And I passed her off to a security guard to deal with."

"Hey." Harrison got out of the chair he'd been sentenced to, hoping his sentence had been lifted at least enough that he could join Cash on the loveseat. "Don't beat yourself up over this. It's not your fault."

"Tell me what we do about it."

"We?"

"Yeah, *we*. If you need an in at Hell's Bedroom, you've got it. Whatever you need to get to the bottom of this, you've got it. I'm at your disposal. You could've told me the truth from the beginning."

"I had to consider you a suspect." Even though he never really had. "And you know so many people there. If it wasn't you, it could've been one of your friends."

"I get it. I hate the thought of it being someone I know, but that's what makes it so important to find out. BDSM is all about trust." He gave Harrison a look that had him flinching again.

"You *are* mad at me."

"Not because you didn't tell me about the case."

"Because...?"

"How much were you faking, Harrison? All of it?"

"I think you know what I was faking and what I wasn't.

142

I swear you have some kind of internal lie detector. At least when it comes to me."

"I told you what my kink is. I just can't with a disinterested partner. It's like ice water in my veins."

"Then you already know the answer to how much I was faking it."

"So the other day with the TENS unit—"

"All real, all me. And that first time with my nipples? That was me too. And some of those other things we've talked about that I said I wanted to try—I do want to try them. With you. It's just been weird because it was a job. And because I was lying to you. And because..." he trailed off, not quite ready to explain Sir Magnus.

"Is that why wouldn't kiss me? Or touch me?"

He nodded, hoping he was reading Cash's cues right as he slid closer. "It wouldn't have been right, not while I wasn't being honest with you. But could I now? I don't know where this leaves us, but if you're willing to give me another cha—"

He hadn't even finished the sentence before Cash crashed into him, fusing their mouths together with a hunger that spoke of deprivation. Harrison felt another pang of guilt over the abominable way he'd treated this honorable man. He couldn't regret blowing his cover. Only not having done it sooner.

He gave himself up to the demands Cash's mouth made as he sent his hands over the body he'd denied himself till now. Cash was strong and steady, with mountainous shoulders that felt incredible to cling to, but Harrison wanted to do more than grope some shoulders. He pushed, and Cash straightened up with a frantic look of concerned disappointment.

"Let me do you," Harrison said, taking a quick nip at Cash's mouth to reassure him he wasn't running away this time.

"Okay, but remember—"

"I know. You get off on getting me off. But I'd really like

to suck your cock. I haven't even *seen* your cock, except—"
He wasn't going to remind either of them of what he'd seen earlier because he could feel Cash's cock wedged against his hip now, hard like it ought to be. He wanted it out and in his hands. "Please let me touch you."

Heat flared in Cash's eyes. Harrison intended to keep it there by making it clear every step of the way how into this he was, how into *Cash* he was. He seriously owed Cash some truth in that regard.

He got down on the floor between Cash's legs. It was exactly like at the club except it was completely different, with Cash's eyes soft and his dick hard as Harrison worked the fastenings on his jeans and tugged down the front of his briefs to reveal the beauty beneath them.

"Ooh, Daddy."

"I didn't think that was your thing."

"I'm not calling *you* Daddy, just showing some respect for this beast you've got in your pants. Come on, let's get these all the way off. I need to see the whole snake."

Cash laughed shakily, but he assisted in the process of getting him undressed. "You're sure you want to—"

"Cash. I want to." He licked a stripe up one of the most beautiful cocks he'd ever seen. Not cartoonishly big but plenty big, perfectly proportioned with the sweetest vee at the head and a pair of shaved balls below. "Here, I've got an idea." He popped to his feet to shuck his own clothes. "Check that out," he said as he thrust his pelvis forward for Cash's inspection.

"Happy to." Cash leaned down, his mouth already open, but Harrison put a hand on his forehead to hold him back.

"Check it out with your eyes," he corrected. "See how hard I am." He stroked himself, coaxing out a drop of pre-come which he offered to Cash on his finger. "Taste how much I want you."

Cash licked his finger, his eyes flickering closed as if the taste were ambrosia. "I love how wet you get."

"Okay, so now you can see I'm turned on, that I want

this. If you're not sure at any point, just look down here." He got back into position between Cash's knees, leaving one hand on his cock to give Cash a show and getting back to the business of covering Cash's pretty dick with saliva, claiming every solid inch of it as his own.

He might not have a fetish like Cash did, but he enjoyed pleasing his partners, and he had the skills to do it. Sucking cock was one of his favorite activities. Normally he put all his attention into his technique, holding back his own enjoyment to enhance his partner's, but for Cash's sake, he kept his hand moving over his own cock fast enough to get close, working himself to orgasm as he worked Cash to orgasm and allowing his moans to seep out around the flesh in his throat. He stopped right on the edge—where it was difficult to stop—to catch some of the pre-come dripping off his cock and offer it to Cash's eager mouth.

"Do it," Cash urged. "Make yourself come. Let me see it. God, let me help. You're killing me here."

"In such a hurry," Harrison chastised. "I'm going to blow a really big load for you. When I get around to it."

Cash groaned "Fuck, I'm so turned on."

"I can see that."

Cash's dick was diamond hard, producing the occasional drop of pre-come itself—not as much as Harrison's produced, but he could catch a quick burst of flavor when he dove deep. Cash thrust his hips up, but he didn't come, and his eyes were open, sighting down to where Harrison was working himself.

"You want me to come first, don't you?" Harrison had never thought of himself as a tease, but it was fun teasing Cash with his own orgasm, fun to have a partner this focused on him even as he was getting his cock sucked.

"Please," Cash begged. "It feels good?"

"So good. Your cock hits the back of my throat just right. Triggers something in me." He sucked it down hard, forcing Cash all the way down this time and letting his orgasm swamp him at the same time. He'd never come with

145

a cock in his mouth before, but he liked it. A cock in his mouth, a cock in his hand, both of them spurting out their loads as Cash joined him in orgasm.

"Shit," Cash said faintly as the tension left his legs. "That was the best blowjob I've ever had."

"Yeah?" He wiped his mouth with the back of his hand and staggered to his feet to plop down onto the couch.

"They're not my favorite thing. Getting them, I mean. They're usually missing the mental stimulation I need. But that was amazing."

"I've been listening," Harrison told him. "I've been lying, but I've been listening."

Chapter 16 Cash

Cash hooked a hand around Harrison's neck to keep him from popping straight up. "Are you anti-cuddling or only anti-aftercare?"

"I'm not anti-cuddling," Harrison insisted, but he stayed rigid against Cash's side like he didn't know how cuddling went. "And what's aftercare?"

"When the top takes care of the bottom after a scene. Whenever I try it, you dash for the door like you have bees in your pants."

"Guilt in my heart." Harrison burrowed in just a touch, reluctantly consigning himself to the cuddling.

Cash was a cuddler. A cuddler and also one of those guys whose energy nosedived after an orgasm. If Harrison would let Cash pet him—maybe fall asleep with him—they could dispense with formal aftercare.

He dropped a kiss on top of Harrison's head. They were half-reclined, drifting toward his side of the loveseat as his ability to sit up fled. That'd been fantastic. He could only come from a blowjob when the guy was really, really into it, which in the BDSM world meant using his dick to choke someone with a choking fetish. And that required him to remain conscientiously in control so that no real choking happened. This had been nice—letting Harrison take the reins, being able to let go completely.

"Have you ever been paid for sex?" Harrison asked, clearly not as drowsy as Cash was.

"You put in for those hours we were scening?" The idea amused him more than concerned him.

"Well, no. Not that I'm expecting to make much either way." Harrison frowned, which Cash used as an excuse to wrap him up more securely, easing him into a reclining position on the loveseat, which was a tight fit for two. They should move to the bed.

"Then you weren't being paid," he said with a yawn. "Can we worry about it later? I'm all endorphined out here." Part of his job as a top was dealing with over-endorphined subs, but tonight he was the one who'd gotten his mind blown, leaving him even sleepier than usual.

Harrison rotated around in his arms so they were facing each other. He brushed Cash's bangs out of his eyes and pressed a kiss to his mouth which hung slightly open from relaxation.

"Sure, babe. Sleep if you want." He shifted as if he were about to leave.

Cash tightened his arms. "Stay. Please." If this was honest between them now, if they were going to have any chance at a real relationship, then he needed to see a difference. "Let me nap for half an hour and I'll make you dinner."

"All right, but could we move somewhere more comfortable? My ass is half off the couch."

Yes! Cash bounced to his feet with a sudden surge of energy at the prospect of having Harrison in his bed. The majority of his space was either garden or living room, but he'd crammed a king-sized bed into his tiny bedroom and he was excited to share it with Harrison.

"All naked," he insisted as he helped Harrison shuck his clothes. Then he tugged him down into the unmade mess of jewel-toned bedding and wrapped him up like an octopus.

"Um."

"Just go with it. This is me. Unless you really don't like cuddling?"

"I'll learn to like it." Harrison settled onto Cash's chest, melting in slow degrees as Cash stroked over his back and flanks. "I think... it won't be hard to learn to like it. You're going to teach me a lot of things."

"Still up for that?"

"I told you I wasn't faking anything. Not anything you didn't catch as fake anyway. I've always had a fascination with the stuff I saw on BDSM sites, just couldn't figure out how to reconcile what I wanted with who I am. But what we've done, I've liked. The things you said I would like, I've liked. So go ahead. Be my Dom."

"I'm not a Dom," Cash mumbled, as he lulled himself to sleep with the sweep of his hand over Harrison's back.

"But you can be mine," he heard Harrison say, right before he stopped hearing anything.

HE WOKE TO THE SOUND OF CLANKING coming from his kitchen, confused about what Sandi was up to out there before he remembered it would be Harrison puttering around. Nevertheless, he pulled on a pair of athletic shorts before leaving the bedroom, and it was a good thing because both of them were out there.

"Harrison was kind enough to answer the door," Sandi said, "since you were apparently dead."

"What time is it?"

"Late enough that I got hungry," Harrison said. "I didn't have dinner before our, uh, date." He flashed a look at Sandi, who was leaning against the counter watching him cook. There was a skillet on top of the stove and a mess of food products spread across the counter—way too many ingredients for what looked like grilled cheese. "You want one of these?"

"Sure." Cash rubbed a hand over his bare stomach. Though both Sandi and Harrison had seen him shirtless before, there was something more intimate about being bare-chested in front of them together. In his kitchen. After he and Harrison had fallen asleep together. "What are you doing here?" he asked Sandi.

"Nice."

"You know what I mean."

"I came down to see how it went at the club. I guess it went pretty well." She arched an eyebrow at him.

"We cleared up some miscommunications." He wasn't sure how much Harrison would want him to say about the investigation.

"I already confessed I'd been lying to you."

"You did?"

"She's a tough negotiator. I thought I was going to get brained."

"Did you tell her *why* you'd been lying?"

"He told me he couldn't tell me why. Top secret. I suspect he's a CIA agent. He says he's not, but that's exactly what a CIA agent would say."

"I promised her I wouldn't lie to you anymore, and she agreed to let me live."

Damn. All that had gone on while he'd been sleeping. He really *had* been out of it.

Harrison turned off the flame under the skillet and served up two plates of grilled cheese. He parked Cash at the table with one but ate his own standing up, leaning against the kitchen counter as he dipped it in a puddle of ketchup. When Cash bit into his sandwich, he understood the spread of things across his countertop. The sandwich was laced with tomatoes, onions, jalapenos, and...

"Are there capers in here?"

"Genius, right? Beats peanut butter and jelly, which is the only other thing I can make."

"It's good." Now that he'd recovered from the shock of it. "Spicy."

"Yeah, well, turns out I like things spicy." Harrison winked at him, and Cash felt his ears go warm. Sandi knew he was in the scene, but again, the two of them sharing his

150

secret together was another level of intimate. Nice, but weird.

"So tell us about you." Sandi wasn't eating, but she'd taken a seat across from Cash at the table. She had a glass of wine in front of her, something she must've brought with her because Cash didn't think he had any.

"I'd rather not go into the details of what I do for a living," Harrison said.

"But you're apparently not a tattoo artist."

"No, that's my sister. She's got a place in Harvard Square, did all of what you see here." Harrison had put his shirt back on, but his tattoos crawled out from beneath both sleeves. "She and I sort of get along and sort of don't. We're less than a year apart in age. It's been a lifelong battle for dominance."

Sandi snorted at the word.

"Not that way," Harrison qualified. "Although she probably gets some of the credit for my resistance to the concept of being dominated in general."

"All right, one bossy sister. What else? Any pets?"

"A fish."

"You have a fish tank?" Cash liked all animals.

"There's a tank, but only the one fish in it—a murderous red molly."

"Red mollies aren't murderous."

"Tell *her* that. I used to have a bunch of fish, but she did them all in. I only keep her because I'm afraid to get rid of her. It's more like being held hostage than owning a pet. If I feed her regularly, I'm allowed to live."

Sandi snorted. She liked Harrison, Cash could tell, which suggested his judgement wasn't totally off. Maybe this could work.

"What's the fish's name?" Sandi challenged.

"You think I named her?"

"You must call her something," Cash protested.

"You think I talk to her?"

"Cash talks to an imaginary hamster who live in his

walls," Sandi snitched.

"Ellie isn't imaginary, and I already told Harrison about her.

"He did." Harrison came over to scoop up his empty plate, bending down to press a kiss against his cheek as he did. He was so light now, smiling even. "I believe in Ellie. I also believe she's a rat."

"She's not a rat," Cash muttered. It was sweet, the two of them ganging up on him, this little promise of what life could be like. It almost had him teary.

"Well, I think I may have used up all her cheese. You'll have to buy her more." Harrison dumped the dishes in the sink with a clatter. He cooked the way a tornado gardened, and he left dishes in the sink instead of putting them in the dishwasher, but if those were his worst faults, Cash could live with them. He went over to wrap his arms around Harrison from behind, snuggling down into the warmth of his neck and inhaling the contented smell of him.

"I guess that's my cue." Sandi picked up her wine glass, now empty, and carried it to the front door. "Nice to meet you, Harry."

"That's not nice," Harrison yelled after her. "You told her about Harry, didn't you?" he accused Cash as Sandi thumped the door shut with a chuckle.

"Guilty, but I didn't know Harry was a top secret undercover identity at the time. I just thought you were a flake."

"I was a total flake. I don't know how you stuck it out as long as you did. You're sure you're not pissed?"

"Nothing I can't get past, but I wouldn't mind going over some of the details again." They'd rushed through the explanation to get to the makeup session, but now that his brain was awake and his dick was asleep, he had questions. "Tell me again about those interviews you had with the Doms who signed them in."

"One Dom. The other was a sub as it turned out. Bob Jones."

Right. That was the guy Harrison had asked about before. Not because Harrison was shopping for a better Dom—as Cash had convinced himself at the time—but because he was investigating a missing persons case.

"I think I know who you mean, now that I'm thinking about subs. Our age, a little campy with a beer belly?"

"That's the guy."

"I'm not surprised he would've signed Arlo in. He's kind of a mentor to the younger subs. They call him Uncle Bob. He said Arlo was looking for twenty-four seven, huh?"

Harrison nodded. "I hired a uniform to back me up while I was undercover, and by a weird coincidence, it turns out he's in the scene. Guy named Brixby. Know him?"

Cash shook his head.

"Anyway, he tried to explain twenty-four seven to me, but I still don't understand what it means exactly."

"It means different things to different people, but it sounds like Arlo wanted something permanent. Permanent and intense."

"Intense how? Whips? Knives? Metal rods stuck down his pee hole?"

Cash laughed. "He might or might not want any of that. I meant intense in terms of submission, not pain. Fulltime, maybe a live-in thing. That Popinjay guy said the same thing about Jessica, right? That she wanted to stay with him? That's what Arlo and Jessica had in common. They were both looking for a master."

"Kneeling and crawling all the fucking time. I don't get it."

"No, you don't." He leaned in to give Harrison's pursed lips a kiss. "That's why you were so bad at playing sub. But your inability to understand the submissive mindset is keeping you from getting into the minds of your victims. I've got a lot of practice understanding my, uh, victims isn't the right word, but you know what I mean. I need to understand them so I can give them what they're looking for."

"All right." Harrison's eyes were serious, challenging.

153

Cash felt certain this was the real Harrison in front of him now. "Tell me what Arlo and Jessica were feeling."

"Frustrated, I would guess. There's something they want that they've read about or seen other people practice, and they're not allowed to have it. And since they're not allowed to have it, they've romanticized it. 'If I had a master. I'd be taken care of.' Fed, clothed, housed. They were both on the edge of homelessness, right? That's another thing they had in common."

Harrison nodded. "Arlo was couch-surfing. Jessica made money stripping, but she had a drug habit to support, and we haven't been able to track her to a fixed address, so she might've been on the street too. Popinjay says he always picked her up at the club when he met her."

"Master might equal parent to them—someone who'll love and care for them, with the benefit of sex. A person who's romanticized the twenty-four seven lifestyle probably imagines it's unendingly sexual. It's not, of course. Total power exchange can turn even the most mundane chore into an act of service, but mundane is still mundane."

"But you're saying people want that?"

"People want it." He tousled Harrison's hair, gently chastising him for the judgement in his voice. "I could arrange for you to talk to Francesca and Ilona, but you'd have to curb that attitude. I'm not going to subject my friends to someone who's sneering at them."

"I'm not *sneering*." Harrison corralled his features into a more neutral expression. "I'm just trying to understand."

"Well, understand that total power exchange is a valid and consensual form of BDSM and that yes, some people want it."

"But *you* don't." Harrison used his finger to draw a line down the ridge of Cash's forearm, his gaze focused there instead of on Cash's face.

"Dominance is an act for me—not something I could keep up twenty-four seven—but I get where they're coming from. Francesca has an attentive partner who caters to her every whim and thanks her for being allowed to do it. Ilona feels deeply owned and perfectly supported. If that's what Arlo and Jessica wanted, they might've been willing to do a lot to get it."

"So they went looking for a Dom who would keep them fulltime and maybe found one. Am I supposed to congratulate them on their luck and walk away? Arlo's seventeen, Jessica's nineteen and an addict. Neither of them is in a place where they can make that kind of decision."

"I'm not arguing with that. We should find them." Cash didn't like the fact that Arlo hadn't been in touch with anyone. Even if Arlo were over eighteen and perfectly content in a total power exchange relationship, he should be allowed to contact his friends. Any Dom who cut their sub off that completely was a dangerous one.

"I should get going." Harrison levered himself away, but Cash clung to him, trying to haul him back in.

"Do you have to?" This all felt so tenuous, like if he let Harrison go, this particular version of Harrison would never come back. He would either get Harry the pretend sub or Harrison the private investigator who only cared about his case. He wanted *this* guy—the one who treated him like a boyfriend, not a tool.

"I don't *have* to," Harrison said with a smirk. "Depends what you're offering."

"Anything. Anything at all."

Harrison inserted a hand between their bodies to find and pluck at one of his own nipples. "I didn't get a blowjob earlier."

"Fuck, yeah." He bundled Harrison out of the kitchen and into his bedroom. One blowjob with nipple stimulation coming right up.

155

Chapter 17 Harrison

His nipples hurt. Again. He kind of loved it. He had to keep reminding himself not to rub them as he waited in the Hell's Bedroom lobby for Knight to okay his visit. Last night, Cash had broken out a devious rubber tube which he'd said was for suctioning venom out of snake bites but which he used for an entirely different purpose, namely to suction pleasure out of Harrison's cock via his nipples.

When Cash had squeezed the tube and applied its open end to a nipple, forming a vacuum seal around it, the resulting combination of pain and pleasure had sent Harrison levitating off the bed. His nipples had been twice their usual size by the time Cash had finished sucking him off—ruby red, as hard as his cock, and throbbing with the same energy. *Touch me, touch me.* God, he loved Cash touching him. And now he could enjoy it without conflict.

After the orgasm Cash had wrung out of him, which had practically warped the fabric of the space-time continuum it'd been so intense, Harrison had fallen asleep in Cash's garish bed. It was the second time he'd slept in Cash's bed in a single day, but a nap was one thing. Spending the night was another. Their relationship was moving at a speed that frightened him.

"Fisher," Knight said when Harrison had been shown into his office, decidedly more cool than he'd been the last time. "I thought we agreed you were done asking me for favors."

"There's another incident I need to talk to you about."

"Another underage patron? No one's been turned in since you were here last. I've been keeping an eye on the logs."

"No, not underage. That is, she might've been underage. I don't know yet. The point is she was screaming."

Knight smiled. "We get a lot of that around here."

"Screaming for help. Being chased. One of your members reported it. He doesn't remember the exact date, but if I give you his name, can you look it up that way?"

When Knight turned to his computer with a resigned nod, Harrison spelled out Cash's full and legal name for him. Cassius Minton. He should be as easy to find as Nicholas Popinjay.

"Don't see any reports under his name," Knight said after he'd clicked around for a couple of minutes.

"Can you see if there's anything about a woman being chased around the club?"

"In the entire month of May?"

"How many reports of women being chased do you get?"

Knight huffed out another sigh and turned back to his computer screen. This time it took more than a few minutes but he finally shook his head. "No women screaming for help, no one being chased. Not in May or in the months before or after May. Are you sure this incident got reported?"

"I heard it straight from the guy who reported it. He doesn't remember the name of the guard who took his report, but he was Hispanic. Short beard, about my height."

"That would be Paul." Knight picked up the phone on his desk and spoke to someone. "Paul's a solid employee. If he took the report, he logged it."

A knock on the door heralded Paul. He looked like the man Cash had described—shorter than average and medium-complected with a neatly trimmed beard and mustache.

"Yeah, I took that report," he said after Knight explained

157

why he'd been called in. "The Dom said they'd been playacting, that she had a safeword and hadn't used it. I confirmed it with her, then wrote him up for non-consensual involvement of bystanders."

"You talked to her without the Dom there?" Harrison remembered how the guard had separated him and Cash when he'd had to be cut out of the ropes.

"Sure. Followed protocol all the way. What's the issue?"

"I can't find it in the logs." Knight waved Paul over to the computer, and the two of them peered at the screen together. "Here, log in as yourself. We can look through your incident reports." He tilted the keyboard in Paul's direction.

Harrison couldn't see the computer screen between the two bodies crowded in front of it, but the conversation wasn't reassuring. No sudden *aha* to signal they'd found what they were looking for. He tapped his fingers on his knee while he waited, steeling himself not to touch his nipples to see if touching them would hurt. It would hurt.

"That'll do then, Paul." Knight's voice was oddly shuttered.

"You found it?" Harrison asked as Paul left the room. "What does the report say?"

"Everything was handled according to protocol, just like Paul said."

"Can I get the names of the people involved?"

"We have an obligation of confidentiality to our members. I assisted you previously because you were here about an underage non-member, but in this case, I'm afraid there's nothing I can tell you." He rose dismissively.

"Wait." Harrison rose with him. "Can you—?"

"There's nothing more I can tell you."

"Let me give you my card," Harrison said as he found himself being herded out of Knight's office toward the front door. "In case you—"

"I have Officer Brixby's card. He gave it to me the last time you were here. But I won't have a reason to use it. Good morning."

158

And with that, Harrison found himself in the lobby with a receptionist who'd obviously been told to make sure he didn't stick around. If getting the bum rush was supposed to convince him the incident in question was unimportant and had been handled according to protocol, well. It hadn't worked.

A FRUSTRATING DAY OF WORKING on a non-Arlo case while totally failing to have any genius ideas about Arlo's case ended with him sitting in his office staring at his phone and wondering if it would be okay to text Cash. Not so they could go to the club. Or maybe so they could go to the club. Fuck, he didn't know what step to take next, either with Arlo's case or with Cash.

Before they'd parted ways this morning, Cash had said something about a volunteer gig he did on Friday evenings, so why text him? Harrison didn't have anything to say except "I've had a rough day and could use a distraction," which Cash didn't owe him.

What he normally did on Friday night was go out to a bar. Pick someone up, find a place to get off with him, make quick work of it. Afterward, he would go home, drink beer, and binge-watch *Murder She, Wrote*, snarkily making fun of Jessica Fletcher while secretly wishing he had half her success rate. As coping mechanisms went, casual sex and television were better than some options but not nearly as good as letting Cash teach him new things about his body.

He rubbed a hand across his chest, brushing his palm over his nipples. The throb had faded. Or maybe he'd just worn it out by activating it too often, like the way he used to scratch his scratch-and-sniff stickers until he couldn't smell them anymore. He missed the sensation, the reminder of what they'd done, how hard he'd come and how happy it'd made Cash to see it. He wanted to make Cash happy like that again, but his conscience was telling him he should think of something to do for Arlo.

His phone rang before he could make a choice—duty or Cash. Figuring his phone had made the choice for him, he answered the call, but it was only his sister.

"There's someone here who wants to see you," she said without preamble.

"Here where?"

"At the store. Where else am I going to be? He's more interested in you than a tattoo, but I think I've got him talked into a tattoo." She laughed, then ticced, then laughed again. Behind her, Felix ran through his litany of fucks.

"You've got random guys walking in off the street asking for me?"

"Apparently. Big Black dude. Shaved head. He said get your ass down here. Okay, gotta go. He's in the chair." Taylor hung up before Harrison could ask any questions, but what would he ask? If Knight was waiting for him at his sister's shop, he'd better get his ass down there as ordered. He just hoped Taylor would pick a nice big design because it was rush hour, and getting out to Cambridge was going to take some time.

He fought his way onto a train and braced himself against a post, trying to keep his body angled so no one would make contact with the gun strapped to his lower back. He hated wearing a gun on public transportation, but it beat going weaponless in booty shorts. He hopped off at the stop for Harvard Square, then pushed through pedestrians to get to his sister's place, convinced Knight would be gone before he got there or that it wouldn't be Knight after all. But it was him, all right, sitting in Taylor's chair with a stoic expression, watching as she applied the gun to his right arm.

"What're you getting?" Harrison asked him.

"My kids' names."

Harrison peered around his sister to see Tabitha, Jeremy, and Calyx stenciled out along the length of Knight's arm. Tabitha was already mostly filled in.

160

"Back off," Taylor complained. She jostled Harrison with her free arm in what he was pretty sure was an intentional move, not a tic. Sometimes she got away with that. He positioned himself on Knight's other side.

"Guess you should've taken my card."

"If I had, would it have mentioned that you aren't really a cop? Or does your card lie as much as you do?"

Taylor snorted.

"Hey, now," Harrison said, giving Taylor the evil eye to let her know he didn't need her opinion about his truthfulness. "I never said I was a cop. I flashed my PI license at your receptionist, and she assumed."

"And you didn't correct her."

"Would *you* have? I needed your help." He opened his wallet and handed over one of his cards. "Harrison Fisher, Licensed Private Investigator," he read off it, tapping the words for emphasis.

Knight pushed the card away. "Yeah, fine. You never lied to me directly, just stretched the truth."

Harrison shrugged and returned the card to his wallet. Those cost him money. "Stretching the truth is how we do what needs to be done." That'd been true when he was on the force too. "You were a cop."

He was guessing, but Knight nodded in confirmation. "Which is why I didn't need any card to track you down. Had your name, found your sister, figured I'd drop in on her and wow you with my detective work."

"And let her ink you up?"

"That wasn't in the plan, but your tats are quality work, and she's a good salesman."

Taylor let out a bark just then. When the resulting cacophony had died down, Knight raised his eyebrows at Harrison, then shrugged when Harrison didn't answer the unspoken question.

"Don't move," Taylor complained.

"Yes, ma'am."

"So why not call?" Harrison said, returning to the

subject at hand. "If you could find my sister, I'm sure could find my phone number."

"DDD owns my cell phone, which I'd never considered a problem before, but maybe I do now. Walls have ears. Phones can have ears too."

"Does that mean you think DDD is in on whatever's going on?"

"It means I want to talk to you about it. But maybe not in front of a civilian." Knight nodded his head in Taylor's direction.

"Yeah, well, you're stuck with me for another hour," she said. "Unless you want two of your three kids to feel like they not worth more than an outline."

Harrison ran a hand over the stubble on his chin, thinking fast. "I want Brixby to hear what you've got to say anyway." And Cash too. Because Cash had been there when the incident in question took place, not just because Harrison was looking for an excuse to see him.

He went out to the street and arranged for Brixby to stop by his apartment as soon as he could extricate Knight from under Taylor's gun. Then he texted Cash to invite him over too. When he didn't get an answer after a few minutes, he went inside and tried to prod Taylor into finishing faster.

"If you rush me, it'll take even longer." Her shoulder gave a jerk that was definitely a tic, reminding Harrison that tics were aggravated by stress, which meant she was right. If he rushed her, it would take longer. Still, it was weird hanging out in her space with a guy he didn't really know and no place to even sit. He amused himself by chewing on his nails because he knew it bugged her.

"All done," she said finally. Knight had a layer of plastic wrap over the names marching down his arm and an aftercare instruction sheet. The word aftercare made Harrison think of Cash, so he checked his phone, but he still hadn't gotten a response.

Knight had a car, but he didn't seem excited about having Harrison in it, so Harrison made another T ride back—this one slightly less crowded. He beat Knight, probably because Knight was circling the block trying to find a place to park, but Brixby had the cruiser right out in front, and Cash came strolling down the sidewalk on cue. Harrison couldn't help beaming at him.

"You made it."

"Just finished up at the library and figured I'd pop over." Cash leaned down to give him a kiss, as if this were normal for them—getting together at his place after work. It made Harrison wish it were.

Brixby had done some surveillance on Cash, but the two of them had never formally met, so Harrison introduced them to each other and brought them both inside. His place was kind of a wreck since he hadn't been expecting company, and he left Cash and Brixby to get acquainted while he did some clutter relocation and inventoried what he had in the way of refreshments, which was beer.

"This must be your fish," Cash called out to him from the living room while he had his head stuck inside his empty refrigerator. "You said her name is Molly?"

"I said she's a red molly who doesn't *have* a name."

"Well, we'll call her Molly."

When Harrison came back into the room, Cash had his face pressed to the glass like he was trying to commune with the fish. She'd swum over, probably because she wanted to eat him. Harrison tapped a few dashes of flakes into the tank to dissuade her from it.

A light rap on the door heralded Knight's arrival. Harrison offered the beers around, then brought everyone over to his dinette set.

"Wasn't expecting a club member," Knight said with a questioning glance at Cash as he took a seat.

"He's the one who reported the incident we were discussing. I assume there's more to it than what you said in your office this morning."

"Can't tell you anything about the incident itself, but what I *can* tell you is that it was erased. There's an entry in

Paul's log with the incident number but nothing else. If you click on it, you get a message saying it was deleted."

"By who?"

"Admin."

"Which is?"

Knight shook his head. "No idea. If I close an incident, it's shows my name. But this incident isn't just closed, it's gone. And I've never seen anything tagged as Admin before. After you left—"

"After you threw me out, you mean."

"I thought it best if I didn't appear to be accommodating you any longer. And that was before I learned you weren't even really a cop." Knight shook his head, obviously still a little raw on that score. "But after you left, I paged through every incident that's been reported in the last year."

"Let me guess," Brixby said. "That wasn't the only one that'd been deleted."

"You got it. There aren't a lot of them. Only five, in total. But they all happened in the last six months, and they were all deleted by an anonymous admin. All I can see are the stubs—the incident numbers—and not a goddamned other thing."

Chapter 18 Cash

Cash knew who Aldous Knight was, though he'd never had any reason to speak to him directly before. Knight usually radiated an assuring air of confidence, as though he could handle anything that might be thrown at him, but he was rattled now, and Cash could hardly believe what he was hearing. Was Hell's Bedroom itself complicit in what'd happened to Arlo?

"But those incidents we talked about before," Harrison said. "Jessica, Arlo—those are still in there?"

"So far."

"Why delete some and not others?" Brixby asked.

Harrison had mentioned his uniformed backup/ unofficial partner who was also a Dom, but he'd never mentioned Brixby's startling blue eyes or the fact that, in his uniform, he was every sub's wet dream, almost too hot to be a real cop. More like a Chippendale version of a cop.

"I've been thinking about that," Knight said, "and it seems to me deleting the record has to be a worst-case scenario. It breaks protocol and looks suspicious."

"Right." Harrison tapped his fingers on the table. "Arlo's incident shows Hell's Bedroom in a positive light. He was identified, removed, and the member who checked him in had nothing to do with his disappearance. The deleted incidents probably don't look so good, maybe even implicate the club." Harrison turned to Cash. "What do you remember about that Dom?"

165

"Almost nothing." He shook his head, frustrated with himself. "I'd never seen him before. White guy dressed in black leather, which describes maybe seventy or eighty percent of the Doms there. I wasn't paying much attention to him."

It was the woman he'd been watching. She'd torn past him, barefoot and stumbling, words that were convincingly terrified tumbling from her lips. A man had caught her and carried her off. Cash had searched out a security guard to send after them. He'd even checked with the guard later to make sure everything was okay, but once he'd been told it was, he'd mostly forgotten it.

"The woman had light brown skin and curly black hair past her shoulders. Curvy, with big breasts and wide hips. Sorry," he said to Harrison, who was looking at him as if he'd been intentionally ogling the woman. She'd been running naked. Things had bounced. Just because he didn't find breasts sexually appealing didn't mean he couldn't see them.

Harrison went back to tapping the table. "Can you get the entries back?" he asked Knight.

Knight shook his head. "I don't think anyone can get them back. I checked the manual, and deleted is deleted. You have to click an acknowledgement to that effect when you do it. I don't even have the option to delete an incident, only close it."

"Right, so who does? Luke Olsen? That's the manager's name, right?"

"He's *our* manager, yeah, but Hell's Bedroom is a single branch of a bigger conglomerate. Maybe Olsen has the admin password, but I'm guessing he doesn't. I told you before—he's a pencil pusher, a numbers guy. From a corporate point of view, he's no one."

"So we're talking about someone in headquarters," Brixby said. "Someone who's monitoring your incident reports and deleting the ones that might tell on them."

"That's why I'm here with you-all instead of going

166

through channels. We've got something bigger going on than one missing kid or a single, rogue Dom."

"Had to be more than one Dom," Harrison said, positively jiggling with restrained energy. "Jessica's a straight woman and Arlo's a gay man, so unless we've got a bisexual Dom assembling a harem, there's more than one buyer involved."

"Buyer?" Cash questioned. How had they leapt to buyers?

"If someone's kidnapping people, they're either using them for their own purposes or they're selling them. To sell, you need a buyer. Those missing incidents—those are our buyers. The product they bought was trying to escape."

"You're saying the woman I saw screaming for help might've been trafficked?" Cash felt sick to his stomach. He'd known something was off, but the worst he'd imagined was a newbie Dom operating with insufficient training, that lines were being crossed out of ignorance or arrogance.

"It's a possibility we have to consider," Harrison said. "Someone's been using the security system to bury the very issues it's meant to highlight."

"And I'm not standing for it," Knight said. "You don't give me a protocol then subvert it. We need to shut these fuckers down."

"Yeah, but, um, how?" Everyone turned to frown at him for asking the question, but he wanted to know. "The records are gone, Arlo's gone. How do we find whoever's behind this? They're not necessarily even in Boston, right? Where's headquarters for DDD?"

"San Francisco," Knight supplied.

"But Arlo and Jessica disappeared from Boston," Harrison pointed out, "so we've got a local conspirator, and that's where we start." He leaned across the table to speak to Brixby. "Let's take another stab at figuring out where Arlo and Jessica went after they left Hell's Bedroom. I don't know what we haven't followed up on already, but we'll find something."

"And I'll talk to Paul again," Knight said. "Maybe he can ID the Dom from that incident. We see a lot of faces, so I can't promise anything, but I'll work on him."

"What are the chances Paul's involved himself?" Harrison asked.

"He logged the incident," Knight said. "That speaks to his innocence."

Harrison nodded. "Just be careful who you ask what. If you get the wrong people worried, they might do worse than fire you."

"I can take care of myself." Knight rose to his feet. "Gentlemen." He offered his hand around to each of them in turn, then let himself out.

Brixby rose too. "I should get back out on the beat."

"Hey," Harrison fished under his shirt and pulled the bronze medallion he'd been wearing off over his head. "You want this back?" He extended it toward Brixby.

What the—? Why was Harrison wearing Brixby's necklace?

Cash scowled at Brixby as he said, "Nah, keep it. We're not out of the woods yet. You still might have to go back in there, and now we know I was right to be worried."

"Yeah, but I've got Cash now. He's not going to let anything happen to me."

Damn right. Cash sat up straighter, using all the height his accident of birth had gifted him with to demonstrate how safe Harrison would be in his care.

"Keep it," Brixby insisted, pushing Harrison's hand away. "Anytime you've gotta be without a weapon, I want you to have a backup. Don't do anything I wouldn't do, boys." He gave them a mock salute and left the apartment.

"What is it?" Cash picked up the medallion Harrison had dropped on the table. Not a token of affection, he hoped. Not a collar.

"There's a GPS welded to the back of it so he can track me using an app on his phone. He's a worrier." Harrison disappeared into the kitchen as Cash flipped the medallion over to look at the back. Now that he'd been tipped off, he could spot the extra disc. Harrison came back with two more bottles of beer and carried them into the living area. Cash followed him there.

"Well, I'm glad someone's been looking after you." He re-hung the medallion around Harrison's neck, even though he hated it. "So this is your place, huh? Very single-guy-lives-alone."

Windows covered in horizontal mini-blinds, unrelieved white walls, a fish tank without a castle, and a fish with no name. Cash couldn't help equating Molly with Harrison himself—a fighter who didn't know how to relax enough to be loved.

"It's not as nice as your place," Harrison admitted. "No garden, just a little balcony off the back I never use. The view's not exactly soothing—brick walls and a tiny patch of grass that gets sun for an hour a day."

Cash knew he'd gotten lucky with his place, but more could be made of this one than was being made. The floors were bare, the furniture utilitarian. No pictures, no cushions, no color. And apparently no food, he discovered when he offered to make dinner and Harrison only laughed.

"Pizza?" Harrison suggested instead.

"Yeah, sure. Pizza." Nothing wrong with pizza, but Cash wished he could magically transport the two of them over to his place where he had food and foliage, but he wasn't going to complain about having been invited to Harrison's. He'd been pleasantly surprised to find Harrison's message waiting for him when he'd finished his session with Mr. Jackman because it'd answered the question of how many days he was supposed to wait before reaching out himself.

A pizza was ordered and received, additional beers were consumed, and Cash ended up with Harrison's head in his lap, giving him a scalp massage while a baseball game droned in the background. Most people liked getting their heads rubbed, and Harrison liked being rubbed just about everywhere in Cash's experience. He had his eyes closed, not even pretending to watch the game, and was making soft sounds of contentment as Cash worked around his ears to the back of his skull.

"How are your nipples?"

"Fuck," Harrison said, which wasn't exactly an answer. Cash brushed a soft finger over one of them, and Harrison shuddered. Cash's cock grew chubby at the response, causing Harrison to grind his head down into it with a laugh. "You liked that, did you?"

"Uh huh," Cash answered honestly. "Thinking about what I can do to you next. How are you on ass play?"

"What kind of ass play?"

"We've got quite a few options. Figging? Milking?"

"I have no idea what either of those are, but I'll let you shove food up my ass if you promise to suck it back out."

"So that's a yes on rimming." Cash filed that information for future reference, then explained figging and milking.

"So I can have my ass burn with internal fire or have all the come squeezed out of me one drop at a time? Those are my options, just so we're clear."

"It's not an either-or question. You can do both. Maybe not on the same day."

Harrison laughed.

"You can also do neither," Cash qualified. "It's always okay to say no."

"Yeah, I get that. I'm not into the whole 'yes, sir' thing, remember? If I don't want you to stuff a piece of ginger up my ass, I'll flat out tell you not to stuff a piece of ginger up my ass. So if you want to do it, you're going to have to explain exactly why I would want you to. Slower this time."

"It's sensation. Painful sensation, but pain without injury or marks. And it's intense. You seem to be a fan of intense."

"What about the other one?" Harrison blinked up at him, more curious than concerned.

Cash hedged, trying not to give away how much he

170

loved milking because he only loved it when his partner was into it. "You might feel helpless. But also, hopefully, safe."

"Like when you restrained me for the e-stim? I had to let you be in charge because otherwise I'd ruin it."

"Like that, yeah. It's a slow process, which means if your dick gets impatient—"

"Ha! My dick's name could be *Mister* Impatient. I'm starting to realize I've never gotten as much out of it as I could've because I've been letting it run the show. From now on, you can be in charge of it. Even when you blow me, the time you take with it... wow. Explosive."

"Edging," Cash said, his voice rough because fuck, he would spend every minute of every day edging Harrison if he could work out how to keep them fed. "You might like being milked then. It's like endless edging."

"Can we do it now?"

"Unfortunately, no." In addition to not having the basic comforts of home, Harrison's apartment didn't have a collection of sex toys. Considering how much time Cash wanted to spend making Harrison melt into a puddle of come, he would never be able to manage it with his fingers alone. "But rimming is on the table." Toys or not, he would find a way to rock Harrison's world tonight.

"Maybe in a bit." Harrison stretched lazily. He zapped the television quiet but didn't get off Cash's lap. Though Cash's dick was hard from all that talk of milking, Harrison's wasn't, so Cash rubbed his stomach instead of his cock.

"Still thinking about the case?"

"How can I not? Let's say DDD really is selling subs. Where do the buyers come from? Who are they? What do they want?"

"Complete control, real life fantasy. A slave without a contract, someone whose needs don't have to be considered. Mind you, most Doms wouldn't want that even if they could get it. I doubt the percentage of Doms who are abusive is much higher than in the general population, but it's not any lower, and when the two things are combined..."

"You end up with someone chained in a basement," Harrison finished, which was exactly what Cash was afraid of. Cross a Dom with a sociopath, and he didn't want to think about what might be happening to the subs who'd gone missing.

"What about your friend Francesca?" Harrison asked. "She'd be the type to want a slave like that, right?"

"Definitely not."

"Don't stop rubbing." Harrison complained, because Cash had picked up his hand in response to Harrison insulting his friend that way. "I'm just saying she does the twenty-four seven thing."

"She does, but it's all consensual. She and Ilona have a contract, which Ilona could terminate at any time. And Ilona doesn't get chained in a basement, I assure you. Or maybe she does, on occasion, but briefly for defined periods while Francesca monitors her from nearby as part of a game they're both enjoying. I don't know that much about their sex life, but I do know Francesca would never kidnap anyone."

"All right, I'm not accusing your friend of anything. But someone at your club is guilty of something."

Cash hated that it was true. Even though he couldn't personally vouch for every person at Hell's Bedroom, he wanted to be able to vouch for them on principle, to say "no one in the BDSM community would do this thing." But someone had done something or DDD wouldn't have bothered to cover it up by deleting incident records.

"I need someone who can play the role of buyer," Harrison mused. "I should've gone undercover as a Dom."

"Why didn't you?"

"I had a secret desire to be whipped." Harrison's grin said the joke wasn't really a joke.

"We could do that too." Cash's dick, which had dozed off, perked back up, but Harrison was still wholly focused on the case.

172

"If I'd gone in as a Dom with a bad attitude, I might've attracted attention from our sellers."

"We could pull in Francesca. I know I just said she wouldn't want an unwilling sub, but whoever's behind this wouldn't necessarily know that. On the surface, she's the sort of Dom they're looking for."

"Would she help?"

"I think so. Francesca would hate that the club is being used to target vulnerable subs as much as I do."

"And we can trust her?"

"Definitely." He was as sure of Francesca as he was of anything.

Chapter 19 Harrison

Harrison had never risen high enough in the department to spearhead an investigation, and he was too much of a loner to be called a leader—bossy, Taylor would say, as if she weren't just as bossy, but not really the managerial type—but now he had a squad.

They were all gathered in Cash's garden, strewn about on camp chairs and impractical wrought-iron things Harrison suspected were meant to be purely decorative. Francesca had brought Ilona, because she didn't go anywhere without Ilona apparently. Knight and Brixby were there, of course, and since Tripp was nominally Harrison's client and most definitely an involved party, he'd been invited too.

Everyone held a frosty glass of a sparkling fruit drink Cash had made out of actual fruit because he loved to fuss over people. Whatever. The drink was good. Harrison took an appreciative sip, then set his glass down and called his team to order.

He had Tripp start by describing the text Arlo had sent saying he'd scored an invite to Hell's Bedroom, after which he'd never been heard from again. Tripp had waited longer than he should've to report Arlo missing, but Harrison understood why. Arlo might be underage, but Tripp was only nineteen himself—Arlo's friend, not his guardian. It spoke to how much Tripp cared that he'd not only gone to the police but sought out a private investigator when the police wouldn't listen.

Tripp's knowledge of what'd happened to Arlo ended with that text, so Knight took up the narrative from there, describing how Arlo had been reported and eventually tossed. Then Brixby summarized the interviews they'd had with Bob Jones and Nicholas Popinjay. Tripp confirmed that Bob Jones, a.k.a. Uncle Bob, was a sort of mentor to the younger, less-experienced subs in the scene and that he often signed subs into the club to get around Hell's Bedroom's membership restrictions.

Harrison was inclined to agree with Jones that the club's policy wasn't fair. It forced subs into a position of dependence, as if they weren't vulnerable enough. Knight explained that the policy was intended to guard against what would otherwise be an imbalance between subs and Doms, but really? Doms were in greater demand? Harrison shook his head. So many people looking to have someone treat them like shit.

To finish summarizing the status of their investigation to date, Knight caught everyone up on what they knew about the deleted incident reports, which wasn't much. In his second interview with Paul, he'd learned that the Dom involved wasn't even a member of Hell's Bedroom.

"So the sub was a member?" Harrison asked.

"No, neither of them were. We have a reciprocal visitor agreement with the other DDD-owned clubs—one of the perks of premium membership. Paul remembers that the Dom in question was a visitor but not which club he'd come from or his name."

Not anything useful in other words.

Francesca listened to the whole story, alternately sipping from her glass and holding it up for Ilona to drink from. Ilona knelt next to her on a cushion Cash had brought out to soften the stone of the patio. She wore one of those things women called rompers, decorated in bright pink flowers splashed over a lighter blue background. Her bare arms and legs were chubby, and her hair was swept up off

175

her neck into a high ponytail. With her head tilted so determinedly down, Harrison couldn't see much of her face beyond the slope of her forehead and the tip of her nose. He barely knew what she looked like, he'd seen so little of her, and he wasn't sure whether he ought to be looking or not. When he did, he felt like he was gawking, but when he didn't, he felt like he was treating her like an animal or an object.

Cash nudged him, breaking him out of his thoughts. He'd stayed on his feet so he could fidget his way through this commander-of-the-SWAT-team role, but Cash was sitting close enough to touch him, which he did on a regular basis, as if checking to make sure he was still there.

"Right." Harrison clapped his hands together to recapture everyone's attention. "We haven't had any luck tracing Jessica or Arlo after they left Hell's Bedroom, assuming they went anywhere. It seems more and more likely that they disappeared from right in front of the place."

"I told you!" Tripp exclaimed. "Didn't I say Arlo had been captured by a human trafficking ring? That's what I said the very first day."

"And maybe you were right," Harrison acknowledged. He'd never had any trouble believing there was a shark at Hell's Bedroom, or even that the place hosted a whole pool of sharks, but something more coordinated than individual bad behavior was going on. "The question is how to move forward. Trying to plant a sub—namely me—didn't get us anywhere. I probably don't come across as the kind of victim they're looking for. So either we start over with someone else or we work the buyer angle. Which is why you're here, Francesca."

Francesca inclined her head. Harrison needed an imperious Dom, and he couldn't do better than Francesca. She exuded an expectation of obedience.

"You most closely match what we think their target buyer would be," he told her. "You're an established Dom, known for her dedication to the lifestyle. If you were to suggest you were in the market for something... less consensual, my hope is that the market would find you."

Francesca stroked a graceful hand over Ilona's head. "Hush, pet," she said, even though Ilona hadn't made a noise or even so much as twitched as far as Harrison had noticed. To Harrison, she said, "Of course I'll help. However I can. But everyone knows Ilona and I are devoted to each other. Not to mention that we live together. We would have to appear to have broken up for it to be believable, and where would she go?"

"She can stay with me," Cash offered. "She can have the bedroom. I'll sleep on the couch."

Francesca's hand tightened in Ilona's hair. Even Harrison could tell Ilona was distressed now. "I'd like to bring my girl inside for a moment if I may." She went over to the sliding door with Ilona crawling next to her on hands and knees—which made Harrison wince—and disappeared through it.

"Maybe we should come up with another plan," Brixby said, "if this is going to upset Ilona."

Harrison shot him an annoyed glance. It wouldn't kill Ilona to sleep at Cash's place for a few days while they planted a story about Francesca's search for a new, more subjected, sub.

"We can let them make that call," Cash said. "Francesca will say no if she means no."

Harrison hoped she wouldn't say no because he was out of other ideas. He watched the sliding door avidly, only realizing he was being too obvious about it when Cash tugged him down onto the bench. When the door finally opened, Ilona was walking upright—no leash, no guidance. She still wore the silver latticework collar around her neck, but otherwise she'd thrown off all appearances of being subservient. Now Harrison could see she had a bow mouth, bright blue eyes, and cheeks so fat they tempted his fingers to pinch them. A little like a female version of Arlo.

"Ilona is going to join the conversation," Francesca said.

"She'll need to have a say in what happens. Sit, pet." She patted the spot next to her on a cushioned wicker loveseat and Ilona sat down like an actual human person. Harrison appreciated the change, honestly. Their vibe creeped him out.

"Welcome to the team," he said to Ilona.

"Thank you." Her voice was reedy, hesitant.

"You're certain you're all right with this?" Brixby asked her.

"I'm not happy about being separated from Mistress or her saying she wants a different sub, even if she's lying, but I understand how important it is to figure out what's happening."

"I think it'll work best if we set up a scene at the club," Harrison said, re-focusing on their plan. "I don't mean a BDSM scene. I mean, like, an argument. Ilona disobeys Francesca, and Francesca fires her."

Ilona blanched.

"You needn't be disrespectful," Francesca said. "I'll flog you for some supposed misbehavior, and you can call red."

"Maybe Francesca doesn't listen when you call red," Harrison suggested, earning a hard look from both Cash and Brixby. "What? The point is that Francesca wants someone she can abuse. Let's get her written up, bring her to the attention of whoever at DDD is deleting those incident records."

"I can make sure she gets written up," Knight said. "I'll tell one of my guards we've had complaints about her, ask him to keep an eye out."

"Perfect. So Ilona calls red, Francesca doesn't stop, and Security intercedes."

"And the community thinks Francesca ignored a safeword?" Cash asked with a frown. "That's awful."

"It's necessary," Francesca corrected. "Can you do that for me, pet? Say red because I told you to? It won't mean anything. We have our own safewords, don't we?"

Ilona nodded.

"You'll have to tell the guard a good story," Knight reminded her.

"I can do that. I know what it's like to have a safeword ignored. I didn't always belong to Mistress."

"This is going to be triggering," Brixby fretted. "I'm still not sure—"

"Ilona is capable of making her own decisions," Francesca said. "And also of speaking for herself, now that she has permission to do so."

Ilona gave them all a dutifully brave smile. "It's no big deal, right? Say red to Mistress but it's not our real safeword so it doesn't mean anything, lie to the security guard, then sleep at Master Cash's house for a few days."

"You know I just go by Cash."

"Let her say it," Francesca stroked Ilona's neck softly. "She'll need someone."

"Then she'll have someone," Cash said.

Harrison glanced over at him sharply. What did that mean? Cash wasn't going to—?

Cash was watching Ilona, smiling like he was ready to tilt at windmills for her while Brixby could hardly contain his anxiety about upsetting her. This was what a real sub did to a bunch of Doms apparently—turned them all into Don Quixote.

"HOW CERTAIN ARE YOU OF FRANCESCA?" he asked Cash when everyone had left. Cash was at the sink, washing dishes, and Harrison was sitting on one of the countertops. He kept expecting Cash to tell him to get down, the way Taylor always did, but Cash just worked around him.

"Completely certain."

"She weirds me out. Well, not her so much as Ilona."

"I know. You've got to stop making it so obvious you disapprove of their relationship. It's *their* relationship.

179

Leave them to it. Plenty of people would disapprove of ours."

"Why?" Harrison snagged a leftover canape from the plate Cash had been about to empty into a Pyrex container.

"Because you're a brat. They would think I should control you better."

"Hah. As if."

"Exactly." Cash kissed him hard, then went back to the dishes. "You recognize yourself as a person who has definite preferences, but you don't recognize Ilona that way. Yes, her preference is to conform to someone else's preference, but that's still a preference, and she's still a person. You'll have a chance to get to know her better while she's staying here. Admittedly, I don't know her very well myself."

"That's what I'm saying." Harrison drummed his feet on the cabinet beneath him. Cash gave him an unimpressed look for it, but come on, enough with the cleaning already. He'd been promised a whole new sexual experience tonight, and he was ready to get to it. The investigation was moving forward again finally, which meant he could indulge himself without guilt.

"I think someone wants something." Cash took a final swipe around the sink, then dropped the sponge on the ledge and washed his hands with a liquid soap that smelled like his garden. When Harrison leaned forward to get a better whiff of it, Cash caught him around the waist and swung him down to the floor. "What did you decide on?"

"Not so sure about the burning stick of fire being shoved up my ass."

Cash laughed. "Maybe another time. I did buy some ginger, just in case." He opened his crisper drawer and pulled out something that looked like a potato had gone to war with an army of rubber bands and lost.

"This is ginger?" Harrison turned the root over in his hands. If it had magic stinging properties, it wasn't using them.

"The kick is beneath the peel. Did you change your mind about trying it?"

Harrison handed the ginger back with a shake of his head. If anything, the weirdly shaped root had solidified his choice. "I want to try the other thing—the milking." He'd paid extra attention to cleaning his ass in the shower before coming over. As a top, he appreciated a nice, clean ass, so he figured he ought to live up to his own standards. "Are you going to fuck me too?"

"Is that something you'd like me to do?"

"Depends on how good the milking thing is. You'll have to make me want it."

Cash grinned—the sort of grin Harrison had always imagined a Dom ought to have. Not Brixby's continual frown of concern or Francesca's cool stoicism or Sir Magnus's ugly smirk. Cash looked like he was going to enjoy being evil but only for Harrison's own good.

"This is going to be torture, right?" He wasn't sure why that sounded like fun, but it did.

"Mm, should I restrain you for it?"

"Maybe." That was another thing that sounded better than it ought to—the idea of being prevented from interceding on his own behalf. "How much am I in for?" He snuck a little closer to Cash, who was returning the ginger to the vegetable bin.

"All of it," Cash said with a waggle of his eyebrows. "Come on, subby. Let's tie you up." He hauled Harrison into his bedroom and tossed him on the bed, using his body to bully him in a way Harrison didn't mind under the circumstances. They were playing at Dom and sub, and the result was going to be him having one motherfucker of an orgasm.

He wormed out of his clothes and set his gun and holster carefully off to the side while Cash set out what he needed. A pair of Velcro restraints, a pump bottle of lube, three different toys—good God, what had he gotten himself into?—and a box of condoms.

"In case you're inspired to fuck," Cash said as he plunked the last item down on the bedside table.

"Can you take your clothes off?"

Cash was always dressed when they screwed around, and he wanted to change that.

"See, that's where not being bound by anyone else's idea of what a D/s relationship ought to look like works in our favor," Cash said as he pulled his shirt off over his head. "A classic Dom usually stays dressed, the better to exert his authority."

"Well, exert naked authority." Because he liked the view. Cash was hard, his cock sticking straight out in front of him. When he came over to the bed, Harrison gave it a hand, which Cash tolerated for the length of time it took him to wrap a pair of cuffs around Harrison's wrists.

"Okay with me attaching these to the bedframe?"

Harrison looked over his head at the metal bars that formed Cash's headboard. Convenient. He grinned his agreement, and Cash fastened his hands in place. He was free to move around on the bed in almost any way, but he couldn't use his hands.

"You're sure?" Cash asked, probably because he was testing the cuffs, checking to see just how stuck he was.

"I'm good. You'll let me go if I say to, right?"

"That depends. Do you want me to?"

"Um, yeah. Of course."

"Not so quick. Suppose you're all 'make me come right now, you fucker.' Should I make you come, or should I continue with my nefarious plan?"

When Cash winked, a shiver ran down Harrison's spine. He didn't know where those other subs had gotten the idea that Cash wasn't dominant from. Cash not only had Harrison at his mercy but had him wanting to be there.

"Oh, so that's where safewords come in," he said, understanding the concept better now. "I can swear at you and yank my arms around, and you'll keep going unless I say red."

"If that's how you want it, yes. But decide now, because if you tell me we're using safewords, I'm not stopping unless

I hear one."

Harrison's cock voted yes with an urgent jerk. The idea of being unavoidably pleased appealed to him. It wasn't at all like someone controlling him or demeaning him. It was more like having his pleasure shut-off valve overridden. Complete indulgence.

"Let's do that."

"All right then. Still, if something's uncomfortable, speak up. You can say yellow if you need a timeout."

Cash positioned himself between Harrison's legs, pushing his knees up and out of the way so his body opened up to him. The bottle of lube—which was big enough to have Harrison a little alarmed—sat on the bed next to them. Cash pumped a shot over his fingers, then laid himself out long between Harrison's legs and started with his tongue.

Harrison liked being rimmed. Fingered, too. Fucked, sometimes. He enjoyed the sensation of it but not always what it meant—what his partners sometimes tried to make it mean—but when he did like it, he liked being lazy with it. Cash gave him all the lazy. Harrison couldn't be expected to reciprocate, not with his hands attached to the bedframe. All he could do was lie there and enjoy while Cash's tongue and then fingers breached him, loosening and stretching him, sending shivers of anticipation through him. Cash paid just enough attention to his cock to keep him at full attention—no more—until Harrison started to think he should get on with it. He squeezed Cash's head between his thighs.

Cash stopped what he was doing to say, "Don't make me restrain your legs too. You won't like the position I put you in."

Was that a... threat? Harrison swallowed the urge to say "yes, sir" and let his thighs drop open again.

"We're getting to the good stuff here," Cash promised as he finally turned his attention to Harrison's prostate. It responded immediately, already hungry for more than a single finger thanks to all the build-up, but there was more build-up and more build-up and more build-up until Harrison was ready to scream.

One finger became two, but two didn't turn into three. Cash's movements were slow, steady, not exactly light but definitely not firm. Brush and stroke and brush and stroke until Harrison was ready to be fucked already, ready for anything that would be *more*.

"How do I get you to move this along?"

"What do I get if I do?" Cash asked, reaching lazily for the lube again.

"You get to fuck me."

"Do I?" Cash sounded unconvinced. "We'll see."

"Fuck, Cash."

"I said we'll see." Cash dribbled lube over one of the toys, and Harrison relaxed.

Finally something was going to happen beyond this impossibly slow crawl toward an unreachable climax. He'd never had a toy up his ass before, but he hardly gave that a second thought as Cash worked this one in. It was stainless steel—long and thin except for a conical head and a ball partway down the shaft. What a little thing like that was going to do to him, he couldn't imagine, but the first thing it did was make him jump. It was cold. Not ice cold, but not as warm as Cash's tongue and fingers had been.

"Ah," he complained, but Cash only laughed and continued to work the head inside him. The whole length of the toy was cold, brushing through his channel like an icy finger until the head reached his prostate. The toy was so heavy inside him—heavy and foreign. The hard steel ran over his prostate like nothing ever had before. Pure strength and weight, maximum force.

The device reached body temperature as Harrison's body temperature continued to climb. He felt like he was getting the most thorough fucking of his life, but when he raised his head to watch what Cash was doing, he saw that the wand was barely moving at all, only rocking a little. His own wildly thrusting hips were adding motion, but not much motion was needed. The toy hit him right where it was meant to hit—on the one small part of his body that radiated out to all the rest of his body.

"Fuck, I'm going to come."

"Are you?" Cash asked with an evil smirk.

There was come leaking out of his cock, that was for sure. One drip after another splashed onto his stomach. Cash licked up each one as it fell. The sensation of orgasm spread to Harrison's fingers and toes, wrenched his balls tight with expectant pleasure. A contraction hit him, and he threw back his head and moaned as another single drip splashed onto his stomach followed by the soothing wash of Cash's tongue.

"More," he begged.

"Just this," Cash said, not increasing the speed at all, continuing to rock, rock, rock the wand over his engorged gland. Each contraction spit out another plump drop, one blending into the other, delicious but insufficient, like taking an orgasm and dragging it out across all of eternity— pleasure delivered so slowly it became insufferable.

"Fuck me, you fucker."

"Not yet. I'm enjoying this too much." Cash dropped a kiss on the inside of each of his thighs then rocked the wand again, summoning another drop.

"Make it stop," he pleaded. "Oh God, Cash. It's too much."

"Just relax. We've got a while yet."

"How much of a while?"

"Until there's nothing left. I want it all."

Until there was nothing left? It could take days to get it all out at this rate. Harrison wriggled his hips, trying to drive himself harder on the toy and triggering another of those contractions that weren't quite a climax but that left him moaning as if he were having one. The fight dripped out of him along with the come, leaving him more and more limp. Even his cock deflated, but his prostate only got more sensitive, and the pleasurably achy spasms never subsided.

185

"Let's ramp this up a bit," Cash said finally.

"Oh, thank God," Harrison muttered, but when Cash removed the wand, Harrison wanted to scream for it back. He'd become addicted to the pleasure of it. He just needed more—needed Cash to make him spurt for real.

"What are you doing?" he asked when he realized Cash had gone for one of the other toys instead of the box of condoms. "What is that thing?"

"Vibrator," Cash said, sounding amused by the prospect. The device in his hand was v-shaped, vaguely reminiscent of the ginger but made out of soft rubber instead of potato skin. One side of the V was dildo-esque, but the other side had stranger bumps and edges. It was the dildo side Cash worked into him, but when it was fully seated—the head of it pressing against his prostate, of course—the other side lay along his perineum, snuggled up under his balls with its two tickly antennae.

Cash picked up an egg-shaped thing, making Harrison wonder where *that* was going. But it didn't go in him. Instead, Cash pushed a button on it and everything started vibrating.

"Shit," Harrison grumbled as the vibrations ramped up in intensity, drumming his already-too-sensitive prostate. The antennae along his perineum had his dick plumping back up, though how he could get hard when he'd already been drained of all life force, he didn't understand. But apparently he still had more life force because it continued to ooze out of him, the drips coming faster and thicker as Cash dialed up the speed.

Vibrations rumbled, deep and lasting, coming in a wave and then dropping off long enough for him to catch his breath before starting again. Moans fells from his mouth as fast as come ran from his cock—strings of them, one after another.

"Shit," he begged. "I need to come."

"You've been coming for half an hour now," Cash said smugly. He was sitting back on his heels, holding the egg-shaped remote in his hand and otherwise only watching. His cock stuck straight out in front of him, one tiny drop of pre-come at its tip. Harrison wanted to teach him what it would feel like to have that one drop replaced by another and then another and then another, but he was tied to the fucking headboard and didn't have the energy for lessons anyway.

He ground his hips into the bed, but the vibrator didn't respond to his wriggling. It delivered steady sensation in long, heady bursts then stilled while his body vibrated with its own rhythm before beginning again.

"*Really* come," he said, forcing the words out through a throat gone dry from too much moaning. "I need to *really* come."

"You sound thirsty." Cash put down the egg and helped him raise his head so he could sip from the glass Cash held to his lips.

"Not thirsty," he complained between sips. How was he supposed to drink with convulsions wracking him? But his throat felt better for the water, allowing his focus to return to those parts of him that were pleasure-soaked and thrumming. "Need to come. Please, Cash. Please make me come."

"Don't know if I can," Cash mused, running a hand over Harrison's shaft. It felt so fucking good. His cock was all the way hard again, dying to be touched. "I'm not sure there's anything left in you."

"Need it. Need it so bad." He thrust his cock through Cash's fist, groaning at the glory of it. He could feel it—one last big surge waiting inside him. "Want you to fuck me until I come. I can do it. It's going to be so big. Oh God," he muttered as another spasm shook him.

In the back of his mind, he knew there was a word he could say that would stop all this, but he didn't want it to stop. He wanted it to finish exactly the way it was meant to finish, with Cash tearing him apart from the inside out.

"Fuck, *now*." He squirmed in Cash's grasp, feeling it

coming, trying to hold it off so Cash could get in him first. "Fuck me."

Cash released his cock, making Harrison groan with the loss. He'd descended too far into madness to understand that he was finally going to get what he wanted. Cash was putting on a condom. Cash was dialing down the vibrator, removing it, and then, ah!

"Yes!" He bucked his hips up to accept Cash's cock, taking all of it in a single motion that had Cash groaning with him. "Come on. Come on." He could only maneuver so much with his hands fastened over his head, but he set the pace, drove the intensity. It was out there—that explosion he'd been chasing—and then it came.

Pleasure washed over him as his body wrenched in a contraction harder than anything he'd ever felt before. Outwardly, the contraction only produced a few weak drops of whatever was left inside him, but inwardly, it wracked him from fingertips to toes. He screamed into it, throwing his head back and letting everything go until there was literally nothing left.

"Holy shit," Cash said.

Harrison tried to focus on him. "Did you..."

"Holy shit," Cash repeated. "Holy shit, holy shit, holy shit. I think I just came my brains out."

"I definitely did." He tugged on the cuffs, wanting them off now, and Cash reached over him to undo the Velcro, then flopped onto the bed next to him.

"Holy shit."

"You said that." Harrison's body was soft. Soft all over. Soft and happy.

"You have no idea, Harrison. You really have no idea."

Chapter 20 Cash

"Help me, Sandi. I'm totally in love."

That'd been too much last night, too absolutely perfect. Harrison, flushed and demanding, giving himself up completely, only wanting Cash to make him come. And Cash had—had made him come for a solid hour, every minute of it feeling like he was coming too. It'd been so good to pump himself into Harrison, to finish them both off in a mutual climax.

Perfect. Harrison was perfect. So tense and edgy, so willing to be relaxed out of it. So strong and commanding, so nervous about letting go of even the smallest strand of control, and so beautiful when he did.

"It's too soon to feel this way, right?"

"You feel what you feel." Sandi's voice was warm, even over the cold distance of a cellular connection. "Are you sure he's there with you, though?"

"Not so sure, no. He's kind of a closed-up person. He opens up during sex, but the walls go right back up again after." He still hadn't been able to get Harrison to submit to anything like aftercare. Last night, Harrison had shrugged off all his attempts to cater to him, instead staggering into the bathroom on weak legs to clean himself up.

Cash was accustomed to enjoying a period of ownership after a session, where the man in his arms felt very much his, where he could pretend that it wasn't just for tonight. He didn't get that with Harrison, but maybe what he did get would last longer. After cleaning himself up, Harrison had come back to bed and curled into Cash's still-limp body, apparently fine with cuddling, just not with being coddled. It wasn't so bad, getting to be the one taken care of after a scene instead of always doling it out.

"Regardless," he said to Sandi as he moved through the people crowding the sidewalk. "I should probably stop giving you details about our sex life. This isn't like my usual hookups. You have to be able to look him in the eye. Wednesday, right?"

They had a getting-to-know-you dinner planned. Sure, Sandi and Harrison had met before—the evening she'd barged in while he was napping off his sex haze—but this was different. This was the actual, intentional introduction of his best friend to his... boyfriend? Could he use that word? Love might be too far, too fast, but boyfriend wasn't a stretch.

"I'm going to lose you in a minute," he warned as he jogged down the stairs into the station. "About to get on the T."

He was scrambling, racing from the library over to Hell's Bedroom. Francesca and Ilona were going to do their big breakup scene tonight, and he needed to be there to scoop up Ilona and bring her back to his place after. In order to meet Harrison on time, he'd had to ditch out of his session with Mr. Jackman fifteen minutes early. Not that Mr. Jackman had minded. Anything relating to Cash's new... relationship, Mr. Jackman was all in favor of.

Cash, on the other hand, tried to dodge the subject as much as possible—using gender neutral words, avoiding Harrison's name. It felt awful. Like lying. He'd never had to worry about it before because why would his sex life come up in a literacy lesson? But Harrison already meant more to him than sex, and Mr. Jackman was practically a friend.

"I'll see you Wednesday then," Sandi said. "If not before. I'll bring—"

The call dropped before he could hear what she was

190

planning to bring, but he could guess it was some form of cocktail. He tucked his phone into his pocket and let his thoughts return to last night as the T hurtled him through the dark tunnel.

Harrison looked damned good with cuffs on. Cash didn't have a bondage fetish, but a tough guy shooting knives with his eyes while helplessly begging for release? So fucking hot. He probably shouldn't be thinking about it on public transportation.

Harrison was already waiting in front of the club by the time he made the six-block walk-jog from the T. Despite the temperature being in the nineties today, he was lurking outside in loose-fit jeans and a tight t-shirt with a Red Sox cap pulled low over his eyes, studiously ignoring the valet who thought everyone ought to arrive in a car.

"The lobby's air conditioned," Cash said as he swooped in for a quick kiss. He had to duck to get under the bill of the hat.

"The last time I was here, Knight had me thrown out. That was the day shift, but I don't know if they've got a picture of me at the front desk. Hopefully, Knight has taken care of it, but here"—he thrust a driver's license at Cash— "you can get me checked in. I'll keep a low profile."

Cash went over to the reception desk with Harrison lurking well behind him like a genuinely dutiful sub. Harrison kept the bill of his hat pulled down until they got to the locker room.

"Harry Carter," Cash said as handed him back the ID. "Is your last name really Carter?"

"Shit, no." Harrison threw the ID into a locker along with his hat. "It's Fisher. Sorry about that."

"Eh, we've covered it. Nice to know my boyfriend's real name though. Boyfriend, right? Are we good with that?"

"Yeah, sure." Harrison dropped his jeans. Beneath them were those shiny booty shorts. Apparently Harrison only had one set of club wear, but that was okay. Cash wasn't ever going to get tired of this particular look. Then

191

Harrison pulled his t-shirt over his head and Cash's eye was drawn to the medallion lying between his pecs on a dark bed of hair. The medallion he could live without.

"So boyfriend means exclusive, right?" He knew the medallion was a security device, not a token of affection, but it didn't hurt to be sure.

"Are you asking or telling?"

"Asking. I'd like to be exclusive. I'm falling for you, Harrison. I hope this means more than work to you."

"Cash." Harrison stopped messing around with his locker and turned to him. "Or should I say Cassius? I do solemnly swear, all right? I'm trusting you with a lot here. Yes, you're helping me with a job, but if I didn't have... feelings for you, you wouldn't even know what my job was, never mind be helping me with it. Exclusive works for me."

That was probably as romantic as Cash could expect Harrison to get. He pulled him in for a kiss, using his bigger size to hold him tight for a moment, to command the closeness he needed.

"Thanks. You ready to obey me, boy?" He released his boyfriend before he got decked by him and ushered him into the playroom.

Francesca and Ilona would be rolling in a little later so they could play out their argument to a maximum capacity crowd. For now, there was nothing to do but wait and drift. Cash nominally led, Harrison trailing slightly behind him. There were a few good scenes running, but the one that captured Cash's attention had a woman laid out face up on a bench with her pussy spread wide and glistening while her Dom flicked a crop against it.

The light taps probably didn't hurt much, but the Dom was getting a reaction. A little sting and the wet slap of leather seemed to be exactly the stimulation the woman needed to get off. She tensed against her bonds, thrusting her pussy up to meet the crop, quivering and whimpering when her partner teased her by brushing it—wet with her juices—across her nipples in between slaps.

Cash guided Harrison around in front of him so he could lean into his body and observe his response to the scene, but Harrison didn't seem to be getting much out of it, so Cash maneuvered them away again, making another circuit of the space to see if Francesca had arrived yet.

"There she is," Harrison said, pointing with his chin. "They just walked in."

Ouch. Francesca was leading Ilona on a leash, which wasn't unusual, but the way she was yanking on it was. Ilona scrabbled along behind her, the tears on her face as believable as the anger on Francesca's. If this was an act, it was a better one than Harrison had ever put on. And it was breaking Cash's heart.

"They're heading for the stockade," Cash said in an undertone. "Should we go over?"

Harrison shook his head. "Let's not seem interested. Maybe check out... whoa, what's going on over there?"

"The whipping? You've seen someone whipped before."

"Right, I remember. Come on, force me in that direction like you're threatening me with it. It's close enough to the stockade."

Harrison didn't need to be forced, but Cash curled his hand around the back of his neck and gave him a yank to make it look good. As they passed the stockade, he caught a glimpse of Francesca threading Ilona's head through the bars and heard Ilona promising to be good. The two of them had attracted an audience already. Francesca was normally so controlled, Ilona normally so obedient. This had all the earmarks of a good scene, in both senses of the word. They were about to put on a show. Cash just hoped it really *was* a show, that nothing had gone wrong at home as a result of their being asked to take part in Harrison's investigation.

Over at the next station, a man had been strung up by his hands with his feet tethered to the ground. Between those two points of suspension, he was free to swing around, which he was doing in response to the rhythm of the whip. The top was landing his strokes carefully, and the bottom was clearly eating it up with lots of yummy shrieks of gleeful agony. When Cash had first gotten involved with BDSM, he hadn't always been able to hear the *want* behind the screams, but his ear was better tuned now.

He and Harrison watched the scene together, their backs to Francesca and Ilona but still able to hear them, even over the sounds of the whipping. Francesca was spanking Ilona, and Ilona was making a fuss. *All part of the act*, Cash told himself. He threw a worried glance over his shoulder but only saw the top of Ilona's head.

He turned his attention back to Harrison, snuggling him in front of him as he had before so he could scan for signs of arousal. Yeah, definitely aroused. That was a nice bulge he was rocking in those shorts. Cash ran his hand down Harrison's side and wrapped it around his thigh, just under the bulge in question, but he held off on going further. This was Harrison's job—something he hadn't understood the last time they were here.

"I think you're going to like being whipped," he whispered in Harrison's ear.

"Mm, maybe. More than being spanked probably." Harrison turned a bit, trying to see what was going on behind them. Cash swayed their bodies in that direction, giving them both a peek at Francesca swinging a glove-covered hand at Ilona's naked bottom. "Spanking is kind of infantile."

"Well, that's part of the appeal for some people—the humiliation aspect. But I can see how it wouldn't be for you." He titled them back in the direction of the whipping so their interest in what was going on behind them wouldn't be too apparent.

"You know how to use something like that?" Harrison asked with a nod forward. The whip in question was a bullwhip, like the one Sebastian had been using on Harrison's first visit—a long heavy thing made to deliver a serious zing.

"Yeah, but my apartment doesn't have the clearance for

it. We'd have to come here."

Harrison tilted his head back to look up at him. "Not sure I'm comfortable playing at the club, all things considered."

Cash understood the sentiment, but it made him sad. Hell's Bedroom had been a safe space once, a place where beginners like Harrison could experiment, knowing the community would keep an eye on them. Their community had been replaced by a system, and the system was corrupt. Whatever it took to make Hell's Bedroom a community again, Cash intended to do it.

"We'll figure it out." He pressed a kiss to Harrison's cheekbone. "We'll get you whipped, if you want to be whipped."

"Maybe," Harrison said again, but Cash could hear the yes in his voice.

Some louder vocalizations from Ilona had him turning in her direction again. The two women had attracted enough attention that it was reasonable to show interest now. Ilona was making a giant fuss, nothing like her usual demeanor on the rare occasion she got punished. She kicked backward and managed to strike Francesca in the thigh. The look on Francesca's face almost made Cash laugh. She seemed so genuinely shocked.

"You little fucker," Francesca said. "You're going to pay for that."

Someone to Cash's right inhaled sharply. Cash turned to find Sebastian watching the scene, his face aghast. Whether Sebastian was aghast at what Ilona had done or what Francesca had said, Cash didn't know. Both were unprecedented.

"You didn't like my hand?" Francesca asked Ilona. "Well, you're *really* not going to like this." She went to over to the rack and pulled out a cane, swinging it so it made that sharp, swishing sound only a cane could make—as if the air were literally being cut in half. Ilona winced, which wasn't an act. Ilona was no masochist. She wasn't going to

195

like being hit by a cane.

You can call red at any time, Cash tried to telepathically communicate to her.

"What the hell is Francesca doing?" Sebastian asked.

Cash shook his head as if he didn't understand it either.

"What could Ilona possibly have done? This isn't—" Sebastian stopped talking when the cane landed on Ilona's buttocks and Ilona *howled*. And no, that wasn't arousal. Every muscle in Cash's body tensed as Francesca pulled her arm back again.

Any time, he begged Ilona.

Next to him, Sebastian had his jaw clenched and his hands in fists. "Cash," he said, as if asking him why he wasn't doing anything.

"Ilona hasn't called red," Cash pointed out in answer, and then, thank God, she did.

"Red." The word was choked, quiet. It would've been hard to hear except most of the noise in the normally frenetic room had died away, leaving the two women at the center of attention. Despite the call of red, Francesca landed another blow.

Sebastian stepped forward, but Cash grabbed his arm to hold him back. "Let Security handle it," he said, even though he'd just been thinking about how important it was for the community to police itself. Tonight they needed Security to intervene so a report would be filed.

"Red," Ilona said, louder this time, screaming it out. Francesca pulled her arm back to swing again.

"You deserve this, you little shit." The cane whistled, thwacking Ilona's thighs with a sound too loud for Cash to believe Francesca was pulling her swings. Every bit of this was real, and it was killing him.

"Where the hell *is* Security then?" Sebastian wrenched his arm out of Cash's grip. "I'm stopping this."

Cash let him go. He buried his face in his hands, unable to watch and wishing he couldn't hear, as Francesca swung

196

the cane again.

"She has a real safeword," Harrison reminded him in a low voice. "And Sebastian's stopping it. He took the cane away from her. Here comes Security. It's over, Cash. It's okay." Harrison patted his back. "Go on and get Ilona."

Cash bolted for her. Sebastian had Francesca backed up several feet away from the stockade, the cane in *his* hand now, gesturing with it as if he were threatening to use it on her. Francesca was managing to look unrepentant, but Cash knew this had to be one of the worst moments of her life—to have hurt Ilona, to have been seen doing it, and to not be able to defend herself.

Cash detoured around Francesca, Sebastian, and the guard trying to come between two charged-up Doms, and went straight to the stockade to free Ilona. He pulled her into his arms, scanning down the back of her body to check for damage and finding only superficial marks. Painful, undoubtedly, but not permanent.

"Get me a blanket," he barked at a second guard who'd come to hover over them. Cash would let him do his job, but he needed to do his too. Ilona had a report to make, but she was also a sub who deserved proper aftercare. "You did so good," he whispered as he cuddled her in his lap on the floor. "You're so brave, such a good girl. We're going to take good care of you, little one."

Francesca stalked away from Sebastian to come stand over Ilona with a scathing expression on her face.

"I'll take this." She undid the clasp on the silver collar around Ilona's neck and pulled it free. "You don't deserve to wear it. If you can't obey me unconditionally, I'll find someone who can."

That was enough for the guard, who dragged her away by the elbow.

"What the fuck?" Sebastian ran a hand over his face. "I don't understand what the hell just happened here."

Cash cut his eyes up at him, trying to tell him now wasn't the time. Ilona was sobbing in his arms, the tears from having her collar removed way too real. She had to be their first priority.

"Miss?" The guard Cash had sent in search of a blanket handed one to him. "I'm going to need to take a statement."

Chapter 21 Harrison

Harrison shifted his butt six inches to the right. Wherever he situated himself, he seemed to be in someone's way. Cash's kitchen wasn't big enough for four people, though only he and Cash and Sandi were truly *in* the kitchen. Ilona was more lurking around the fringes of it.

He should probably go keep her company in the living room instead of parking himself on Cash's countertops, but he wanted to be where Cash was, and the point of this dinner was for him to get to know Sandi. Plus, Ilona still made him uncomfortable. When it came to women, he was accustomed to Taylor, who always gave as good as she got and would never let him see her cry. Ilona cried every damned night.

He felt bad for her, of course. No question that scene had devastated her, and even though she and Francesca Skyped daily as a reminder that this was only temporary and only pretend, she seemed really rattled. Adrift and anxious. Harrison wished she weren't finding the whole thing so traumatic, both for her sake but also because Cash refused to leave her alone. Which meant that if Harrison wanted to see him, he had to do it here. Cash's place was more comfortable than his in basically every way— including the way where Cash cooked really good food—but the lack of privacy was brutal.

When Sandi brushed him out of the way again, he bit back a sigh. It wasn't Sandi's fault. It wasn't Ilona's fault either. He was restless and irritable because he wanted the investigation to move along, and he couldn't *make* it move along. It'd been five days since the big scene, and Francesca had gone down to the club every night since then, but there'd been no contact. Just a lot of shunning. Her Skype sessions with Ilona grew longer, and Ilona emerged from them even more despondent. Neither one of them was doing well, and Harrison had put them in this position without being able to do anything to get them out of it.

Sandi turned off the faucet where she'd been washing... was that the ginger? Harrison cleared his throat and looked away. The ginger had never gone anywhere near his ass. It was fine.

"So," he said, in a forced force attempt at being social. He felt like a pretty shitty detective these days, but he could be a good boyfriend. "Are you queer, Sandi?"

"Depends which letters you include in the rainbow."

"All of them, of course."

"Then yes. I'm heteroromantic and demisexual. I've never been involved with anyone sexually, but I feel like the potential is there, though I'm generally pretty happy with platonic relationships." She beamed at Cash who was at the stove stirring a skillet of creamy sauce that smelled amazing.

"Demi and straight? That means Cash would be right up your alley."

"Possibly. If he'd ever been interested in return." She dumped the ginger she'd been mincing into Cash's skillet and returned to the chopping board.

"And you're gay?" Harrison asked Cash. "I was wondering if you were bi or pan. You were watching that woman the other day."

"My voyeuristic streak is pan, but if I'm going to be taking action, I'd rather take it on a guy."

"You've never played with a woman?"

"No, I have, which is how I know that. It was fine but"— Cash shrugged—"I like men."

200

"Me too. Gay." He pointed at himself as he said it. He hadn't gotten anything out of the scene Cash had stopped to watch since he didn't have a pussy to be spanked and didn't want to spank one, but he hadn't missed how much it'd turned Cash on.

"I'm a lesbian." Ilona had drifted right up to the edge of the kitchen where fake wood transitioned into fake tile.

"Yeah?" he turned toward her with an encouraging smile.

"You sure you don't want something to drink, Ilona?" Sandi asked. "These cocktails are my signature item. Watermelon basil."

"They're amazing." Harrison waggled his glass at her. Ilona had previously turned the cocktails down, but she nodded now, so he hopped off the counter and poured her one.

"You two could wait out in the garden," Cash said, pushing back with his ass to give Harrison's a tap. "It's crowded in here."

"Yeah, okay. It's nice out. What do you say, Ilona?"

Ilona looked like she wanted to say no, but she gave him another nod. Harrison led her outside, determined to do a better job of getting to know her without judging her. She was making a big sacrifice for him, after all. He asked about her job, and it turned out she was a graphic designer, just like Cash. That made an easy transition to tattoos. She showed him the two she had in publicly visible spots, both of which she'd designed herself.

"This is my mistress."

The tattoo gracing her calf was a floral motif, not a person or anything Harrison would associate with BDSM. Ilona stroked it with one finger, then her hand went to her neck in a gesture that'd become familiar. Harrison hadn't liked having something wrapped around his throat, but as strange as he'd felt wearing a collar, Ilona seemed to feel just as strange without one.

He unfastened Brixby's medallion from around his

neck.

"I know it's not the same," he said as he held it out to her, "but you could wear this. It's Brixby's. He gave it to me to keep me safe, so it could be kind of a symbol of a Dom who's looking out for you."

"Don't you need that?" Cash asked as he stepped onto the brickwork carrying a platter of chicken breasts in one hand and a bowl of that scrumptious cream sauce in the other.

"I'll borrow it back if I need to go undercover again, but it seems like we've done what we can do at the club for now."

Sandi's appearance on the patio stifled further conversation on that topic. Harrison didn't know how much Cash had told her about who Ilona was and what they were up to, but there were already too many civilians involved in the investigation.

When his phone buzzed, he gave it a quick peek, jolting out of his reverie when he saw it was Francesca.

"Hey." He brought the phone up to his ear as he moved inside to get some privacy. "Something happen?"

"Got an email from a friend—their word, not mine—who asks if I'd be interested in an alternate—again, their word—way to find a sub."

"Oh, you're definitely interested." Harrison's skin tingled with excitement. This was it. Contact had been made.

FIRST THING THE NEXT MORNING, he and Brixby dropped in on Gina Harlow, the department tech who'd added the GPS to Brixby's medallion. Francesca had already received an answer to her reply, but the follow-up email hadn't contained much—just a link and a login ID. As far as cyber investigating went, Harrison was already in over his head, so they were coming to Gina for help.

"No can do," she said once they'd explained what kind

of help they needed. "I do device tech, not cyber tech. You want my partner."

"I didn't realize techs worked in pairs," Harrison said.

"Not that kind of partner. This kind." She tapped a ring on her left hand. "Come on, he's just down the hall. But I warn you, he's sort of a geek."

How much more of a geek could Gina's partner be than Gina was herself? But even having been warned, Harrison wasn't prepared for the full-on pocket-protector nerd who grunted in response to Gina's greeting without raising his eyes from the screen of the laptop in front of him, as if she might go away if he ignored her. Well, that was a sex life Harrison didn't care to imagine. The two of them probably scheduled their encounters through a Google calendar and pre-diagrammed their moves with flowcharts.

"That's Lance," Gina told them. "Lance, this is Officer Brixby and some PI who's helping him work a case."

"Harrison Fisher," Harrison put in, not that Lance appeared to care. He was a bulky man—tall and carrying some extra weight—with the pallor of someone who never saw any light except what came from a computer screen. His office, in complete contrast to Gina's, was empty enough to suggest it was hotel space, but his name was on the door. Lance Harlow. He would make a hell of a D&D character.

"It's an interesting case," Gina said in a singsong voice, like she was trying to tempt a cat to eat a medicine-laced treat.

"Interesting how?"

"Human trafficking? Deep web?"

"Deep web?" Lance raised his head at last. He made a come-in gesture with his fingers.

Harrison took one of the seats in front of him and Brixby took the other.

Lance scowled at them. "What have you got?" He made the come-in gesture again, but this time Harrison understood it was actually a gimme gesture so he handed over his phone with the two emails Francesca had received. When he tried to explain the background, he got a distracted wave.

"The data tells its own story." Lance pushed a few buttons on the phone then handed it back and turned to his laptop.

"Should we—?" Harrison started, but another gesture cut him off.

"I think we just sit here and wait," Brixby whispered.

Why did tech people have to be so weird? Did their ability to understand computers interfere with their ability to relate to people?

"If you'd come to me earlier, I could've inserted a tracking pixel in her response," Lance said a few minutes later. Harrison wasn't sure what a tracking pixel was, but it sounded like a lost opportunity. "Then again, these are the kind of people who would've detected a tracking pixel, so maybe we dodged a bullet there."

"Yeah, that's what we were thinking." He was so smart, knowing better than to insert a tracking pixel. Totally.

"Not much more we can do with that first email, but this invitation is interesting."

"Gina said something about the deep web?"

"What do you know about the deep web?"

Harrison considered his options and decided to go with the truth. "Literally nothing."

"Good. I don't have to de-educate a bunch of bullshit out of you. The deep web a.k.a. the dark web isn't a physical space. It's a term for the part of the web you can't find your way to by accident. Hence this invitation."

"The link, you mean?"

"Yes, the link. It'll take you to a site, probably hosted on a server outside the U.S. What do you expect to find there? People for sale? Gina said human trafficking."

"That's what we're hoping for, yes."

"This would definitely be the best way to sell a person," Lance said, as if he'd already considered how best to sell a

204

person. His laptop pinged. "I've activated a tracker, but don't get your hopes up. I can trace the traffic through our established monitoring points until it disappears from the public grid, but that won't get us anywhere. Anyone who's set up a storefront on the deep web has taken steps to safeguard their location."

"Then why run a trace?"

"You never know," Lance said with a smirk. "Sometimes people aren't as smart as they think they are. Okay, here we go. You want to watch this?" He beckoned again, and this time his gesture really did mean come here.

Harrison moved around to the other side of the desk to watch Lance log in to a page that was more basic than anything he'd ever seen on the net. No flashing ads, no suggestions for additional content they might enjoy, not even a link to click if they'd forgotten their password.

"Can they trace our session back to the squad house?" Brixby asked.

"First, good question, because yes. But also, stupid question, because I've already thought of that and made sure they can't." Lance's fingers moved faster than Harrison could follow as he typed in the login information Francesca had been provided with and clicked to validate it. The login screen disappeared and what looked like a product page appeared. Except the product was a woman.

"Hello, Kim," Brixby said.

Kim appeared to be in her early twenties. She had heavy eyebrows, dark hair past her shoulders, and a deeply tanned complexion. The stats gave her height as five foot four, her weight as a hundred and forty-five pounds, and her cup size as C, though there was no need to list her cup size given that her boobs were right there. She faced the camera like she was having a mug shot taken. A naked mugshot. No smile, no life in the dark eyes, her expression carefully blank.

"Can you save the photo?" Harrison asked Lance. "Brixby can run it through Missing Persons, see if they can tell us who she is."

"This whole session is being logged, but here. I'll pop it off for you right now." In a few swift clicks, Lance had forwarded the picture to Missing Persons with a request for an expedited reverse image search. "She's American?"

"Native American maybe even," Harrison said, considering the strong cheekbones and proud nose. "But yeah, this is a domestic human trafficking ring, as far as we know."

"So what do we do with this website?" Brixby asked.

"I'll examine the traces, figure out which country they're hosting their servers in. If we have any reciprocal agreements with the local authorities, I might be able to get closer, but probably the fastest way in is this." Lance pointed at a greyed-out button on the screen that read Bid. "Auction starts tomorrow, three pm Eastern Time. Win Kim, and you've got yourself a witness."

"Little problem with that," Harrison said. "Starting bid is thirty thousand dollars. My client is a college student who's yet to pay me a dime." Not that Harrison had submitted a bill. At some point, the job had become personal. "Would the Boston PD cover it?"

Lance snorted. "My budget doesn't extend to human trafficking money. I'm lucky I can afford to keep up with the latest decryption tools. What you want is the FBI. This is beyond Boston PD jurisdiction."

"We don't have time for the FBI. Auction starts in less than twenty-four hours. If we don't buy Kim, who does?"

"Selling people is illegal," Brixby said, as if anyone in the room might be confused on that subject. "Let's just bid on her and then stiff them. Fuck paying for her."

"You think they'll release her before they've got cash in hand?" Harrison shook his head. Sometimes Brixby's lack of experience showed. The only thing bidding without the cash to back it up would do was delay Kim's sale until whoever was behind this website could set up a fresh auction. And then Francesca would be poisoned as a

206

contact.

"We're going to have to think about this," he told Lance.

"Damn it. I wanted to bid on a lady." Lance snickered to himself before adding, "Don't tell Gina I said that."

They left him alone with his questionable sense of humor, heading out onto the street together, though they had nowhere in particular to go. Thirty grand. Wow. Obviously a person was worth more than that, but it was too deep for Harrison's pockets.

"I'll kick in what I can," Brixby said as he fixed his sunglasses in place. "Do you think they take credit cards on the deep web?"

"I appreciate the offer. I feel the same." But their combined fortunes wouldn't be enough to buy a quality sex doll, never mind a person. "I don't see any choice but to bring in the FBI."

Chapter 22 Cash

"But what's Ilona supposed to do in the meantime?" Cash asked Harrison. The three of them were in his living room—he and Harrison next to each other on the loveseat with Ilona in one of his moon chairs. She had her head buried in her phone as if she weren't listening, but he knew she was.

"If Francesca's going to continue to be seen as a viable point of contact..." Harrison trailed off, but his meaning was clear. Ilona and Francesca had to continue to live apart until the FBI could follow up on the next auction opportunity.

"I don't think we considered how open-ended this situation would be when we asked Francesca and Ilona to get involved."

"I know." Harrison rubbed a hand over his face in frustration. Cash couldn't help reaching for his shoulders. He hated seeing Harrison tense, much as it seemed to be his natural state. "I can't figure out how to get Francesca and Ilona out of this, but they're not obligated to continue either. Ilona can go home at any time."

Ilona didn't raise her head, but she swallowed convulsively, as if she might start crying. She cried every night. Cash tried not to listen, because he couldn't fucking do anything about it. She didn't want the consolations of a random Dom and certainly not those of a gay service top. She wanted her mistress.

"Ilona," Harrison said, prompting her to finally look up.

"I'm okay. We have to. Now that we know there's really people—" She choked to a halt, her body language tiny and miserable. "I'm going to take a walk."

"I can't stand it." Cash got to his feet to watch Ilona's legs cross in front of his window, then lingered to give Mr. Moo's chin a scratch. Mr. Moo rolled up to offer his belly, and Cash rubbed it, glad he could make at least one being feel better.

"I don't know what else to do," Harrison said.

"I know. I'm not blaming you."

"If I had thirty thousand dollars..." Harrison snorted. "Never mind thirty thousand. That's only the starting bid. God knows what it'll get up to."

"What if I knew someone who did have that kind of money?"

"Who? You?"

"No, not me. I wish." His salary barely covered his living expenses. He definitely didn't have a person-sized rainy day fund. "You remember Sebastian? Brooding, dark-haired guy in leather."

"I remember Sebastian."

Of course. No one forgot Sebastian. Cash swallowed back how much he hated the idea of Sebastian being the savoir his boyfriend needed. This wasn't about him. It was about Kim and Arlo and Jessica. "Sebastian works for the State as a prosecutor, but he comes from money. Went to Harvard Law, Yale for undergrad, lives in one of those high rises on the Waterfront. If anyone's got human trafficking money, it's him."

Harrison shook his head. "I don't know. We've got too many civilians involved as it is. The sensible thing to do is go to the FBI."

"For Kim's sake. *Kimi's*," he corrected, because Harrison had told him they'd identified the woman in the picture. Kimi Cota, an Algonquin who'd been reported missing two months ago in Chicago. She'd already been in captivity for two months, and they were supposed to let her disappear again, off to whoever bid the most? His confidence in the FBI wasn't high enough for him to feel certain Kimi would ever be found if they didn't take the opportunity to rescue her now.

"Are you sure Sebastian's not the type to buy a slave for real?" Harrison asked. "He seems like an ass to me."

"An ass yes, but an ethical Dom. You saw how he reacted to that scene."

Harrison frowned in consideration. "I'd love to wrap this investigation up. I'm frustrated. In more ways than one."

He cocked an eyebrow, and Cash got it. It would be nice to move the investigation along so their relationship could move along. Having a permanent third hanging around— one who was suffering from heartbreak—put a real damper on their sex life.

"There's a hundred good reasons to do it," Cash said. Sex was the least of them, but it still counted.

"Call Sebastian."

"Really?"

"Yeah, really. Whatever we have to do. Arlo, Jessica, Kimi—we've got to bring them all home."

"A HUNDRED EVEN," Lance read from his screen, as if they couldn't all see the answering bid right there in plain black numbers on a plain white background.

Cash didn't complain about the redundancy because he was lucky to be there at all. This was Lance's office, Harrison and Brixby's investigation, and Sebastian's money. Cash was just a very interested bystander.

"What's our limit?" Lance asked.

"No limit," Harrison answered from his spot next to Lance. He had his neck craned forward and an eagle eye on the screen. "That's a fucking person. She's worth anything."

"Sure, in a metaphorical way. In a more practical way,

you need the funds to back up your bids."

"I have the funds," Sebastian said. "But that doesn't mean we need to let them know that. We're broadcasting our eagerness by responding too quickly. Let that bid sit a bit."

"Like I just said," Harrison grumbled, "she's a person."

"And I'm not going to lose her, but as long as we keep bidding, they'll keep stringing us along. You see these other accounts?" Sebastian indicated the other two bidders listed on the auction page. "They're not bidding against each other, only against us."

Sure enough, the top bid hadn't changed while they'd been discussing strategy. It currently belonged to one Madame X. The other bidder—Lady Mia—wasn't responding, but the last time Lance had put in a bid, she'd topped it quickly enough.

"You don't think Madame X and Lady Mia are real people?" Cash asked.

"I think they're here to keep the bidding moving," Sebastian said, "to see what we're willing to pay. Realistically, how many female Dommes are out there looking for a fulltime slave at any given moment? We know they've had Kimi for a couple of months already. If they'd had a buyer for her before now, they'd have sold her."

"I still don't get why they're respecting her sexual preferences," Harrison said. "They kidnapped her, they're selling her into slavery, but if she's a lesbian then by God she's a lesbian? It doesn't make sense."

"Even sick fucks want to believe their victim finds them sexually attractive," Sebastian said. "It's part of the fantasy."

Harrison looked at Sebastian like he was a fucking fount of wisdom. Well, what did Cash know about the noncon side of BDSM? Nothing. Why would he?

"I suppose they've got an interest in keeping their customers satisfied," Harrison agreed finally. "Wouldn't want one of them running to the police."

211

"I wonder what their return policy is," Sebastian said with an inappropriate smirk. He was enjoying this too much, bouncing on the balls of his feet as the bid clock counted down on the screen.

"Guys?" Lance prompted. "What am I doing here?"

"Leave it to the last minute," Sebastian told him. "Let them sweat. Then bid one twenty."

"One twenty?" Cash questioned. They were only at a hundred thousand and had been going up five at a time.

"A long wait followed by a big jump telegraphs that this is your last bid," Sebastian said. "Classic bidding mistake. A real opponent would immediately bid us up, knowing we're out, but these aren't real opponents. The sellers are freaking right now that they may have accidentally pushed Francesca over her limit. They'll let our next bid take it. Wait and see."

And of course he was right. Their next bid sat uncontested for the full fifteen minutes, and then the auction ended. Rather anticlimactically, in Cash's opinion. There was no gavel, no fireworks, just a greying out of the bid button and a single line of unadorned text that read, "Congratulations. Please visit our payment page to complete your transaction."

"That's it, huh?" Harrison looked similarly unimpressed. "You get anything useful?" he asked Lance.

"I'll dig through the traces, but I'm guessing we'll end up in the same place that email led us to."

"Who knew Switzerland was such a douchebag."

"Neutral is kind of another word for douchebag," Cash observed. If you weren't against evil, you were in favor of it, and apparently Switzerland looked the other way on all kinds of cyber shenanigans.

Sebastian and Lance hunched over Lance's laptop, working through the intricacies of buying Bitcoins and transferring them to whoever was behind the auction. Lance had three giant monitors arrayed on the credenza behind him, but he seemed to do everything on this one tiny laptop on his desk.

"Instructions for claiming our prize will be delivered." Sebastian straightened up with a hand to the back of his neck. "Tell Francesca to check her email."

Cash wondered if they'd just gotten scammed out of a hundred and twenty thousand dollars, but apparently the kidnappers were ethical, as far as kidnappers went, because Francesca called Harrison before the two of them had even made it all the way out of the building. She was now the proud owner of a woman named Kim who would be arriving by Greyhound bus at South Station early tomorrow evening.

"Hot damn," Harrison whispered as he grinned at his phone. "We've got them now. We're going to have that place staked out so hard. Gotta go, babe." He popped up on his toes to give Cash a kiss, then darted back off to find Brixby.

Hopefully, this was all about to end. For Ilona's sake, for Kimi's sake, for Arlo's sake, and for his own.

"THEY'RE BRINGING KIMI HERE," Cash warned Ilona the next night. She was curled up on the loveseat reading something on her Kindle, probably about ready for bed.

"Here? Why?"

"Everyone's coming." He tucked his phone away and set to putting on a pot of coffee and scrounging through his cupboards for refreshments. Would Kimi be hungry? She'd been in captivity but was apparently unharmed. Harrison had just texted to say she'd cleared a medical check and didn't need to be admitted.

So that was the good news. They had Kimi. The bad news was they hadn't captured any perpetrators. Kimi had shown up at South Station unaccompanied, disembarking with a backpack and a hand-lettered sign that read simply "Francesca."

"Why *here* though?" Ilona asked.

"It's a neutral place everyone knows. Sebastian's coming. And Brixby. You like Brixby."

Ilona closed her hand around the medallion hanging from her neck. "Mistress is coming?"

"Yeah, Francesca too."

Ilona disappeared into the bathroom, probably to put on her face. Cash went back to trying to rustle up refreshments for half a dozen people with zero notice. Sebastian made it to the apartment first, followed by Harrison and Brixby arriving together. Brixby went over to talk to Sebastian, while Cash detained Harrison at the door for a kiss.

"Where's Kimi?" he asked in a low voice.

"Francesca's bringing her." Harrison glanced at Ilona, who'd dressed herself up as if she had a job interview. "She's very attached to Francesca."

"Kimi is? Already?"

"It's weird. The whole thing is weird. She came all the way from Chicago by herself. Multiple stops. She could've gotten off the bus at any point, asked someone for help, disappeared into the crowd at South Station. Instead she willingly stood there and waited for Francesca to claim her."

"We knew these guys were working with people's kinks," Cash reminded him. "Arlo wanted a lifestyle Dom. If they told him he was getting one, he wouldn't have run away from him. He'd have run toward him."

"This fucking sucks." Harrison ran a hand over his short crop of hair. "Human trafficking isn't a kink."

"No one's arguing that."

The next buzz of his intercom heralded Francesca, wearing a dramatically long raincoat and holding the arm of a woman who was underdressed for the cold summer rain.

"Kimi, honey, can you say hi to Master Cash for me? He's our host."

When Kimi looked up to say hi, Cash caught a peek at her eyes—a little dull, a little scared.

"Is she on something?" he asked Harrison as Francesca introduced her to the rest of the room. Brixby and Sebastian had Ilona on the long sofa between them, as if to buffer her.

"Generic Valium. We found the pills in her bag. But the doc says it's not enough to make her act irrationally, just soothe her anxiety."

"Kimi, this is my submissive, Ilona." Francesca had skipped Ilona on the first round of introductions, but she dropped the bomb now.

"*I'm* your submissive," Kimi said with an angry look at Ilona. Ilona smiled in response—the first smile Cash had seen from her in days.

"We need to talk about that." Francesca steered Kimi to the only remaining empty chair and sat her in it.

Cash scrambled to pull in extra chairs from the dining area so everyone could have a seat. He handed around the drinks and snacks he'd pulled together, making a point to press them on Kimi, but she looked more nervous than hungry and refused everything.

"Why is she here?" Ilona challenged.

Harrison dragged a hand over his head again. "We weren't sure where else to bring her, to be honest."

"Where do you want to go?" Cash asked Kimi. Seemed like it was her choice.

"With Mistress Francesca."

"Yeah, that's not going to happen," Ilona said.

"Ilona," Francesca chastised. "No one asked your opinion."

"If I'm not wearing your collar, I don't need your permission to talk. Is *she* wearing your collar?

Kimi put a hand to her throat, the way Cash had watched Ilona do repeatedly for the last week. Neither woman wore one.

"You said this would be the end of it," Ilona said bitterly to Harrison.

"We thought it would be. We didn't expect her to show

215

up alone. You're sure there was no one on the bus with you?" he asked Kimi. "No one watching you? No one at all? Did they threaten you?"

"I *told* you," Kimi said. "I was coming to my mistress."

"*My* mistress," Ilona insisted.

"She's mine. She won me."

"So you knew you were being sold?" Sebastian asked. "How do you feel about that?"

Kimi shrugged. "Proud."

"Interesting." Sebastian stroked his chin, where he seemed to be testing out a short goatee. It made him look particularly Satanic.

"I wanted a mistress. Now I have one." Kimi beamed at Francesca with obvious approval.

Cash could understand the approval. Francesca had removed her raincoat to reveal a white silk blouse with a fluttery neckline and a pair of black flared-leg lounge pants. With her bright red lips and long, dark hair, she looked like something from a classic 1940s Hollywood film—a lesbian submissive's dream. But there were shadows under her eyes that didn't used to be there.

"So you see the problem," Harrison said in summary. "Kimi wants to go home with Francesca. Francesca has Ilona.

"Who also wants to go home with her," Ilona said pointedly.

"And we can't just dump her on the street."

"So you figured she could stay here?" Cash asked, finally understanding why Harrison had brought an entire party of people to his house at eleven o'clock at night.

"Do you mind?"

"Of course not." He did, a little. He wanted his apartment and his boyfriend to himself, but his needs were nothing compared to what Kimi needed. Most of which, unfortunately, Cash couldn't give her.

Chapter 23 Harrison

All Harrison wanted to do was crawl into Cash's arms and let Cash take care of him. He didn't even mean that sexually. Some fussing would go over really well at the moment, like how Cash would stroke his arm or rub his stomach or play with his hair. Cash was good at soothing, and Harrison needed it. Because tonight had sucked. He'd never had an investigation go belly up in such a big way.

Brixby's precinct had sent half a dozen officers to stake out South Station, ready to pounce on whoever Kimi showed up with, only to have her show up alone. Francesca had approached her while they scoured the area for someone observing the transaction, but no one had been observing it. Kimi had been put on a bus with a sign. She'd gotten off the bus with a sign. She was there to be claimed. She'd been claimed. She was so thoroughly complicit in her supposed kidnapping it made Harrison and Brixby look like alarmists. What should've been a newsworthy arrest to launch Brixby's career and bring some good PR to Fisher Investigations had fizzled into embarrassment.

"Do you have a copy of the contract you signed?" Sebastian asked, like the attorney he was.

Kimi shook her head.

"Do you remember what it said?"

"I didn't really read it."

"Of course not. No one ever reads anything. They just sign." Sebastian made a scrawling motion with his hand.

"Can she really agree to be sold?" Harrison asked. He was pacing behind the chairs Francesca and Cash were sitting in, wishing he was within touching distance of Cash but too wired to actually make that happen.

"No, definitely not. Selling people is illegal, which means there's no contract you can sign to make it legal. If they're smart, the contract doesn't say she's being sold. It probably reads like an employment agreement."

"She'd been doing housekeeping," Harrison told him. "They were keeping her in a motel where she was cleaning the guest rooms in exchange for room and board."

"Were you having sex with anyone?" Sebastian asked her.

Kimi shook her head. "I stayed in my room. Cleaned during the day and watched television at night."

"Was your door locked from the outside? Were you restrained in any way?"

She shook her head again.

"And no one forced you to do anything you didn't want to do?"

"This is what I *wanted*," she answered with another covetous look at Francesca.

"Frankly," Sebastian told Harrison, "you've got a tough case here. Kimi's of age, and she did everything voluntarily. That online auction site didn't make any promises about what they were delivering. The sellers could argue they were selling a photo or brokering an opportunity for Francesca to meet Kimi in person."

"You're acting like they're running a kinky matchmaking service. Does no one except me see why this is fucking wrong? Arlo wasn't of age when he disappeared."

"But he is now," Sebastian said, because Arlo had turned eighteen a week ago with nothing to mark the occasion except one more tick in the running total Harrison kept of how many days he'd been missing. "For all we know, they fed him milk and cookies and sent him to school until he turned eighteen. I'm not saying what they're doing is

218

right. I'm just saying I wouldn't want to be the one prosecuting it."

"Well, you don't have to worry about prosecuting it if we can't catch anyone. Tomorrow, Brixby and I will go over everything Kimi remembers about where she's been the last two months and the people who put her there, but we still have to figure out what to do with her tonight. Kimi, Cash says you can stay here."

"I don't like men."

"It's just a place to sleep, somewhere you'll be safe."

Kimi shook her head. "I belong with my mistress."

"She's *my* mistress." Ilona went over and knelt at Francesca's feet. Francesca put a hand in her hair, but it seemed perfunctory. She had a tired air about her that Harrison could sympathize with. They'd spent an hour at the bus station, followed by another couple of hours at the hospital. They were all ready for bed. It was just a matter of figuring out who was sleeping where.

"Kimi," he started, but before he could ask her to please stay here because otherwise he was going to have to rent her a hotel room he couldn't afford, she started bawling. And what was he supposed to do about that? He was bad at women having emotions.

Francesca watched Kimi with concern, obviously wanting to go to her, but Ilona was watching Francesca just as avidly, as if she might physically prevent Francesca from doing it if she tried. Harrison liked seeing Ilona willing to fight for what she wanted. Personally, he would put up a hell of a stink if Cash decided to play at being someone else's Dom.

Brixby crouched down next to Kimi, trying to console her, but she only cried harder, pushing him out of the way with a sharp elbow. "I don't like men. If I can't be with mistress, I want to go home."

"Maybe we should have Brixby arrest her," Harrison said, half to himself.

"What?" Cash's voice carried more vehemence than

Harrison was accustomed to from him. "How is that fair?"

"She can't go back to Chicago. The kidnappers will know we're on to them, and the whole investigation will be jeopardized. We'll never find Arlo."

"If you force her to stay here, you're no better than a kidnapper yourself."

"She's not the only one involved, and she's clearly not thinking straight. This lifestyle business is a form of Stockholm Syndrome, if you ask me. Maybe I could get her a psych eval, put her on a seventy-two hour hold."

"Holy-fucking-wait-a-minute," Ilona protested. She'd been looking like she approved of the plan to either arrest Kimi or send her back to Chicago, but she was pissed now. "Wanting a mistress doesn't make her mentally ill."

"Signing her life away makes her mentally ill. You heard her. She didn't even look at what she was signing. And now she'd rather live with a strange woman who's going to make her walk around wearing a fucking leash than stay with Cash. It's sick."

"Harrison, stop." Cash grabbed for his hand, but he couldn't stand still long enough to allow it. "Could we try to involve Kimi in the conversation more?"

"All I've gotten out of Kimi is 'I don't like men.'"

"Do you blame her?" Ilona asked.

"Everyone needs to control their subs," Sebastian said with a significant look at Cash that had Harrison bristling.

"Fuck off. I'm not anyone's sub."

Sebastian snorted. "What was I thinking? You've got too much fire in you to be tamed by the likes of Cash." He winked, which made Harrison want to punch him even harder.

"Get this straight, asshole. This is *my* investigation and *my* relationship. No one asked for your opinion."

"Only my money."

"Fine." Harrison flung his hand toward Kimi. "You bought her. What do you want to do with her?"

"I don't like men," Kimi said for at least the third time.

"Yeah, we get it. You don't like men. Well, too bad for you because the people who were supposed to be hooking you up with the perfect mistress actually sold you to a sick fuck named Sebastian."

Kimi cried harder, Sebastian rolled his eyes, and even Brixby gave him the stink-eye.

"No wonder she doesn't like men." Francesca pushed Brixby out of the way to wrap her arms around Kimi. "No one is giving you to Sebastian. I promise."

"No one's giving her to anyone," Harrison said. Because really. That was the point he'd been trying to make. People couldn't be bought or sold or given. Calling it kink didn't make owning humans legal. Or right.

"But why do I have to stay *here*?" Kimi cried. "I want to go home with you. I've been waiting and waiting, with no friends and nothing to do, just work and wait, but I believed and then it happened. But you were lying. You were all lying." She cried harder, now trying to push Francesca away too.

"You don't have to stay here," Harrison told her. "And I won't have you arrested or get you locked up in a psych ward. That was just... threats." That he shouldn't have made. "But I don't know what to do with you. Can you pick something? Something besides going with Francesca or going back to Chicago."

When Kimi shook her head, Harrison threw up his hands and went over to sit on the loveseat next to Sebastian where Brixby had been. That gave him a good view of Cash's face, which was set hard. So much for Cash comforting him. Cash was pissed at him.

"She can go with Mistress," Ilona said. "I'll stay here."

"Really?" That wasn't at all what he'd expected to have happen next.

"I can wait. Kimi needs her more." Ilona wrapped her arms around herself, forlorn but resolute. Francesca beckoned her over and pulled her down onto her lap so the three women huddled together.

221

"You won't forget about me, will you?" Ilona asked her. "And have her instead?"

"Never, pet."

"If Kimi could go home with Francesca, that would be great," Harrison said. Not only would Kimi be somewhere she could be monitored, but it furthered the ruse of Francesca having bought her. "We might still be able to use the channel of communication between Francesca and the traffickers for something."

"Am I going to be acquiring a harem?" Francesca asked through a mouthful of Ilona's hair.

"You could let it be known you're open to more. If we get invited to another auction, it would give us a second chance to find the people behind it." And rescue another captive sub, although Kimi was starting to feel less like someone they'd rescued and more like someone they'd taken hostage.

"Let's play with that idea," Sebastian said. "Suppose Francesca takes both Kimi and Ilona home with her. Ilona's been forgiven for not toeing the line, but her punishment is playing second sub to the new girl."

"That's pure mental sadism," Cash grumbled.

"Psychological torture is my favorite weapon," Sebastian agreed without a hint of shame. "I'm a mindfuck Dom," he explained to Harrison. "I enjoy keeping my subs unsettled."

Harrison shook his head. He couldn't even be surprised anymore. They were all a bunch of sick fucks, each with their own sick specialty.

"Well, that'll finish off what's left of my reputation," Francesca said with a sigh.

Sebastian mumbled his way through an apology for the way he'd treated her before he'd been let in on their secret. "I should've had more faith in you," he finished.

"No, you really shouldn't have," Cash said. "We need to call each other out when we see shit like that. No more minding our own business. This *is* our business. We're lucky Knight has been willing to help us, but we shouldn't have needed his help. We should've been paying attention ourselves."

"The cat minding the pigeons," Harrison said. "Y'all *need* external security."

"Or a good psych eval, right?" Sebastian rose with a glower. "Don't bother thanking me for funding your operation. Since we've arrived at a resolution, I'll see myself out."

"We have a resolution?" Francesca asked the door Sebastian had closed with an implied bang.

"Seems like it," Harrison said with a sigh. So Sebastian was mad at him too. So what? "Bring them both home. If you talk to anyone, tell the story Sebastian came up with. I'll come by tomorrow to interview Kimi after we've all gotten some sleep." And everyone had chilled the fuck out.

Ilona removed the medallion from around her neck and handed it Brixby. "I'll have Mistress's collar now," she said with a hopeful glance at Francesca.

"As soon as we get home, pet." Francesca herded her charges out the door, both of them clinging to her. Which was a lot of woman hanging off her tiny frame.

Brixby dropped the medallion on the television stand.

"You don't want that back?" Harrison asked him.

"Hang onto it until we've got Arlo back. Just in case." Brixby and Cash shared a look Harrison couldn't define. "Are you going to talk to him or should I?"

"I've got it."

"Got what?" Harrison asked, but Brixby didn't answer, just gave him a slap on the back and let himself out.

"What?" Harrison repeated as Cash started bussing dishes into the kitchen. "Hey, we've finally got the place to ourselves." He was so tired he couldn't imagine doing more than cuddling, but Cash's unusually steely demeanor was making him wish the cuddling would commence. "Do we have to talk tonight?"

"Yeah, I think we do." Cash returned the dining room

chairs back to their places around the table while Harrison shadowed him.

"What then? Tell me."

"You know what. We've talked about it before."

"Fine." Harrison heaved an exasperated breath. "I'm sorry I didn't use the politically correct terms to describe everyone's kinks. I'm tired, I'm frustrated, and it's late."

"You called us sick, Harrison. And you're one of us."

"Whoa there. Don't lump me in with people like Kimi. And don't lump yourself in with people who think it's okay to own a slave."

"I don't. But I do lump myself in with Sebastian and Francesca. There's a difference between what the kidnappers did to Kimi and what Francesca does with Ilona, just like there's a difference between what I do to you and if I went up to someone on the street and shoved a metal rod down his dick. I need you to understand the difference because you're not only insulting my friends, you're insulting me."

"Come on, you have to admit that what Kimi wants is sick."

Cash shook his head. "Someone took advantage of what she wants in an awful way, but you don't get to say that what you want is normal and what someone else wants is sick. You just don't. Kimi might be very happy with Francesca if Francesca didn't already have Ilona."

"But Francesca wasn't the one who bought her," Harrison pointed out, his voice rising, despite the fact that Cash was being very calm. "Kimi only ended up with someone who might be a good mistress to her because we interceded. Anyone buying a slave in an online auction is unethical by definition. Which means Arlo, Jessica, whoever else is out there—they're not living a dream come true. They're in the hands of a maniac."

"No one's arguing that," Cash said. "I'm asking you to see the difference between a maniac and people who practice safe, sane, consensual BDSM."

"I'll agree there's a difference if you'll stop acting like the kidnappers aren't doing anything wrong."

"I didn't say the kidnappers aren't doing anything wrong. I'm just pointing out how they're using people's kinks to manipulate them. Whoever's taking these subs must be in the scene." Cash sat down wearily on the loveseat.

Harrison could see how much Cash hated admitting that the perpetrator must be one of them. Obviously *Cash* wasn't sick. He was the most decent guy on earth. But Harrison wasn't ready to say the same about every person who practiced BDSM.

He sat next to Cash, who stretched his arm across the back of the loveseat and curled it around his shoulder. He'd been forgiven apparently. He hadn't even gotten around to apologizing yet. Cash was just too nice. But it was that very niceness that made him finally regret his words. If what he'd said had hurt Cash, then he was sorry for it. Cash had shown him that his early experience with BDSM wasn't the only sort of experience to be had, but those memories were still lodged hard in his heart, coloring the way he saw everyone and everything else.

"I guess I never mentioned I'd dabbled in BDSM before."

"What?" Cash turned to him. "No, you never mentioned that."

"I was young. Arlo's age. I'd been toying with the idea for years. You know—watching videos, hanging out in online forums, trying to hit myself and totally failing at it. But I thought I'd like it if someone else hit me, so I arranged to meet this guy." Harrison swallowed. "Sir Magnus."

He waited for Cash to laugh, to immediately know how thoroughly stupid he'd been, but Cash didn't laugh. Not at all.

"What happened?" he asked fearfully, as if whatever Harrison was about to say was going to hurt him as much Harrison had been hurt.

"He hit me, with a whip. What you'd call a carriage

whip, I think." He hadn't known any of the terms then, but he knew them now. "And I liked it. I did. But there was more. Names, insults." Words like the ones that woman at Hell's Bedroom had thrown at the man drinking piss. And worse words, words like runt and Munchkin and weak.

"He mocked me for liking it until I stopped liking it, but he kept hitting me anyway. He got off, I didn't. He let me go, and I left. He thought I'd be back." Harrison shook his head. "Who would go back? I don't understand it, Cash. That scene fucking broke me." He put his hand to his chest where he could still feel the ache of it. "I was so young I hardly knew what self-respect was. It took years to get it back."

"Oh, Harrison." Cash wrapped him up hard.

"Who chooses that?" he asked Cash's chest. "And why?"

"Whew. Where to start? You've been fighting to prove you were good enough your whole life, haven't you?"

Harrison nodded. Between Taylor and his height, he'd always felt like he had to.

"So the humiliation play, which I suppose is what Sir Magnus thought he was doing, felt awful to you, like a repudiation of who you were trying to be. But for some people, humiliation play assuages their imposter syndrome, allows them to stop trying so hard, to be comfortingly worthless for a while."

"You're kidding me." He couldn't even imagine.

"Not kidding," Cash said. "It's not universal, but it's common, and I have no right to judge. But I do have a responsibility to make sure it's what my sub wants before going down that road, which apparently Sir Magnus didn't do."

Harrison shook his head. Before Cash, he'd assumed subjugation was inseparable from pain, that he had deserved one by asking for the other, but Cash treated him with respect, like an equal, despite the difference in their heights and the fact that he held the whip.

Except once.

"Oh God, Harrison," Cash said, apparently remembering, as Harrison was doing, the night Cash had called him a worthless worm named Harry. "I'm so sorry. I never should've veered into humiliation without permission in the first place, but realizing now what a trigger it was for you—" He sank his face into his hands.

"Hey, come on. Don't beat yourself up over it." He took Cash's hands away from his face and pressed them between his own. "I sort of forced you into it."

"Not an excuse," Cash said. "Can you forgive me?"

"Of course." He had to laugh, even though it'd been far from funny at the time. "After everything you've forgiven me for? I'd be a hypocrite not to. And Cash? You taught me I can have this without hating myself for wanting it, so thanks for reintroducing me to kink the right way, for showing me how it can be different."

"It's been my pleasure. But please let other people have what they want without judging them for it. Even if it's something you wouldn't want for yourself, like humiliation or subservience."

Harrison sighed. "I still think Kimi needs help, but I understand what you're saying. As long as the people involved are consenting adults, it's none of my business what they do. I'm sorry I called Kimi sick."

"Thank you."

"But what about the way Sebastian fucks with people's minds? That's not consensual."

"The subs he plays with enjoy it."

"You don't."

"I'm not his sub."

"But he fucks with you. He fucks with everyone."

"That's a good point," Cash said slowly. "He's an ethical Dom though. If you're looking."

"Why would I be looking? I thought we made up. I even apologized." Which wasn't something he did a lot. "Are you still pissed at me?"

Cash shook his head. "I'm not pissed at you."

"Good." He snuggled deeper into Cash's embrace. "I don't want you to be pissed at me."

Finally the rubbing started. Cash's hands moved from his shoulder to his temples, as if he knew where the pain was—right there in his muddled mind.

Harrison had a fucking headache from all this, but Cash's hands soothed it away, and as the throb receded, the importance of what Cash had been saying started to come through. Not about the kink shaming—which, fine, he would do better with—but the other part, the part about how the kidnappers were working with the victim's kinks.

Imagine if Francesca had bought Kimi for her own purposes. What would she have done with a slave who was, at least temporarily, willing? Taken her home and integrated her into her life, which might include bringing her to down the club.

So maybe Arlo wasn't locked in a basement. Maybe he was kneeling at the feet of the man he'd been sold to, right out in the open in the public play space of his captor's club.

HARRISON STARTED THE NEXT DAY running on all cylinders. A night alone with Cash helped, and so did having a plan. Or at least the start of a plan. He texted Knight first thing, using the new phone number Knight had acquired to keep his transmissions more private, and asked for a list of DDD locations. He also asked which members of his ad hoc team had a premium membership that would allow them to visit the other clubs.

"Sebastian, of course." He showed Brixby the list Knight had texted back. They were in Brixby's squad car, parked out in Charlestown where Francesca lived because they'd just finished interviewing Kimi. "And Francesca, but not Cash. Bummer. I was hoping Cash and I could take one club, and you and Sebastian could hit up another. I don't suppose you'd like to play sub to Francesca?"

"You know I would if it would help, but how can we ask her? She's got two needy subs to look after already."

"True."

The whole time he and Brixby had been trying to interview Kimi, Kimi and Ilona had been competing for Francesca's attention. Exhausting. And fruitless. Kimi had had very little direct contact with the people who'd been keeping her because they hadn't really been keeping her. They'd promised to find her a mistress and, as far as she was concerned, they'd found her one. In her mind, she was more a happy customer than a victim. The only thorn in her side was Ilona.

Brixby examined the list of clubs Knight had sent. "I could get into this one," he said, indicating a club in New York. "I grew up in Jersey. This was one of my first play places. I don't think it was owned by DDD at the time."

"You're still a member?"

"No, but I know people who are. I can find someone to sign me in."

"Ooh, you could play sub for Cash." Harrison didn't know what kind of Dom Brixby was, but he could guess what kind of sub he'd be—an uncomfortable one. Ha! Brixby's turn to see how it felt.

But Brixby had an excuse to get himself out of it. "They know me there, which means they know I'm a Dom. Cash would have to play the sub role. Or how about I bring Tripp? He'd have the best chance of spotting Arlo."

"Yeah, all right. Good plan." That left Harrison with Sebastian, which he already knew he was going to hate. He gritted his teeth and made the call.

"Harry!" Sebastian greeted him. Not because Sebastian didn't know better but because he *did* know better. Reacting would only make it worse, so Harrison didn't respond until Sebastian corrected himself. "Harrison. Do you have something to say or did you just call to breathe at me?"

Since he had a favor to ask, he decided to start with an

apology. "I'm sorry I called you sick."

"Not wholly inaccurate, but I appreciate the apology. Is that it or do you need another hundred and twenty grand? I have to warn you I don't keep that kind of money in my sock drawer. It might take me a couple of days to pull it together, and I'm not impressed with what my money has bought me so far."

"I don't need money." How did Sebastian manage to make Harrison so completely not sorry about taking his money? Or calling him sick either. "I want to go down to XXXtasy in Philly this weekend to look for Arlo. I was hoping you could sign me in."

"Hang on." Muffled voices in the background were followed by the soft thud of a door being closed before Sebastian's voice came back on the line. "So you'd be my sub for the weekend?" he asked gleefully.

"I'd *pretend* to be your sub."

"And I'd get to call you Harry?"

"At the club, you could call me Harry."

"That might be worth a hundred and twenty grand. I'm in. When do you want to leave?"

"If you could take Friday off, we could get down there in time to hit up the club Friday night."

"Now you're really asking for a favor. Hang on." This time it sounded like Sebastian dropped his phone altogether, but after a long period of silence, he came back. "Schedule cleared. See you Friday. Oh, and Harry? I'll drive."

"Fine," Harrison told his phone screen, which indicated that Sebastian had already hung up. "He's going to make me hate every second of this." That comment was for Brixby.

"Glad it was Cash you stumbled on at that party and not Sebastian, huh?"

"I wouldn't have made it." He might enjoy physical pain, but he had no tolerance for psychic pain. "Tripp wasn't wrong when he said Cash was my best choice. He really is."

"I'm glad you found someone."

"I just hope I can make him happy. There's this... imbalance."

Brixby leaned back against the driver's seat and tilted his sunglasses up so he could make eye contact. "There often is in power exchange relationships."

"Right, but that's a problem, don't you think? I've always tried to be a good partner. Totally failed at it, but tried. Cash just... takes care of me. Constantly, in a hundred ways, and what do I do in return? Lie back and enjoy it, basically. Every time I try to do something for him, it ends up being all about me again. I love it, but I also feel like a total shit."

"You're giving him what he wants," Brixby said. "And, no, you don't get to decide what that is," he continued before Harrison could butt in to say that what Cash wanted was ridiculous. "A good Dom is all about his sub, no matter how it might look from the outside. Why do you think there are more subs than Doms anyway?"

"I was wondering."

"Now you know. Whether we're using a whip or a leash, a Dom has his entire attention focused on figuring out how to send his sub flying."

"Even Sebastian?"

"I gotta believe it, yeah. Somewhere in the great, wide world of kink, there's a sub who wants what Sebastian has. And Sebastian wants to give it to him."

Chapter 24 Cash

Cash was in the process of shutting down his workstation for the day when Harrison called to say he was in Charlestown. "No sense jamming onto the T during rush hour, so I'm going to head over to my sister's and wait it out. You want to meet her?"

"I'd love to," he answered without hesitation. Cambridge was just across the river from his office, and the offer was confirmation that Harrison saw a future for them. Hope fluttered like a wild thing in his chest.

"Cool. And we can have dinner after. Let me take you out before I disappear for the weekend."

"Before you—"

"I'll explain later." Harrison made a kissy noise into the phone and hung up, leaving Cash to scramble to get out of the office. It was a lovely summer day, not gruesomely hot, so he walked up to the river before hopping the red line for the trip into Cambridge where Harrison was waiting for him outside a hipster-looking tattoo place. The shop might be hipster, but Harrison's sister, Taylor, was very much not. She was dressed all in black with deep red lips worthy of Francesca and a parrot hanging from a gold loop over her head like she couldn't decide whether she was a vampire or a pirate.

"So you're the guy," she said, eyeing him up and down like he was going to need her permission to date her brother. "Harrison says you don't have any tattoos."

"Not yet."

"Good answer." She pointed at him with a blunt-tipped fingernail. "I'll give you half off. Family discount. What are you thinking about getting?"

He hadn't been thinking about getting anything. He threw Harrison a quick glance, asking for help. Harrison was kicked back against the customer side of the reception counter, while Taylor leaned over it from the other side. The two of them were pretty obviously brother and sister with the same green eyes and strong nose. Same intimidation factor too.

"How about my name on your ass?" Harrison suggested with a smirk.

"Um."

"No names," Taylor said with a dismissive flick of her hand. "That's what I tell everyone, not just men who are dating my little brother, but *especially* men who are dating my little brother. You know he's never managed to maintain a relationship for more than a few months, right?"

"You're one to talk," Harrison crossed his arms over his chest like maybe the jab had hurt, so Cash moved in closer to him.

"It takes two to maintain a relationship. And if I'm being honest, I've never been with anyone long-term either."

"What?" Harrison shook his head. "How's that possible? I swear, people have such poor taste. Leave him alone," he told his sister. "He doesn't need a tattoo if he doesn't want one."

Cash felt another flutter of hope. Maybe Harrison's name on his ass wouldn't be such a bad choice. It was beginning to feel like they really had something here.

Taylor opened her mouth to say something, but what came out instead was a bark, like she was imitating the Rottweiler she reminded him of. Or possibly cueing the parrot, which Cash only just now realized wasn't stuffed because it said fuck and then a whole bunch of other things he couldn't understand.

233

"Don't ask," Harrison said with a long-suffering roll of his eyes, but once they'd said goodbye to Taylor and were out on the sidewalk together, strolling Cambridge in search of somewhere to eat, Cash asked.

"She has Tourette's," Harrison explained shortly. "The barking sound is a tic, and the parrot is a distraction."

"Huh. Cool solution. Hey, maybe I should get a parrot. For the garden."

"You'd have to clip its wings though," Harrison said, as if he already knew Cash would never be able to do that.

"I guess not then. You and your sister are a lot alike, huh?"

"You mean the eyes? Everyone always says that, but I don't wear nearly as much mascara."

"I meant the attitude. I guess you both had battles to fight growing up."

"I was fighting *her*," Harrison said. "What was *she* fighting? Oh." He stopped moving. They were in front of a place with outdoor seating and an appetizing smell, but Harrison wasn't looking at the restaurant. "You think that's why she's so fucking bossy? Because of the Tourette's? Because she's trying to prove something?"

"I would guess. Or, you know, it's just the way your family runs."

Harrison snorted. "Yeah, we're all about as bad as each other, but I never thought about how the Tourette's might've affected Taylor's self-confidence. You scare me sometimes, you know that? That kink of yours is like a superpower."

"I just pay attention to people and—"

"Care. I know. Don't pretend that's not special." Harrison leaned up to kiss him, right there on a sidewalk in Cambridge, and Cash had never felt more special. But then, over dinner, when they'd each had two glasses of wine and were stuffed with seafood and feeling pleasantly relaxed at a table on a sidewalk in the beautiful gold of a setting sun, Harrison told him what was happening this weekend.

CASH HATED EVERYTHING ABOUT THIS NEW PLAN, from the major fact that Harrison was on his way to Philadelphia with Sebastian to the relatively minor fact that he'd been wearing Brixby's medallion when he left. He particularly hated that Sebastian was a fucking premium member and he wasn't. Which meant Sebastian could get Harrison where he needed to go while Cash was left standing on the curb, watching his boyfriend drive away in a low-slung German sports car.

Sure, Harrison had kissed him goodbye, but it would be Sebastian he knelt to tonight, dressed in booty shorts with Brixby's medallion like a collar around his neck, play-acting at being Sebastian's sub. Or maybe not play acting. Harrison was a curious guy, and Sebastian swung a good whip. Would Harrison think whipping fell outside their agreement for exclusivity?

Cash had wanted to clarify before letting Harrison drive away, but he hadn't because Harrison needed to be free to do whatever he had to in order to find Arlo. Including getting whipped. Harrison was just doing his job. But did he have to do it with Sebastian?

By the time Cash met Mr. Jackman at the library after work, Harrison and Sebastian would already have made it to Philadelphia, would have checked into a hotel and would be showering before changing into their club clothes. Sebastian would've teased out Harrison's kinks on the drive down, would know by now exactly how to play him like the master he was.

"You're distracted today," Mr. Jackman observed.

"Sorry." Cash refocused on the screen Mr. Jackman had been reading from—a story about recent changes to immigration law that Cash hadn't heard a word of.

"Things not going well with that new girl of yours? You've been so happy the last couple of weeks."

235

"No, it's fine. We should get back to this." They were there for a literacy lesson, not a gripe session.

"Not so fine," Mr. Jackman said with a slow and knowing shake of his head. "What's gone and happened? She mad at you over something?"

"No, just traveling for work. With a guy. A co-worker. It's fine."

"Ah ha!" Mr. Jackman stabbed a finger into his side. "Green-eyed monster got you. I know how that feels, but a person's gotta do their job. Doesn't mean anything."

"No, I know. He wouldn't—" Cash broke off, trying to figure out how to reword what he'd been about to say.

"Don't interrupt yourself on my account. Finish your sentence."

"He wouldn't cheat on me," Cash finished. "It's a man. I'm gay."

"Huh." Mr. Jackman pursed his lips for a moment in consideration. "You know, I thought that might be how it was. There's a woman over there. You see her?"

Cash looked in the direction Mr. Jackman was indicating. A woman with light skin and short, brown hair ducked her head as soon as he glanced her way. "Sure. What about her?"

"She's there every week. Watches us."

Cash squinted in her direction. She did look vaguely familiar, like she might've passed by and said hi a few times.

"I was beginning to think you needed some lessons in *sexual* literacy," Mr. Jackman said with a deep chuckle. "My man's got no game. But I get it now. You don't like the ladies. That's aiight."

"It is?"

"Why? You asking my permission?" Mr. Jackman chuckled again, like all this was a joke. "Man, you *are* gloomy today," he said when he'd finished snickering. "If you don't think your guy's going to cheat on you, what's the problem? Just missing him?"

Cash couldn't go into detail, but he couldn't get

Harrison off his mind either, so he wasn't sorry for the opportunity to talk about him. "I feel like the guy he's traveling with can do things for him I can't. I have certain... limitations."

"Like you can't get it up?"

Cash rolled his eyes. They'd gone from pronouns to impotence in a matter of minutes.

"All right, all right. You don't gotta tell me. Doesn't matter what it is anyway. My Margaret, she was the only one who ever knew I couldn't read. Least, that's what I thought until my grandson Bill—see, I know that there says William now—he bought me this phone, and I told him nah, son. I don't want no fancy phone, and he said Grampa, Imma teach you to use it, and he did too. Real patient, like he knew I couldn't read what it said, but he saw how even though I couldn't read, I could figure things out." Mr. Jackman tapped his temple. "He taught me in a way I could understand."

Mr. Jackman had been already been able to do a lot with his phone by the time Cash met him, using a combination of pattern recognition, memorization, and very careful matching of letters in print to the letters on the keypad.

"See, Margaret never learned to drive, and I never learned to read, and that worked just fine. She held the map and I held the wheel. What I'm saying is, people who love you, they see past what you can't do. They see how you work with what you *can* do. Whatever it is you think some other man can do that you can't, if your guy loves you like you deserve to be loved, it won't matter none. He'll hold the map while you drive."

That was just really, um, sage. Harrison was a terrible sub, but the things that made him a terrible sub also made him perfect for Cash. Wasn't the same true in reverse? The two of them had a relationship that worked for them, based on their specific strengths and interests, just like Mr. Jackman and his wife.

He'd been a fool to let Sebastian and Harrison go off together. Not because something might happen between the two of them, but because he could've gone with them instead of sulking about not being rich enough for a premium membership. He could've been there for Harrison, to give him a blowjob or a backrub or whatever he needed when the day was done.

Cash checked the time on his phone. "You mind if we wrap this up early?"

"There you go." Mr. Jackman clapped him on the back. "You go fight for what's yours."

"I will. Thanks for the story."

He had to rent a car, and by the time he got on the road, the GPS said he wouldn't arrive in Philadelphia until three in the morning. He didn't even know which hotel Harrison had checked into, and he would be at the club now without access to his phone, so Cash just headed for Philadelphia at large.

He was well past New York City, starting to droop and grateful that the endless traffic and sudden lane closures kept him alert, before his phone pinged with a message from Harrison. The quick flash of Harrison's name superimposed over the GPS screen flooded him with relief. Harrison had made it out of XXXtasy and still wanted him.

At the next rest stop, he pulled over to plug in the address Harrison had sent and buy another cup of coffee. Maybe it was selfish of him to chase Harrison down, but he itched to tell him this thing he'd realized.

"You don't want a Dom," he said before they'd even had a chance to properly greet each other. Harrison had a room all to himself. He wasn't sharing one with Sebastian as some of Cash's more ridiculous fears had suggested might be the case.

"I thought we figured that out on our first date." Harrison was dressed in nothing except boxers and had obviously been sleeping. The spikes of his short hair were matted down, and his eyes were heavy. He yawned and

238

headed for the bed.

"I had a hard time believing it," Cash told him. He wanted to shake Harrison awake because this was important. "The men I've dated in the past have always wanted me to be something I couldn't be."

"What's that?" Harrison asked as he crawled into bed. He patted the space next to him. "Loving? Attentive? Super-sexy-skilled?"

"A Dom."

"But you *are* a Dom. Will you get in bed already? It's three in the morning, and I was at the club until one."

"Right, sorry. How did that go?"

"No, keep telling me whatever you were trying to say. But get in bed to do it."

"See, that's not how you talk to your Dom." Cash stripped down to his shorts and climbed in next to him.

"I get it. You're not really a Dom, and I'm not really a sub. But we knew that. Why the sudden reveal in the middle of the night?"

"Because I just realized it's okay."

"Now who's kink shaming?" Harrison gave him a sleepy kiss then rolled over onto his side, reaching back to arrange Cash around him the way he liked. "You're *my* Dom. And if Sebastian ever makes another crack, I'll fucking crack him back. Now go to sleep. We'll talk in the morning."

Cash pulled him in tighter and went to sleep. As ordered.

HE WOKE TO SEBASTIAN'S VOICE outside their door. "Knock, knock," Sebastian shouted. The thud of what sounded like a kick accompanied his words.

Harrison grumbled himself onto his feet and staggered over to the door to open it. "God, what time is it?"

On the other side of the door, Sebastian stood picture-perfect, already showered and dressed, holding a cup of coffee in each hand. "I figured we should recap."

"Where's my coffee?" Cash asked, snickering a little when Sebastian nearly dropped both cups at the sound of his voice.

"When did you get here?"

"Around three," Harrison answered. "Which is why it's really fucking early to be pounding on our door."

"I didn't realize there was pounding going on last night." Sebastian set the cups down on the table in the corner and took a casual seat in one of the chairs next to it. "Don't trust your boy with me, Cash?"

"I trust Harrison just fine," he answered as he stepped into the jeans he'd left on the floor last night.

Harrison, still wearing nothing except boxers, took a sip from the cup Sebastian had handed him, then passed it to Cash to share. "Little sweet for your taste," he warned.

"Because I didn't get it for Cash," Sebastian said. "I got it for you."

"And you know how Harrison takes his coffee?"

"A Dom learns things about his sub."

"Stop being such a fuckwit," Harrison grumbled. "God, it's too early for this." He wandered over to the suitcase he'd left on the luggage stand and began searching through it.

"You know what they call Cash down at the club?"

"They call me something?"

"The Kitchen Sink Dom. Little bit of everything, all slopped together." Sebastian chuckled cruelly. "Perfect name for him, isn't it? Cash has always been best with leftovers."

Harrison stopped rummaging through his suitcase and turned to Sebastian with a t-shirt in one hand and the other hand balled into a fist. Cash intercepted him, pushing him back to approach Sebastian himself.

"Red."

"What?"

"I didn't agree to accept your mind fuckery. Save it for people who consent to it."

"Oh, come on, Cash. You know I'm teasing you."

"I don't give a fuck what you think you're doing. It hurts in ways I don't find pleasurable. So are you going to quit it, or am I going to quit you?"

Harrison came to stand next to him. "I'll find a way to finish this investigation without you if I have to."

"All right, all right." Sebastian held his hands up. "Wow, kind of sensitive this morning, aren't we?"

"You're still trying to fuck with me."

"I'm not— *Okay*," he said when Cash continued to glare at him with his arms crossed, using every inch of the bulk he had. "I'm sorry I teased you in a non-consensual manner.

"Harrison and I are allowed to have whatever relationship we want to have."

"Obviously."

"And play whatever roles we want to play."

"I'm just saying—"

"*Whatever* roles." Cash knew how to do the intimidation thing in the context of a scene. It just hadn't occurred to him to use his skills on Sebastian.

"I have no problem with switches," Sebastian muttered.

"What's a switch again?" Harrison asked.

"Someone who plays both Dom and sub roles," Cash reminded him.

"Oh, right. Well, I'm not a switch. Being a Dom seems like a lot of work."

"It can be. It's not with you, though."

"Aw." Harrison went up on his toes to peck him on the nose, then wriggled free. "So he's the Dom, I'm the sub, and we don't care if you don't like it," he said to Sebastian. "I'm going to take a shower." With that, he disappeared into the bathroom, leaving Cash with Sebastian and a cup of overly sweet coffee.

"I'm an asshole." Sebastian played with the cardboard cozy on his own cup of coffee.

"Sometimes."

"It's not like I don't know it. I just can't always contain it."

"Try harder."

"I will. I'm sorry." He managed to look genuinely contrite this time, so Cash sat down across the table from him.

"It's at least fifty percent jealousy," Sebastian said after a moment. "You guys seem good together, made for each other even. Whatever labels you put on it, you mesh."

"You're one of the most sought-after Doms at the club."

"Sure, for a little play here and there. If someone's feeling particularly masochistic one night, they come looking for me. But I'm a bit much for most subs."

Just like Cash had never been enough. He got it. And him telling Sebastian to be less of an asshole was like all the people who'd told him to be more of one. They were at opposite ends of the Dom spectrum, but being anywhere other than the middle could get lonely.

"Your guy is out there," Cash promised.

Sebastian shrugged, unconvinced. A month ago, Cash would've been equally unconvinced. He needed to hold on to Harrison really hard, to appreciate what had stumbled into his life.

"So I take it you didn't find Arlo?" He and Harrison hadn't talked about what'd gone down at XXXtasy last night, but he assumed if Arlo had been spotted, that news would've preempted any other subject of conversation.

"No sign of him," Sebastian confirmed. "Or Jessica either. And we didn't scene, if you're wondering. We walked around, introduced ourselves to people, watched a few scenes. Your boy's definitely interested in whips."

"He's not my—"

Sebastian held up a hand to stop him. "Your boyfriend. Your Harrison. Whatever you want to call him. He's interested in whips."

"I know." And he would make sure Harrison got the experience he was looking for when they had the time and

242

space for it.

"Come with us tonight," Sebastian suggested. "Put on a show. It'll attract attention."

Cash shook his head. Harrison didn't like being part of a show, and Cash didn't want to distract him from finding Arlo. He was glad he'd made the drive to Philly, but he could wait at the hotel while Sebastian and Harrison went back to the club tonight.

Chapter 25 Harrison

Cash grabbed him as soon he got out of the shower. That was one huggy dude. Harrison kind of loved it. His own exterior was prickly enough that most people didn't fight their way through it, respecting the "do not touch" vibe he gave off without exactly intending to, though it was true enough for the general population. He wasn't one to hug strangers. But Cash had found all the ways and places in which he loved to be touched and worked them on a regular basis.

"Mm," Cash said into his neck. "You smell nice."

"Clean as a daisy. Or something like that. Are daisies actually clean?"

"I wouldn't eat one without washing it first. Speaking of which, I could probably use a shower myself."

Harrison craned his neck around the blockade that was Cash to take in the empty room beyond him. "Sebastian's gone?"

"I got rid of him. We have some time before you go back out, right?"

They definitely did. Time and a bed. They should take advantage of that. "You know," he said. "I'm not a switch, but I am that other thing. Versatile. In fact, I'd almost call myself a top. I don't know if you big, burly Dom-types ever bottom..."

"I can't speak for all big burly Doms, but I bottom. It's not something I get asked for a lot, but you know how my sexuality works."

"As long as I enjoy myself, right?" Fuck Harrison had gotten lucky. "I would enjoy it very much." He cupped one of Cash's hefty cheeks through the denim of his jeans. "I'd love to get in here." He pushed forward, grinding his erection against Cash's groin through the double layers of denim. If he'd known Sebastian had left, he wouldn't have bothered putting clothes on.

"Mm." Cash found his mouth and they made out with increasing urgency, but when Harrison went to lower the zipper on Cash's jeans, Cash pulled away. "Shower first. Let me get clean for you."

Harrison released Cash with a light smack on his ass. He wasn't a Dom, but an ass like that deserved a tap or two.

While Cash showered, he did some frantic digging through his toiletry kit for a condom. His plans for the weekend hadn't included sex, but he was able to unearth a condom left over from some previous trip, and there was a mini bottle of lube in there too. Supplies at the ready, he tore the covers off the bed, ditched his clothes, and kicked back. His dick flagged to half-mast while he was waiting, but it popped straight back up when Cash emerged from the bathroom toweling his hair with one muscular arm and leaving the rest of his body unashamedly on display for Harrison's appreciation.

Harrison gave a long wolf whistle. "Damn, you're a hot piece of ass."

Cash flushed. The guy obviously didn't get as many compliments as he deserved. He tossed the towel onto the vanity outside the bathroom and came to lie down next to him, a little shyly.

"How long has it been since you bottomed?" Harrison asked him.

"God, a while. I can't even remember."

"Nervous?"

Cash shook his head, but it wasn't convincing.

"I won't hurt you. Because you don't like being hurt."

245

"The important thing is—"

"I know. Don't worry. I'm going to enjoy the hell out of this, but I don't need to hurt you to enjoy it, only fuck you starry-eyed, you beautiful hunk of meat. I'm going to bury my cock so deep in you."

"Okay." Cash's eyes were big, and his cock rose in response to Harrison's enthusiasm.

"Let me get in there." He rolled Cash onto his back and separated his legs. "Ooh, pretty. And so clean." He dipped down to give Cash a lick or two, bringing a slick hand up to work Cash's cock into full arousal.

His own cock was definitely ready, and he made sure to position himself so Cash could see it, could see how hot this was for him as he worked Cash open, being careful and thorough and using his mouth as much to describe how he was feeling as to suck Cash's dick.

It was funny. He'd never considered himself much of a dirty talker—more of a grunter—but it was easy to talk to Cash because Cash only wanted to know how he was feeling. It all spilled out in a filthy stream of consciousness: how hot and tight Cash's ass felt on his fingers, how gorgeous he looked splayed open, how eager Harrison was to be inside him. His cock was fucking dripping with eagerness, and he was only managing to hold off because Cash had taught him how good holding off could be.

As he guided his cock through Cash's relaxed sphincter, he offered a silent prayer of thanks to whatever god or fate had put someone in his path who could turn him on to so many new experiences without taking any of his favorite experiences off the table.

"Fuck, baby. You feel so fucking good."

Cash whimpered at Harrison's words, clenching hard around the head of Harrison's cock to squeeze the pleasure right out of him. Cash's cock was leaking a little, courtesy of the attention to his prostate, and Harrison stayed right where he was to give it another encouraging stroke.

"I'm coming in now. That's it, baby. You want me, don't

you?"

Cash nodded, eyes focused hard on Harrison's face, watching him as if he were the most fascinating movie ever. Harrison pushed in slowly, relishing every inch, letting his own eyes flutter shut to narrow his focus down to the spots where he and Cash made contact—his hands on Cash's thighs, Cash's hands on his, the sheathing of cock into ass. A perfect match.

His hip bones came to rest against the flesh of Cash's ass, and all around his cock, warm velvet gripped him so tight he couldn't help moaning. He heard Cash's sharp intake of breath in response and opened his eyes to grin at his lover.

"I've been wanting this so bad." He pulled out and came back in, taking full, deep strokes that swept sensation from the tip of his cock to the root, trying to monitor Cash's reactions even as he got lost in his own. His hips moved faster, answering the call of his desire, and Cash met his every move, perfectly in synch with him.

Harrison gave in to the frenzy, disconnecting from everything except pleasure, chasing the orgasm he knew would be Cash's too. It was almost like they shared a single body. Harrison's balls clenched as he shot his load. He roared with triumphant ecstasy, seeing Cash's load spurt between them through drooping eyes. Cash made a quieter noise of pleasure, and they rocked together, sealing their joining with steady pressure until the spasms passed.

Harrison slumped onto his lover's sturdy frame, leaving his cock buried and shifting his arms to wrap around Cash's upper body. Cash's cock lay warm and wet and still semi-firm between them.

"Can I tell you something?" Cash asked.

"Now's not the time for a critique."

"I don't have a critique. That was perfect."

"So what did you want to tell me?"

"Just that. That it was perfect, that we're perfect. That I love you." He said the last part more quietly, the shift in volume letting Harrison know he wasn't sure he could say it.

Harrison propped himself up on his elbows so they could be eye to eye when he said it back. "You can tell me that any time. Because I love you too."

The relief on Cash's face almost broke Harrison's heart, as if he could possibly *not* love Cash. As if *anyone* could possibly not love Cash. He was the most perfect Dom—the most perfect man—on earth, and Harrison would make sure he never had any reason to doubt it again.

HARRISON STEPPED OUT OF HIS STREET CLOTHES, the action familiar though the setting had changed. XXXtasy was different in appearance from Hell's Bedroom. More closed down, formal almost. The changing room was an actual locker room, and there were two of them, one marked Men, the other marked Women, making him wonder where nonbinary people went and if the club had good policies with respect to trans people.

But he wasn't there to play activist, and he wasn't there with Cash, who would probably know the answers to those questions because he would care, where Sebastian probably wouldn't. Harrison had found the guy offensive from the moment they'd met, but for now, he needed him— needed his money and his gold card or whatever DDD called their fancy premium membership.

He needed Sebastian as a backup too. Though there was no reason for anyone at XXXtasy to mess with him, he felt vulnerable without either a weapon or a phone. He'd gotten accustomed to navigating that vulnerability with Cash at his side, but he wasn't as sure about Sebastian.

"Ready?" Sebastian asked.

"Yeah, yeah." Harrison took his final breath as a free man.

Sebastian had taken advantage of his position last

night. He hadn't done anything overtly sexual, but he'd definitely enjoyed bossing Harrison around—snapping his fingers at him and ordering him to heel or kneel, smirking as Harrison struggled to overcome his instinctive resistance. If Sebastian thought any of that was an advertisement for his superiority as a Dom, he was sorely mistaken.

"Where to?" Sebastian asked as they passed through the door that led into the public play space.

"You're asking me?"

Last night, Sebastian hadn't been so accommodating. Tonight, he shrugged. "I can learn. You're happy with Cash. This is a job."

Harrison only took a moment to process his amazement before snapping into action. "We need to cover the whole space somehow."

The XXXtasy layout with its dozens of nooks and crannies afforded more opportunities for privacy than Hell's Bedroom, but that only made it harder to scope out the whole crowd.

"Split up?" Sebastian asked.

"No, let's stick together. Just keep circulating. We spent too long in one spot last night."

"The whipping."

"Yeah."

One of these days, he was going to let Cash try a bullwhip on him, but watching it happen to someone else wasn't getting him anywhere—either personally or professionally.

They walked together, Harrison hanging back a bit but staying close enough to nudge Sebastian one way or another, and Sebastian took his hints tonight. The club filled as the evening wore on, getting louder and more crowded until people spilled out of the nooks and jammed the hallways.

Harrison had begun to doubt they'd be able to spot Arlo even if he *was* there when a bright flash of blond hair caught his eye. He turned to follow it, unconcerned about pretending to be a proper sub. Sebastian scrambled to catch up to him. His hand ringed Harrison's neck, and Harrison jerked against it.

"Easy," Sebastian said in a low voice. "I'm following you, but it looks like I'm steering you. Where are we going in such a hurry all of a sudden?"

"I may have seen him. There, up ahead. The blond."

"Head full of curls? Could be him."

The blond was slight, shorter than Harrison's five-seven, and walked with the litheness of youth. There was a bulkier man at his side, dressed in a dark suit with short dark hair laced with grey. He had a leash in one hand, the other end of which was connected to the blond's neck, but the blond seemed to be following willingly enough.

"Let's see if we can get around in front of them, confirm the ID." Harrison picked up his pace and Sebastian matched it, muttering angry words at him and shaking him lightly. The sentiment was fake but the words were real and so was the feel of fingers pressing into his throat. Harrison resisted the urge to wrench himself free as he kept moving forward.

The blond and his leash-holder ducked into one of the side rooms. Harrison followed and found himself at the back of a group watching a woman take a crop to some guy's balls. Harrison shuddered. That was a no.

Maybe.

"Where'd they go?" he hissed. The show had distracted him from his prey for a moment.

"Over there." Sebastian gave him a push, and Harrison stumbled in that direction.

The blond was kneeling. His partner stood over him, his leash hand nonchalantly tucked in the pocket of his pants. Harrison made a point of walking right into the blond so he would look up, and there—that was Arlo, all right. Light blue eyes, cherubic cheeks. Their missing angel.

Arlo's captor leaned down and grabbed his chin,

yanking it around toward him. He smacked Arlo across the cheek. Arlo winced at the blow but didn't make a sound.

"You don't look at anyone except me," the man ordered. He squeezed Arlo's chin tight enough to make the tendons in his wrist pop.

Harrison felt a hand on his shoulder—Sebastian holding him back from attacking the fucker.

"Sorry about that," Sebastian said as he pressed Harrison down to his knees. "Clumsy sub. Still in training. Sebastian Gage." He held out his hand, and the man released Arlo's face to take it.

"Zach." Zach used his foot to turn Arlo's head toward the front of the room

Harrison took another quick peek. Yep, definitely Arlo. So now what? Leave Sebastian to watch Arlo and Zach while he ran for his phone to call the local police? Try to wrestle Arlo away? Security would show up, and Harrison wasn't sure whether they'd be on his side or not. They might be corrupt, and even if they weren't, Arlo might say he was happy with Zach, that he didn't want to be rescued.

That display Harrison had just witnessed felt like abuse to him, but Cash had given him too many lectures on the subject for him to be certain. If Arlo wanted to be smacked for turning to look at someone who'd stepped on him, then Arlo got to do that. He was eighteen now, and Harrison couldn't make him come away if this was where he wanted to be. But he needed to confirm this was where Arlo wanted to be, without any coercion or drugs being involved, and he couldn't do that with Zach standing over him.

Sebastian was schmoozing Zach—telling him he was visiting Philadelphia, learning that Zach lived here, getting recommendations for local hotspots. Meanwhile, Harrison knelt next to Arlo and made a discreet catalogue of him.

He was naked except for a collar, which gave Harrison plenty of flesh to catalogue. His body had trauma painted across it in black and blue and red. A constellation of fetid round spots on his inner thigh looked like burns that hadn't

251

healed—the edges red and painful, the centers a disturbing black. Arlo's eyes were cast steadfastly downward, and when Harrison nudged their knees together, Arlo didn't acknowledge it. If this was his idea of fun, Harrison was really, really not getting it.

The hero in him wanted to grab Arlo right now, but his more practical side would prefer to save Arlo without warning whoever was behind the trafficking ring that someone was on to them. Zach was only a customer. He would have an email and a hole in his bank account. He wouldn't know who'd abducted Arlo or who'd authorized his abduction or who'd profited from it. Not any more than Francesca did.

On the other hand, if they let Arlo leave with Zach tonight, they might never find him again. A first name and a description weren't going to be enough to track Zach back to wherever he was holding Arlo.

Track. That was it.

Keeping his movements subtle, Harrison slipped Brixby's medallion over his head. With it secreted inside his fist, he bumped into Sebastian, intentionally knocking him off balance.

"Why you little—" Sebastian jerked him up to his feet. "You did that on purpose."

"Don't hurt me," he pleaded, trying to communicate what he wanted by cutting his eyes in Zach's direction. Sebastian gave him a good shake that forced him into Zach's side, and Harrison grabbed Zach's arm with a frightened, "Help me."

"He really is a problem, isn't he?" Zach asked as he peeled Harrison's hand off his arm without noticing that Harrison was using his other hand to slip the medallion into the pocket of his suit jacket. "You want to be careful, though. The security in this club is over the top."

"Oh, I know." Sebastian took possession of Harrison like he was reclaiming a lost umbrella. "Ours is just as bad in Boston."

"Had to talk to them about this one the other day," Zach said, jabbing Arlo with his foot. "He started giving me grief right in the middle of a scene. I told him if he couldn't behave, he wouldn't be let out of the house, and look how docile he is today. Aren't you, pet?" Zach leaned down and kissed Arlo's cheek as fondly as if he hadn't just kicked him. Arlo didn't respond to the kiss any more than he had to the kick.

"Well, I'd better get Harry out of here and give him what he seems to be asking for," Sebastian said. "Ready for the punishment you deserve, doll face?" Sebastian was so gleeful about it, as if he were genuinely looking forward to doling out some pain, but as soon he had Harrison out in the hallway, he released his hold and turned to face him. "Arlo?"

"Definitely."

"What now?"

"Let's get my phone so I can call Brixby. I planted his medallion on Zach, and I want to make sure he's picking up a signal."

Chapter 26 Cash

Their tiny hotel room hadn't been intended to hold this many people. Harrison had returned with his phone plastered to his ear, too busy to explain what was going on. In the end, it was Sebastian who filled Cash in as Cash brewed one teeny-tiny pot of coffee after another for the people who kept arriving.

They'd found Arlo. And let him go. There was a GPS device on the Dom he'd been with, and Brixby had used it to track them when they left the club. Beyond that, it was all warrants and cross-agency coordination—things Cash couldn't pretend to follow—as cops came and went and strategies were devised and discarded.

The suspect's name was Zach Terzini, and the device had tracked him to a house in a suburb of Philadelphia, which a squad car now had staked out. But what Cash couldn't understand was why no one had busted down his door yet.

"Philly PD got a no-knock warrant," Harrison said when everyone had finally cleared out and it was just the two of them.

"Which means he doesn't have to let you in, right?"

"It means he doesn't even have to be home to let us in. So our plan is to wait until he leaves."

"What's the advantage of that?"

"Stealth." Harrison ran a tired hand over his hair, and Cash regretted questioning him instead of just taking care

254

of him. "We'll pop in, grab Arlo, and get out. Hopefully, Terzini will think he escaped on his own. We're trying to keep the investigation quiet until we get closer to the source. I just hope Arlo is willing to come with us."

"I'm sure he will be." Cash had heard Sebastian's take on what'd happened, and it hadn't sounded good.

Arlo was either too drugged up or too beaten down to differentiate between praise and punishment. A sub who didn't react to praise from his Dom was like a dog who didn't react to being petted by his owner. Something had taught him not to react. Which made Cash iffy on the idea of leaving him to spend another night with this guy, but he understood there was more at stake than a single eighteen-year-old with infected burns on his thighs.

"Sounds like tomorrow's going to be a big day. You should get some sleep."

"Don't know if I can." Harrison was pacing back and forth, his frenetic energy at the forefront. "I shouldn't have had so much coffee."

"Maybe I can put you to sleep."

Harrison looked down at his crotch. "Sex isn't feeling very sexy to me at the moment."

"I have other ways of putting you to sleep. Come here." He pulled Harrison into his arms and wrapped him up tight in an attempt to absorb the energy pouring off him. "How does a massage sound?"

"Kind of indulgent."

"Yeah, well, I'm an indulgent kind of guy."

He got Harrison's clothes off and spread him out on the bed. Harrison was so tense he almost vibrated right back off it, but Cash turned off the lights and put on some meditative music. He coated his hands in complimentary lotion and applied it to Harrison's back, sweeping up and down his spine with soothing strokes. Harrison talked, rehashing everything that'd happened, even though Cash had heard most of it by now, until he'd gotten it all out and his words wound down to contented sighs.

"You're good at that too," he said as Cash kneaded the firm globes of his ass, digging his knuckles in deep to get at the muscle.

"Took a class once."

"You take classes on everything, don't you?"

"Is that wrong?"

"No." Harrison let out another relaxed sigh. "Just honest. And brave."

"Taking a massage class is brave?"

"Admitting you don't already know everything is brave. Putting yourself in a position to learn is brave. I'd never have done this, you know. If it hadn't been for this investigation, I'd have gone the rest of my life wondering about my kinks, too afraid to learn more about who I was."

"That would've been a shame." Cash dropped a kiss between Harrison's shoulder blades, noticing they were nice and relaxed now, lying flat on his back instead of sticking up like wings.

"I know." Harrison yawned. "A terrible shame. Imagine us not meeting."

"I'd rather not."

But there. Harrison was asleep. And occupying the majority of the bed. Cash covered him with a blanket and crawled under it, into the nook of Harrison's arm. He curled up there, tucked into the space his boyfriend wasn't occupying, and joined him in sleep.

IT WAS MONDAY. That was Cash's first thought when he woke up. It was Monday, and his alarm was going off because he was due at work in an hour and a half. Then he woke up some more and realized it wasn't Monday and the sound that'd woken him up wasn't his alarm. He was in Philadelphia and someone was pounding on the door to his hotel room.

He staggered to his feet and over to the door, noticing

as he crossed the room that he was alone in it. The sun coming through the curtains told him it was morning, and the fact that Harrison had managed to slip out without waking him up told him he'd slept hard. He opened the door, expecting to find Sebastian with coffee, but it was Brixby and Tripp.

"Hey." He swiped a hand over his face, wondering how ridiculous he looked with bed head and pillow creases. "I don't think Harrison is here."

"I know." Brixby pushed Tripp into the room, then followed him in. "He's at the stakeout. I just need a place to stash Tripp so I can join him."

"But I want to go too," Tripp whined.

"Why did you bring him to Philadelphia?" Cash asked, a little perplexed.

"We were in New York together. What was I supposed to do—put him on a bus? Anyway, Arlo might need a friend."

"That's why I want to go to the stakeout," Tripp said, but he threw himself onto the bed as if he would just as soon go to sleep. What time was it anyway? The sun was up, but the air was still cool enough to suggest it hadn't been up long.

Brixby ignored Tripp to speak to Cash. "I'll call when there's news, and you can bring Tripp to the hospital."

"Why a hospital? Did you hear something?"

"Just a precaution. We'll do a tox screen on him, have his wounds checked out." Brixby clapped him on the arm in farewell. "Behave," he ordered Tripp before turning to leave.

"Yes, sir," Tripp said, only semi-sarcastically.

But Brixby hadn't even made it out the door before his phone rang. He stopped to answer it. It was obviously business—maybe even Harrison—and Cash wanted to eavesdrop, but he went over and sat on the bed next to Tripp to give Brixby some privacy.

"How was the club in New York?" He would love to see

Tripp with someone like Brixby rather than the edgier Doms he seemed to seek out. Certainly Cash hadn't been enough to make Tripp happy, but he pushed that thought away before he could fall into his old trap of beating himself up for not being enough. He was enough for Harrison. Tripp would have to sort out his own love life.

"Really small," Tripp answered. "I thought it would be huge."

"Maybe people aren't kinky in New York."

"I doubt it," Tripp said with a smirk. "The ones who were there were kinky as fuck. We watched some wicked knife play."

Cash restrained himself from giving Tripp a lecture on being careful about who he engaged in that sort of play with. That was one skill he'd never bothered to learn. The idea of leaving permanent scars didn't do anything for him. Although. If Harrison wanted him to...

"Change of plans," Brixby said as he tucked his phone back in his pocket. He wasn't wearing his uniform today, which made sense since he'd been at a BDSM club last night and wasn't in his own jurisdiction, but even in civilian clothes, he exuded an air of authority. "They've got Arlo."

"Already?" Tripp popped up off the bed.

"Yep. Terzini left, and Arlo wasn't with him, so they took the opportunity to go in."

"Like they knocked and Arlo answered the door?" Cash asked.

"Like they picked the lock and found him in a cage in the master bedroom."

"Fuck." Tripp's breathy exclamation really said it all. "Did he... did he want to be in a cage?"

"Regardless," Brixby said. "You don't leave human beings locked up and alone with no way to call for help or get out in case of an emergency. And no." His voice softened. "I don't think he wanted to be in a cage. Harrison says he's pretty shell-shocked. They're bringing him to the hospital now. Come on, kid. This is why you're with me."

"Me too, right?" Cash didn't know Arlo, but he felt like he did. He felt like they all had a responsibility toward him.

"Yeah, sure. Join the party. Let's go meet the boy who brought us all together."

JUST LIKE THEIR HOTEL ROOM had been too small to hold everyone crammed into it last night, Arlo's hospital room was too small to hold everyone crammed into it now, especially once the three of them were added to the mix. Arlo was dressed in a hospital gown, sitting on the bed that'd been raised to make it more like a chair. He had his knees, which were covered in a white sheet, pulled into his chest, and both arms wrapped tight around them.

A uniformed Philly officer stood on one side of the bed and Harrison stood on the other, next to a woman Cash remembered from the room last night. They were talking in the same rapid-fire, jargon-filled speech they'd been using then.

"Arlo!" Tripp elbowed his way over to the bed and climbed right up into it.

Harrison broke his conversation to acknowledge their arrival with a curt "Brixby." Cash got nothing more than a flicker of his eyes, but Cash saw the affection in them. "This is Detective Ludlow," Harrison told them. "Detective, my unofficial partner, Officer Cade Brixby of the Boston PD." The two of them shook hands.

"Call me Stephanie," the detective said. She looked past Brixby at Cash.

"And that's, uh, Cash," Harrison said. "One of the people from Hell's Bedroom who've been helping us with the case. And also my partner, but of the other sort."

"So how's Arlo doing?" Cash asked in order to hide how widely he wanted to smile. Arlo wasn't responding to Tripp, though Tripp was trying—rocking him and whispering to him.

"We're still waiting on the tox screen," Harrison said, "but he reminds me of Kimi."

"Valium, you think?"

"Maybe. I know you don't like me to say this, but there's something out of whack in his head."

"Under the circumstances, I think you can say it." Cash moved around to the foot of the bed, mostly to get out of the way of the cops but also to get a better look at Arlo. His frail arms extended from his hospital gown, ending in wrists that were too delicate for his frame. Even the billowy gown couldn't disguise how thin he was.

"Should I find him some food?"

"Arlo?" Harrison prompted. "You want something to eat?"

"Anything at all," Cash offered. "I'll go get it."

"How about a Philly cheese steak?" Tripp suggested. Arlo didn't react to either the joke or the offer of food. "Come on, dude." Tripp jiggled him encouragingly. "That's Cash talking to you. He's a Dom. A nice one. What do you say?"

"No thank you, sir." Arlo's voice was scratchy and almost completely lifeless.

"You don't have to call me sir, but let me get you something to eat."

Arlo shook his head.

"Why not?"

A pair of bright blue eyes met his briefly, the fear in them so intense it took Cash's breath away.

"It's okay," he backpedaled. "You don't have to eat if you don't want to." Did Arlo think Cash was going to hit him for not eating? Or was food a reward Arlo was afraid he didn't deserve? "Tell you what, I'm going to buy a few things, and you can eat them if you want."

He went out into the hallway, grateful to escape from the sight of the damaged kid who was hardly more than a boy despite his recent birthday. He went down to the cafeteria and bought anything that looked portable, then juggled it all back up to Arlo's room where he found yet one more cop had been added to the mix—a woman dressed in a suit who appeared to be Detective Ludlow's captain.

Cash deposited the collection of snack items he'd bought onto the table next to Arlo's bed, and Tripp made a few attempts to get Arlo to eat, though it was Tripp who ended up doing most of the actual eating. It reminded Cash that he hadn't eaten this morning either, but he felt weird taking one of the snack items, even though he'd bought them himself. He'd bought them for Arlo.

Finally, Detective Ludlow and her captain left the room, and the officer in uniform went to stand guard outside the door. Harrison plopped down into the single chair, looking like he'd gotten about four hours of sleep last night, which was probably true. Cash went over and stood next to him, not sure if it would be all right to touch him, but Harrison grabbed his hand.

Tripp was happily munching away on a giant whoopie pie, licking filling off his fingers as if he were putting on a burlesque show. For who, though? Brixby's attention was focused on Arlo. He snagged a granola bar from the pile of goodies and sat on the edge of the bed with it.

"Arlo? I'm Officer Brixby. I want you to look at me, please." He said it in a voice any sub would respond to— warm and low, but not meant to be ignored. Like steel covered in velvet. Arlo gave Brixby that same flash of eyes Cash had managed to coax from him before dropping his gaze just as fast.

"Arlo," Brixby repeated with more insistence, pushing past Arlo's reluctance the way Cash never could. Arlo kept his head up this time, though his eyes skittered around the room.

"I'm not going to hurt you. No one is going to hurt you. I'll make sure of that." Brixby handed Arlo the granola bar. "But I want you to eat this." Arlo looked at the granola bar doubtfully. "Are you allergic to anything in there?" Arlo shook his head. "Hate granola bars?" Another shake. "Then eat it. Now."

"Good thing we brought an extra Dom along," Cash said to Harrison when Arlo unwrapped the granola bar and took a bite.

"Not like I was planning to share mine."

Arlo nibbled at the granola bar, visually checking in with Brixby before taking each bite.

"Someone has done bad things to him," Cash said to Harrison in a low voice.

"I don't want to rehash it while he's sitting right here, but the way we found him was pretty disturbing. We haven't been able to get much out of him. Maybe we should let Brixby question him. He seems to have a way with him."

"He exudes a Dom vibe, which is probably what Arlo needs right now."

"If I were Arlo, I'd never go near a Dom again. Tell me this will cure him of wanting one."

Now wasn't the time to remind Harrison to watch his language, so Cash let it go. He watched as Brixby set aside the empty granola bar wrapper and opened his arms. A timid Arlo found his way into them.

Chapter 27 Harrison

"What am I missing?" Harrison looked around the hotel room at the table covered in coffee cups and the tangle of covers they'd slept under, but there were no stray loose ends. No phone charger plugged into the wall or toothbrush left on the vanity. What he was looking for wasn't in the room because what he was looking for was a sense of closure.

Yes, they'd found Arlo, alive and mostly in one piece. He'd been released from the hospital after a few hours of observation with antibiotics for his fever, ointment for those badly healing burns, and a clean bill of health otherwise. He was battered, underweight, and uncommunicative, but he was safe and currently on his way back to Boston with Brixby and Tripp.

What about Jessica though? What about the who-knew-how-many more who might be missing? Now that they had a suspect and a confirmed victim, the FBI had been brought in and detectives were being alerted in every city where DDD owned property. Wheels were in motion. They just weren't Harrison's wheels anymore. He had to leave the case to the Philly PD and the FBI. He had to walk away.

"Everything's in the car," Cash said. "You're just tired. You got almost no sleep last night, and you've been going all day."

It was true. Cash had put him to sleep with that

massage, but his stupor had worn off long before dawn. He'd slipped out from under the sheets to join the stakeout while the sky was still dark, needing to do something, only to find there was nothing to do. Sit in an unmarked car and drink coffee, watch a dark and quiet house remain dark and quiet.

Slowly, the sun rose. The neighborhood came alive around them. Someone cut their lawn, wafting the smell of grass in through the car windows as the morning got warmer. Harrison was debating marching straight up to the door and kicking it down when Terzini finally left. A knock didn't bring Arlo to the door, so they let themselves in, which took surprisingly little effort. Apparently Terzini wasn't worried about anyone breaking in. Or out.

Harrison had half expected to find Arlo on the couch in the living room, watching cartoons and eating cereal and refusing to leave with them, but no. What they'd found—the cage, the boy, the boy *in* the cage—he would never forget it. Was Jessica in a cage somewhere right now?

"Come on." Cash tugged on him, leading him out of the room to the parking lot. "You can sleep on the way back. And when we get home, I've got an idea for how to take your mind off all this."

"I don't want to let the case go."

"Until tomorrow you can. Until tomorrow you need to."

Harrison stopped arguing because Cash was right. They had found Arlo. Tomorrow they would start looking for Jessica.

THEY DROPPED OFF THE RENTAL CAR and hopped on the T, getting off at the stop for Cash's apartment without discussing where they were headed. Cash's place felt like home by now, and there would be food in his refrigerator.

"Just gotta grab Mr. Moo," Cash said after unlocking the door. "Sandi's got him." He went into the kitchen and removed a piece of Pyrex from the refrigerator, then headed for the stairs.

"Payment for watching him?"

"More like a bribe to get him back." Cash ran upstairs with the Pyrex while Harrison dropped onto the loveseat. He'd slept fitfully on the way back but still felt off, a combination of exhausted and restless, like he was trying to forget and trying to remember all at the same time.

Cash came in with Mr. Moo in his arms and pushed the door shut with his ass. Mr. Moo was a two-armed load who didn't appreciate being carried. The moment Cash let him down, he went straight for his usual perch.

"Sandi says he missed us."

"More like he missed his window," Harrison said, raising his voice to follow Cash as Cash moved past him into the kitchen.

"Be with you in a sec," Cash called back. "Just gotta feed Ellie. Sandi refuses to do it, so she's probably starving."

Sandi had some goddamn sense. One night, Harrison had stumbled into the kitchen for a glass of water, and he'd seen it—the rat scrabbling off with a piece of cheese in its sharp little teeth. But that was Cash. He had a cat who bullied him, a hamster who was really a rat, a bunch of plants he babied like they were his children, and Harrison.

Harrison went into the kitchen to watch Cash cut a block of cheese into rat-sized pieces.

"You think you might like a fish?"

"You're not giving up Molly, are you?"

"No, I'm not giving up Molly." His fish had a name now. "You have to take me with her. We're kind of a package deal."

"You mean...?" Cash abandoned his cheese-chopping to come over and grab his hands. "You want to move in with me?"

"I'm not always the easiest person to live with."

"I'll be easy enough for both of us." Cash gave him a kiss that worked pretty well as a distraction from everything he had on his mind.

"You said we were going to have fun tonight."

"And we are." Cash put the cheese chunks down in Ellie's assigned feeding corner and brought him to the bedroom where he rummaged around in a closet that, huh, had a lot of interesting things in it, before pulling out a flogger.

"That's not a whip." He'd been kind of hoping for a whip.

"I know, but I don't have a lot of room for swinging whips here, so let's see if you like this."

"You used that on me before." It'd been all right. Nice enough at the time. It was just that now he knew his pleasure dial could be cranked way higher than nice.

"No, that was this one." Cash pulled out a second flogger.

"What's the difference?"

"Want to find out?"

Once Harrison had taken hold of both floggers, he figured he could guess the difference. The tails on the flogger in his left hand were lightweight and soft, flowing easily between his fingers. The tails on the other were firmer, heavier, and almost seemed to have an edge to them. But why guess when he could learn firsthand? He gave the floggers back to Cash and stripped off his shirt.

Cash flicked his ass with the sturdier flogger, which seemed to mean he should take his pants off too, so he did, adding a pointed reminder that he preferred it when Cash was similarly naked. Maybe clubs had silly protocols about who got naked and who wore a suit, but they weren't at a club. They were in Cash's bedroom, with its wide, inviting bed and the cacophony of color that had seemed like too much at first but just seemed like home now.

When they were both fully undressed, Cash positioned him against the mirrored closet door, giving him a strangely up-close view of his own erection and a pretty nice view of the man behind him.

"Doesn't feel any different," he observed as the tresses

brushed lightly over his shoulder with one soft slap after another. He did like the glowing heat of it, but he'd been expecting more.

"This is a warm up. You'll know when I switch to the other one."

And he did. Even if the slight pause while Cash changed from one flogger to the other didn't give it away, the first blow did.

"Ah." He arched his back when a heavier thud cracked against his right shoulder, followed quickly by a blow to his left shoulder, then one right between the two spots. "That's—"

"Yeah?"

"Interesting." He hadn't sorted it out yet. The sensation came close to pain, like when the TENS unit had been at exactly the right intensity—approaching hurtful without quite reaching it. Intense. Alive. More real than the real world, demanding his focus, clearing his head.

Cash covered him in stripes, always finding a bit of skin where the sensation felt brand new again, the lashings layering on top of each other at different angles and intensities to keep him on edge, not allowing his mind to drift away. He couldn't be anywhere except here, with Cash and his own gloriously alive body. The two of them shared the mirror in front of him—Cash naked and strong, swinging the flogger with powerful accuracy, and his own smaller body absorbing the blows as if he were absorbing Cash's strength with them.

He wished he could see his back—the lines of white, flooding to red—but he could see Cash's face, how caught up he was in the pleasure he delivered. His cock was as hard as Harrison's, swinging with his strikes the same way Harrison's bobbled in front of him. Harrison became nothing but his body, and his body became nothing but his cock, as if the flogger's tresses wound directly around it, until he felt his orgasm gathering at its base, boiling in his balls.

"Now," he called, and Cash dropped the flogger to grab him, finding his cock and stroking it perfectly, exactly the way he'd imagined the flogger stroking it. Cash's arms were strong, his body hot and hard, his breath warm against Harrison's face, and his chest scraped fire over the agony of his back. Harrison pumped into his fist as the sensation boiled down to one great heaving explosion of pleasure.

Come splattered the mirror. Cash's face twisted into a perfect expression of satisfaction that had Harrison guessing he'd blown his load too, but when he sagged back into Cash's arms, he felt a still-hard rod between the cheeks of his ass.

"I can," he mumbled, no strength left in his voice or his spine. He managed to twist out of Cash's arms and sink to his knees, to get himself properly aligned for a blowjob, but his energy ended there. Cash's cock waved in front of him, but his brain was so fried he couldn't remember what he was supposed to do with it.

"Cash," he said. Then more desperately, "Cash!"

He reached up and Cash had him, wrapping him up and half-carrying him to the bed, cradling him as he shook. It all came out—the fear, the responsibility, the inadequacy, the sleepless night and the helplessness of not being able to do more. The pain flaring across his back—it was pain now—and the pleasure that still sizzled through him. The relaxation, the emptiness, the relief of giving it all up. It all came out in a sniveling mess of weakness Cash took from him.

When it was gone, when he became aware again of the vibrant colors of Cash's bedroom and of Cash's body spooning his, Cash's cock was no longer hard, and Cash only shook his head when Harrison rolled over and tried to take it in hand.

"That can't have been very satisfying for you."

"It couldn't have been more satisfying. Physically, your orgasm is my orgasm. I'm happy to share. But I'm even more satisfied here." Cash put his hand on his chest. "I know you don't need to be taken care of, but I want to do it all the same."

"What about you though?" Harrison's chat with Brixby had only reassured him to a certain extent. He really needed to talk about it with Cash directly. "Who takes care of you? Sandi?"

"Is that a problem? Sandi and I have been best friends since college. There's nothing—"

Harrison held up a hand to stop him. "I'm not trying to separate you from Sandi. Or replace what she means in your life. But you take care of me and Sandi takes care of you and I get off scot-free? Is that fair? Brixby says I'm giving you what you want—"

"Well, thank God *someone* understands," Cash said with a roll of his eyes. "How many times do I have to tell you? Don't think you're doing nothing for me because you are."

"What am I doing for you?" He honestly had no idea.

"Wanting me. Wanting what I do to you. Letting me explore you and push your boundaries. Telling me I'm good."

"You're not just good. You're the best." That was too true.

"I've never been the best before, Harrison." Cash swallowed, his eyes a little damp. "I don't need reciprocation. I just need to be the person who gets to see you vulnerable. Let me be your Dom."

"No one else could be."

Cash's face brightened again, a smile breaking through his almost-tears. "Does that mean I can feed you snacks? Give you aftercare?"

"Was that aftercare? What you just did?"

When Cash nodded, Harrison realized he'd been a fool. The physical play was really something, more amazing than he'd ever imagined. But being held afterward—treasured and coddled and seen—that'd been even better.

On the other hand, he couldn't let his reputation for

269

being a stubborn hard-ass go completely.

"I've never met anyone more eager for me to get crumbs in his bed," he grumbled. "But if feeding me snacks is really what you're dying to do..."

"That's what I'm dying to do." Cash dashed off for the kitchen.

"Just don't bring me any of that rat cheese," Harrison yelled after him. Because he was a short, feisty masochist and not at all a sub.

The END

Appendix

As part of a Facebook event one day, I asked the members of Hawthorne's Harem to suggest a plot or character element for a story I was going to write. The suggestions were so voluminous and varied, it was impossible to incorporate them into a single short story. Thus, they became *Kitchen Sink Dom*.

Here are the suggestions I used. Some of them feature prominently. Others are only a passing reference. Can you find them all?

Suggestion	Made by
80s music	Sarah Y
a cat named Mr. Moo, because he has white fur with black spots	Colleen C
A hamster that lives in the walls and refuses to live in the light. The only way they know it's there is it comes out and eats food at night. Flash forward and it's not a hamster, it's a mouse. Hahaha	Amanda S F
Cade	Kathy M
Cassius, alpha male, no piercings, no tattoos	Valerie F
charity work	Helen W
chews nails which drives sister crazy	Nica F
figging	Kelly G
freshwater aquarium with only 1 fish - murderous red molly	Judith S
goes commando	Sandy S
Harrison	Liz T
Harrison is a tattoo artist	Terri H
humiliation fetish	Kate H
oral fixation as a result of quitting smoking	Abigail K
parrot named Felix who only says fuck in 7 languages	Ariana L
peanut butter	Kate H

Suggestion	Made by
pet plant	Samantha T
Philadelphia	Liz T
Philly cheese steaks	Liz T
salt and pepper shakers	Samantha T
shibari	Joscelyn S
smell of fresh grass	Rose H
Tourette's	Steve S
voyeurism fetish	Kathy M

Apologies to those group members whose suggestions I wasn't able to accommodate.

Suggestion	Made by
Daddy kink*	Colleen C
Oh oh can they be switches !!!! Especially if they have any kind of dynamics like daddy/boy and they actually enjoy switching places with the same or different kinds of roles idk do you get that?	Erin R
The more masc/dom of the two loves to wear heels	Kerina L M
hate each other	Nicole N R
enemies to lovers	Bryce W

Book 2 of Hell's Bedroom
Chicken Soup Dom

When Arlo boarded a bus to Philadelphia to turn himself over to a master he'd never met, he thought he was on his way home, that he would finally have both the sex he craved and an authority figure to care for him in a way his parents never had. But what he got was worse. Much, much worse. Now he's been rescued, but where does that leave him?

Officer Cade Brixby immediately bonded with the curly-haired, blue-eyed cherub who needs to be taught the right way to engage in power exchange. But not by him, and not until Arlo has had a chance to process his traumatic past. Brixby's only taking care of Arlo for now. He has no business playing with the boy. Even if Arlo asks. A lot.

Professionally, Brixby is off the case. But he and his band of vigilante kinksters won't rest until every kidnapped sub has been found and the kidnappers brought to justice. Arlo might be able to provide them with some valuable information. Or he might be bait.

Book 3 of Hell's Bedroom

Upsy-Daisy Dom

It's really rude to wish you'd been kidnapped. Especially when your best friend actually was. But Tripp wishes *something* would happen to him. He likes his sex kinky, and he likes his kink on the fun side of risky. Which means he's got his eye on Sebastian Gage, the incredibly handsome, incredibly rich, incredibly dangerous Dom.

Sebastian makes subs cry, and he's not sorry about it. He *is* sorry his bent toward emotional sadism means none of his playmates ever stick around, but he's not going to let any of his newfound friends know that. All they know is he's a cruel Dom and a brilliant attorney, and now's the time to concentrate on the brilliant attorney part instead of getting sidetracked by a gangly young sub with a smart mouth and a penchant for danger.

Because Sebastian will do anything to make sure the perp who's been targeting vulnerable subs gets everything the law can throw at him, maybe even sacrifice Tripp, the only sub who can take everything Sebastian has to offer.

Aftercare

Aayan Denir knows Garrett Hillier was once a high-powered defense attorney, and—thanks to a leaked photograph—he knows Garrett is sexually submissive, which makes him ideally qualified to defend Aayan's brother from the charge of murdering his sub. Aayan would do anything to protect Syed, even if he doesn't understand how Syed could hurt someone he loves. He could never hurt Garrett. He only wants to take care of him—love him, serve him, cherish him. And maybe torture him. Just a little.

Garrett probably shouldn't be dating his client's brother. Right? And what's the use in a confirmed sub dating a guy who doesn't want to be a Dom anyway? The important thing is to get Syed cleared of the discriminatory murder charge he's facing. Aayan is a distraction. But for the first time in the three lonely years since Garrett's husband died, he's feeling hope, ambition, and desire. Can he give up the pain he craves to find the love he needs?

As Syed's trial date looms, Aayan and Garrett explore what a BDSM relationship means for them, and what they mean to each other.

Deep Under

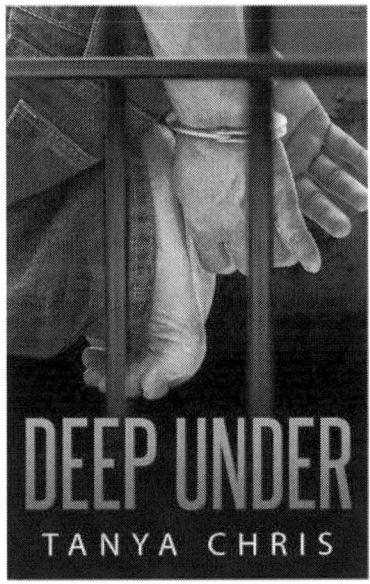

It was a routine traffic stop until the submissive in Jack recognized the Dominant in Maddox. Now Maddox and Jack are walking a dangerous line: on opposite sides of the law by day, on the same side of the bed at night.

Can Maddox trust a man with Jack's past, and does Jack even want him to? One thing's for sure: Jack needs to be punished, and Maddox is just the man to do it.

Manufactured by Amazon.ca
Bolton, ON